# TURNABOUT

By
Lance K. Steele

ISBN    # 978-09827031-6-8

EAN        # 0982703163

## DISCLAIMERS

This story is entirely fictional. All names, places, persons, dates and things are fictional. Any resemblance to real things, etc, is coincidental and entirely unintentional.

In reality, peace officers are always honest, never on the take or in bed with mobsters. They never abuse suspects' civil rights, never grope, rape or beat cuffed suspects.

Neither do they ever 'confiscate' anything during a bust, even though these busts usually take place HIGH UP IN THE mountains in cabins and shacks where they outnumber, outgun and overwhelm the suspects. They never lose exculpatory evidence, never edit their video footage nor otherwise bend the law to get a conviction.

While we're at it; judges never take a cop's word over the average citizen's... And justice is blind.

And, those 'innocent' private-use growers who claim to use all their dope for self-medication... while growing thirty pounds per year? They never sell it, never buy homes or property with the profit.; they smoke that much dope personally every year. Like I said...

It's all FICTION, *GOT IT?*

Good. I'm glad we got that settled.

Now lace up your boots... I'm taking you with me up into the King's Range for a little excursion. Keep your mouth shut, stay in the shadows, and make damned sure where you place your feet.

In a remote meadow somewhere close to the Mendonesia County line, they waited. This was just another burn, in another summer of endless burns in the long, wasteful campaign against Marijuana. Along with the small team of corrupt deputies, four other CAMT agents were on scene.

The huge mound of seized dope stunk to high heavens. But to the average pot smoker, it was a Cheech and Chong mountaintop fantasy. For the Campaign Against Marijuana Trafficking agents, it had been a long day, seizing plants and cracking heads. They could hardly wait to get home.

The dim droning came heavily on the hot evening air. Although he knew the approach route, it took a few minutes before Enrique Talvez spotted the tactical-black chopper flying low... too low, in fact.

Years ago, rural citizens took their grievances to a judge, forcing changes; chopper pilots were supposed to fly at least 500 above the surrounding hills. They were supposed to NOT fly over sunbathers, lovers screwing in the woods or anyone else trying to enjoy forest peace and tranquility. They were supposed to, but it didn't mean dick to the badge-heavy pricks in the helicopters.

Under the aircraft hung a huge net, chock-full of mature plants. It looked like a black bumblebee pulling an Army-Green tennis ball. According to the bean counters whose job it was to justify the costly campaign to the bloated top-heavy bureaucracy, each pound was worth three grand.

Adding this load to the fifteen foot-high pile, the agents would report that they seized four thousand pounds worth of dope; the newspaper scoop would claim that twelve million dollars worth of illicit drugs were seized, somehow making the world a safer place.

In truth, only dried buds were worth much, but the propagandists tallied wet leaves, branches, roots, rocks, lizards, anything else in the bag. It was a lesson learned from Vietnam's infamous body counts; wars were half - won with propaganda. The feds wanted big numbers, to justified increasingly larger budgets the next year.

The chopper quickly established a hover, dropped the load and made for the hangar; maintenance was needed before the next day's raids. Several of the agents posed in front of the pile while others photographed their trophy mound of Sinsemilla.

Deputy Null and Thompkins poured diesel on the perimeter of the musky plants. They lit it while the honest agents headed down the dirt road to their families.

Talvez and Engard were already working the back of the pile, out of sight of departing officers. They quickly pulled the diesel-tainted branches into a smaller pile. Soon only a few hundred pounds of poisoned plants burned. The rest was preserved; a small fortune, this claim-jumped load of new age ore.

Talvez stood in the smoke and took a big hit. Engard didn't smoke; he stayed alert for unexpected returning squad cars. Thompkins joined Talvez. They didn't have to worry about piss tests; whoever secured the fire would obviously be contaminated with THC, so a urine test was pointless.

Two green garbage trucks rumbled up the dusty road. Their innards had been scrubbed, rinsed and towel-dried. They parked with engines running. Everyone pitch-forked plants. Every thirty seconds, the engines would rise in pitch as the compactor units stuffed and crushed each mouthful of contraband into their metal bellies. One driver slipped an envelope to Talvez, who slipped it under his flak jacket. It was over before the sacrificial pyre was halfway consumed. The trucks rumbled off down the hill, headed for the next phase of processing.

The agents watched the fire burn until all the remaining pot was gone. They met at Thompkins' house, around 11:30. After they split the bribe, the meeting broke up. Tomorrow would be another day of raiding plants and cracking heads.

Victor Saldivar was responsible for them becoming deputies; he donated much of the sports equipment they'd played with, as youths. They trusted him.

Long ago he paved the road that now seemed so smooth. His plan worked perfectly; pay the deputies to reclaim his competitors' seized Pot, then have his stooges manicure and distribute it. The cash cow grew bigger each year. Everybody in the loop was happily growing rich.

Certainly the deputies were happy. They couldn't go on every raid or suspicion would mount. Naturally, early raids were worthless, since the pot wasn't mature. If they seized small plants too early, the growers would just replant. But if they waited until harvest time, they could wreak financial havoc upon the growers. So the big money was only available in the late summer - early fall raids. However, the four deputies worked many early raids, to defray suspicion when they seized good stuff later.

Early in the plan, Saldivar counseled them on money management; don't buy fancy cars, upgrade houses, don't flash jewelry or furs. He explained offshore accounts, bearer bonds and so forth. His accountants were available to discreetly help. But Thompkins alone worked through Saldivar's bank. The other three chose to squirrel away their profits in various ways.

## One

# ETHICS

The setting sun highlighted the buck's ears and rack as it fed on acorns and looked for danger. When the head went down, they'd close for ten seconds, then pause for the predictable heads-up safety check. When he lowered the head, they'd resume the stalk.

They first spotted the buck from 300 yards, where a kill would have been fairly easy, but Ted wanted this hunt to be a lesson in ethics, and blazing away from long distance is one of the worst habits any hunter can acquire.

They used a dry creek bed for the first hundred yards, stepping in low spots to muffle the noise. From there, it was uphill across a pasture, dry from the rainless summer, on a cattle trail four inches wide and pounded to dust. This got them under the buck's hilltop buffet.

There was one last problem; the steep slope shielded the buck's vitals. They could see the top of the deer, but a bullet would strike earth before making it to the vitals. They needed to get higher.

One false step would send the little buck off in a flash. Both father and son carefully inched uphill. After ten minutes, they'd moved just fifteen yards. Ted motioned for his son to chamber a round; the first lesson Ted taught him... always keep an empty chamber; safe during slips, falls, and unexpected drops from sweaty hands.

Ted motioned; AJ moved four yards and froze, looking up into the setting sun. He looked at Ted, who pointed at his own chest; a shoulder shot it would be, but due to the steep terrain and the buck's higher position, he needed a steady rest. Ted knelt, plugged his ears and offered his shoulder for a makeshift rest.

The muzzle stabilized; both hunters took a breath and held it. The boy flipped off the safety; the buck heard the metallic click and looked at them. Its ears swept forward, neck craned; they had three seconds before it was gone. The buck was young, not stupid, its survival instincts having been honed by a short lifetime avoiding lions, coyotes, dog packs, poachers and Mexican-American vineyard workers. The rifle roared, the buck lurched and bounded away, its shoulder clamped tight.

"Good shot, son! Did you see him holding that shoulder? I'll bet we find him in a hundred yards or less."
His son feigned objectivity, but excitement bled through.
"Yeah; I held on his shoulder. You think he's down, dad?"
"Oh, if you had a steady sight picture, he's down, alright. We'll let him die in peace, then we'll go find him."

Ten yards from where the forked horn stood, they found splayed hoof prints in the oak duff. They trailed up the hill. Forty yards later the youth's first buck lay still in the meadow. Ted saw the mixture of emotion in AJ's eyes. Every hunter knows that moment, when a long-fantasized goal turns into hard-faced reality. The fanciful thrill of the chase collides head-on with the grim nature of killing an animal; what was once a beautiful, free roaming buck morphs into two cubic feet of freezer space; emotions run strong then. He gave his hunter's thank you prayer.

"Thank you, Lord, for giving us this fine animal, and for guiding the bullet to a clean, humane kill. Bless this meat, as fuel for our bodies. Amen."

Then he turned to the youth.
"You know son, a car could have killed it. Dogs could've hamstrung it in a dry gulch. Grape workers might have gut shot him, so it would crawl away and die a slow death in some deep ravine, where the wardens couldn't prosecute them for shooting it. Or this fine buck might have died from Blue Tongue or Chronic Wasting Disease. I'm sure glad it died a *swift humane death*, right here, aren't you?"

His son looked relieved, eyes pinned on the deer. Ted kept the emotional inertia going.
"Good! Now let's get the truck and get him home."

9

As they walked back, Ted couldn't resist the urge to put his arm around his only son, who was in that strange phase between youth and adulthood. For a change, he didn't object to the hug.

Five years later, AJ was a man. He'd learned countless outdoor lessons. He'd taken six straight bucks and one huge wild boar. All were one-shot kills. Ted was glad to see his teachings took root. He worked hard to avoid the slob hunter image that pervaded much of society.

Later he taught his daughter the same way, then spent his hunting time trying to get his kids in range of game. While it certainly was pleasant, it came at a price; it left no time for the archer to pursue trophy Blacktails with his bow. Still, he was glad for starting his kids out right. He vowed to catch up on his trophy hunting later.

But time is the enemy. His body was getting old. His shrinking window of opportunity forced him to do the unthinkable; to resort to technology.

In the last few years, Ted learned to fly model airplanes. Since his very first flights, he visualized a plane that could fly over animals without disturbing them, while a tiny camera spied on the critters.

He practiced until he thought he was good enough... or so he thought.

# Two...
## NAIVETE

The unseen sun's pastel rays filtered upward, over the eastern face of the coastal mountains adding color, if not heat, to the birthing day. It wouldn't be long before it blazed Ted, on the western face of a distant ridge.

He'd flown the Telemonster a few times; he was confident. Stable at slow speeds and capable of carrying huge payloads, it was perfect for his plan. He knew most of the bucks on the ranch, having watched them grow from fawns to trophies. The variations in their antlers were as familiar as a family member's smile.

Having never flown in steep hills before, he felt a certain nervous exhilaration, but forced himself to stick to the mundane pre-flight routine. He switched on the transmitter, then the receiver. The monitor on the transmitter powered up. Moving the right stick back and forth, a servo whirred and the elevator moved up and down.

He wiggled it right and left; predictably, another servo whirred as the ailerons moved up and down. A grin overtook him when he moved the left stick; the carburetor opened wide and closed, to the hum of a third servo. Finally, he wiggled it right and left; the fourth servo whirred and the rudder wagged right and left. He was good to go.

The monitor showed a monochromatic view of the dirt road in the foreground, bordered by tall wild oats and Harding Grass filled the tiny screen. The distant horizon showed as a series of mountain ranges fading to infinity.

Ted looked up from the monitor to catch the beautiful show of pastels, brilliantly displayed below his mountain peak. He spoke out loud, to drive his point home to himself.
*'Make damn sure; don't point her at the sun!'*

He imagined flying blind while the iris tried to adjust. Forcing his mind from the fantasy crash, he went back to the pre-flight.

11

He split the screen. On the left was the wing cam view, pointing down; just a dark blur since the dirt was too close. The right half gave the forward view.

Satisfied, he shut off the radio to save batteries. He visualized the lift-off, probably fifty feet downhill near a large meadow of tall wild oats; if need be, it would be a great place to put her down without much damage.

Choking the carb, he flipped the prop and saw fuel enter the fuel line. Next, he looked for buzzards. Somehow, they always showed up to soar with toy planes.
*'Climb for buzzards, dive for eagles.'*

Since the birds usually did the opposite, midairs could be avoided. Ted lit the glow plug, flipped the prop; the little four-stroke chugged out a peaceful idle, sipping tiny droplets of nitromethane, methanol and castor oil. He flipped a switch and she obediently went to 'half-flaps'.

After wiping nervous hands on his pants, Ted nudged the throttle, tapped right rudder to cancel torque, the propwash blew dust and gravel. In thirty feet, the eight-foot wing lifted the plane. Ted throttled back, trimming for low-speed flat circles. After a few passes, he felt confident enough to take his eyes off the plane and fly while using just the monitor image. It worked. Each time, he stared at the monitor longer, until he relaxed with this new twist; instrument only r/c flying.

Then he spotted a deer with the down-looking camera; small buck, bedded in the adjacent meadow. Engine vibration blurred the image, so he couldn't count points, but the buck was unconcerned with the buzzing mechanical insect, flying scant yards above him.

Ted let the plane roam a bit, down the canyon. His plane was soon 500 feet below him, and he hadn't even flown over the steep part yet. Although he'd hiked it for years, the airborne perspective was completely different. Ted was accustomed to the slow pace of hiking, but the terrain was going by so fast; he could barely think, much less orient.

The plane quickly reached the base of the canyon, out of sight. The camera was useless for orienting, since the monitor showed only a massive wall of green. Without the light blue horizon, it was impossible to determine if the plane was rising or descending. Of course, the engine gave off clues; rising pitch meant a dive while lowering pitch signals a climb. But the forest canopy absorbed the noise. His fantasy flight morphed into a nightmare; without a horizontal reference it was hopeless.

Fighting panic, Ted tried to recall the terrain down there; on the right, a down-sloping meadow of dry yellow wild oats; there would be room to turn around, if he got lucky.

The fuselage cam  revealed a bright opening on the right. Adding power, he banked right, gave it some up-stick to make a smooth turn. A left bank followed, to cancel the bank, completing the turn. A little up-stick trim for the climb; he hoped to have the plane back, with luck and no downdrafts..

Suddenly the monitor spun clockwise, alternating splotches of bright blue and dark green. Ted gave it down stick, added throttle and crossed the sticks; proper cure a spin, but it kept spinning. Soon the image showed only trees getting bigger and bigger. The image went gray when the plane crashed.

A distant bang drifted lazily up the canyon, but Ted was too disappointed to register it. Somewhere below him, a mile or more away, lay his expensive plane and gear; a gold plated needle in a huge, formidably rugged haystack.

After the shock passed, he recalled hearing a muffled bang; crash noise, probably filtered out on the way back up the canyon, playing out among the noise-dampening leaves, Harding Grass and poison oak.

He thought back; it was about ten seconds from the onscreen crash 'til he heard the bang. Sound travels roughly five seconds per mile; maybe two miles, as the crow flies. Of course, he really didn't know how many seconds passed; he'd been too distracted to pay attention.

Morgan cursed his foolishness; a few more practice flights over flat terrain might have prevented the crash. Failing that, at least it would have crashed where he could find his gear; instead, he faced losing it all to the craggy draws.

Ted swapped his jogging shoes for his hiking boots and his good shirt for his friendly old camouflage shirt. He grabbed his backpack; He never went into the woods without it.

Over the years, he'd been stranded a few times, which highlighted the need for certain items in his backpack. It always held; pistol, brick of ammo, space blanket, rope, first aid, jerky, skinning knife and fire starting kit, which was almost overkill, but when it comes to making fire, there's no such thing. He packed steel wool, waxed matches, magnesium striker and six thick candles.

The last staples were; collapsible cup, small mess kit and of course the most used item of all... ½ roll of toilet paper, easily accessible. Furthest from his spine, his folding shovel formed a hard edge to the back of the pack.

He carried seasonal items, too. It was archery season, so he had four modular arrows of his design; cut in half, fitted with roll pins for backpacking ease. Merely by joining the halves together on the roll pin, four lethal arrows were instantly ready to fly. A tin box held razor sharp broadheads, packed in oiled-soaked paper towel.

The left side pocket held the spotting scope, the right a slingshot and marbles for driving game and topo map. Thirty years of knocking about the woods taught a thing or two about staying alive.

Ted fished out the map, out of habit. Truth is, he knew the country like the back of his hand. The map was already folded to 'his' hunting ranch.

Ted refolded the map to a clean section, neighboring property where he didn't have permission to hunt. All he knew was what his roving eyes told him from afar. For years, he studied and fantasized about the thickly forested forests across the fence, where the bucks were always bigger and the grass greener.

He dreamed of killing "Mr. Big". Three times that big old buck showed on Ted's land, but the buck always sensed Ted before he could loose an arrow into those massive ribs. "Big" would only come out for does during the rut.

He almost wished he'd followed Jo's advice and brought her cell phone. At least he could call the property owners who lived hundreds of miles away, but he HATED cell phones; besides, he didn't have their number... Even if he did, what would he say; 'Gee, I was flying over your land with a spy plane, can I please go get it?"

He scanned the map; four steep slopes comprised the area where his plane crashed. The contour lines were practically touching, indicating hellishly steep slopes. Hopefully he would be able to spot it from his perch on legal land, since both ridges faced each other like skyscrapers.

Ted locked his truck, stowed the map, slung the pack and trudged down the meadow. The bedded buck jumped up and ran uphill. Sixty yards out, he looked back, snorted a few times to warn other deer, then fled.

The slope grew steeper. The grass got taller. Soon the sickening odor of Tarweed coated his throat just like the sticky plants clung to his pant legs. With his ears tuned for rattlers in the deep grass, he scanned the nearby trails for fresh sign of game. As long as his legs were paying the bill, the eyes would reap the data. Soon he spotted fresh hog sign. 'Plane's not goin' anywhere; may as well scout it.'

On the small white oak tree, waist high, was a fresh tusk cut decorated with regurgitated foliage, deposited by the breeding-class boar. The message?
'I'm a real stud, eating well. You could do worse than me.'

Or so Ted liked to think. Who knows *WHAT* pigs think?

The closest spring was six hundred yards downhill, meaning the pig carried wiregrass chum, marking trunks as he went. Ted found the clear hoof print;
*'If you're smaller, stay away. If you're a sow... bring it!'*
He put his nose to the track. He couldn't resist the sweet smell of free-ranging wild boar; like a cross between maple syrup and fresh-roasted almonds.

He started hiking again, to the edge of 'his' property line, sweating hard, although it wasn't much past sunrise. His shirt was soaked in sweat. Sweat trickled down his ass crack. His eyebrows dripped sweat. He dropped his pack and sat in the deep shade of a large White Oak. From the edge of the cliff, he could see the opposing ridge.

Pulling out his binoculars, he began the search. Always the same glass-search; quick-scan the area for movement. Go upper left, search field of view without moving the glass. Go right one f.o.v.; repeat, left to right, top to bottom, reading a big book. After the whole slope was scanned, repeat, since game often moved when the sun shifts.

It was the last place you'd want to hunt for a full-scale Cessna, let alone a tiny model. He was glad he packed the transmitter along, for an old modeler's trick. His thoughts were suddenly busted; just as he started his second search pattern, something seemed wrong.

A buck crashed out of the brushy creek bottom 500 yards below. His ears were pinned back; it headed straight up the hill, without using a deer trail. The huge stag didn't bound, it plodded, head down, like a tired old packhorse. Its breathing was labored and heavy. He was a magnificent three-pointer with a heavy rack, blocky body and short legs; hunters call it a 'brush buck'.

The deer headed straight for Ted. Soon he got in the shade, less than three yards from Ted's outstretched legs. His withers lathered, he breathed hard, with his head turned to the back trail.

16

Ted had never seen a deer breathe so hard. Its ears strained for clues. Both eyes locked its back-trail. Wind carried his scent to Ted; metallic, rank, adrenaline, saddle soap, death. *'No wonder they elude me; they play for higher stakes.'*

Finally the ears swiveled. He turned his head toward the searing heat of the open meadow, which Ted crossed an hour earlier. The buck gingerly stepped over Ted's legs, like two big slippery roots, then walked into the sunshine, pointing its ears back for any sound of pursuers. Once downwind, it caught Ted's stench and instantly plunged into a head-down, weary jog out of sight. Ted couldn't wait to tell his family about the encounter.

Then he heard a distant howl, as he'd suspected. He rummaged for his pistol and the brick of ammo. He loaded the clip, slammed it home and chambered a round; a familiar movement, with a favorite pistol.

They came on at a steady trot. The lead dog, a large Collie bitch with a beautiful shiny pelt, scent-trailed the stag. Behind her was a half-grown Rotweiler. Its body language said the Rot was probably on its first deer run.

Pack rage consumed both dogs. Eager to catch and hamstring the deer, they were totally unaware of the deadly ambush. The trotted into the shade, stopped and sniffed his tarsal scent barely six yards from Ted.

The sights settled on the Collie's chest. He pressed the trigger, then swung on the Rot as the Collie yipped with surprise. The young Rot hesitated long enough for the sights to find his neck. The second bullet dropped the dog without a whimper. Ted swung on the Collie, already running for her life.

Howling and snapping at the lung wound, she sprinted for the open meadow. Ted led the dog two feet and started shooting. The first round kicked up dust behind, sending the canine into full sprint. He swung the sights twelve feet in front and kept firing, taking a larger lead with each shot.

At eighty yards, he connected, sending the deer killer into a dust-raising somersault. Ted reloaded while running.

He found the Collie howling, spinning circles on its side in the Harding Grass. Ted lined up his sights and waited for the right moment. He could hear gurgling and saw a spray of bright orange, oxygen-rich pulmonary blood; the dog would be dead in minutes, but that was too long to let any animal suffer, including deer-chasing dogs. She finally held still; Ted put one through its ear and the dog went limp; she had hamstrung her last pregnant doe.

He hated killing dogs, but when a dog runs deer, it runs them to death. He turned the bitch over and found its red anodized aluminum heart-shaped symbol; *I heart Fifi.*

Fifi was well-groomed, save for a few foxtails and Beggar's Lice. He slit the paunch; sure enough, she had a belly full of dog food. Her nails were done. Someone spent a lot of money on Fifi.

Ted went back to the Rot... it dropped so fast that its mouth was stuffed with leaves. Ted found a bloodless hole just in front of the left ear. He was glad it didn't suffer. The young teenager had a full belly, but no collar or tags. A Yellow Jacket alighted, its mandibles rapidly cutting off a chunk of tongue before it buzzed toward the ground hive.

He slung his pack and started hiking, thinking of the buck's fate. With that much lather, the outcome was dubious. If he could hole up somewhere, he'd make it. But if the buck had to run again from lions, ATV's or more dogs, it would die, but the real cause of death would be Fifi and the Rot, let out by their owners for an 'innocent' romp in the woods.

Soon the steep trail and searing sunshine had him aching for a drink of cool water. He practically jogged the last hundred yards to the creek bed, but it was dry, save for a few holes of still water under the overhanging rocks and cutbanks; stagnant, a last resort. He trudged down the creek, looking for any wet tributary. The second confluence yielded a faint trickling sound, just as a downdraft brought the scent; bugs, frogs, moss.

He climbed the steep, overgrown gully; fifty yards uphill, in the shaded hollow of the past winter's landslide, a pencil-lead sized stream seeped out of the rocks. Running down an exposed muddy poison oak root, the water came to the end and fell eighteen inches, into a pool no bigger than a saucer and certainly no deeper. The clear water didn't run off; it soaked into the gravel, never to be seen again, before it ended in the Pacific Ocean forty miles to the west.

Ted placed his collapsible cup in the stream arc. He sat back to cool his back against the damp, mossy earth. He studied the wall, wondering if the spring would slide closed again next wet season.

His eyes went to the thin stream of liquid life, running from the bowels of the earth, down one tiny root. He was glad he didn't disturb it or he'd have muddy water laced with God-knows what kind of root-living critters.

While waiting for the cup to fill, he munched on a piece of jerky; it was especially good, since it came from a buck his daughter shot. He wondered if he'd ever have such a sweet span of life as when his kids had lived at home. Good times never last.

The cup brimmed over. Ted sucked it down eagerly and replaced the empty cup in the trickle… promising that he'd sip the next one. Ted thought again of the dogs. He disliked killing pets, but it was one of the landowner's rules; *'kill any fuckin' roaming dogs and cats; I can't afford losin' any more stock!'*

He recalled a biologist's report on two radio-collared housecats in Maine; averaging thirteen kills per night, per cat; moles, voles, shrews, amphibians, threatened owls and songbirds, game birds, lizards, snakes and gophers.

More coveys of quail are lost to night roaming house cats than to human hunters. One study estimated 1/3 of the mortality rate of quail are due to house cats and feral cats. Kill rate is higher for wild turkey chicks, which are easier for a cat to spot.

Domestic dogs kill fawns, lambs, calves, sheep, raccoons, opossums, rabbits and wild pigs. In one study three radio-collared suburban dogs in Hollywood killed forty-three feral pigs, seven deer, one cow, two sheep and five skunks in one summer. Considering that these dogs only got out an average of three nights per week, the projected biota impact was staggering.

So, as much as Ted disliked it, when he saw dogs running game or livestock, he would try to stop them. He'd tried once before to inform suburbanites when he returned a hound caught hamstringing a pregnant doe in a dry creek bed. All he got for his effort was some new-age psychobabble about Fido's right to run free, a happy spirit and all that bullshit. They never even thanked him for bringing Fido home.

Apparently, the pregnant doe's rights weren't an issue for the self-described animal lovers. They didn't want to hear about Fido and his two buddies slashing her tendons, eliminating all chance of escape, while they tore off chunks of living flesh. Finally, after an hour or more of harassing her, they rushed in, ripped out the throat of the still-living creature... so that even its last breaths are painful to take.

Most dog packs won't even eat the kill... blood-crazed, they roam to find fresh scent, repeating the macabre scene several times a night. So Ted simply did what many landowners, hunters, deputies, county trappers and game wardens do when they spot game-killing dogs; shoot and keep quiet about it.

The cup filled. He no longer felt thirst, but he'd soon be in the blazing sun again, lungs burning, sweat dripping, so he drank it. This cup tasted not so good. In fact, he could taste critters and flavors.

Ted slung the pack and emerged from the cool grotto into the dry creek and burning sunshine. The contrast of California summer weather hit him; one minute cool and damp, the next, burning hot. He trudged down the main creek, already longing for the cool, sweet water and peaceful music of that grotto.

The canyon walls rose so steeply from the serpentine creek bed that Ted couldn't see the mountaintops two thousand feet above. His plane was up there somewhere, waiting for him. Ted picked the second ridge. He started climbing, slipping, sliding, grabbing roots and vines. He made forty vertical yards in ten minutes. It was always steepest down near the creek bed; so steep that he used the uphill side of a tree to brace his body so he could relax his tired muscles. His lungs burned, pulse pounded like a jackhammer; *"Gettin' too old for this crap"*; he'd been saying it since he was 23, But now it was less joke and more reality.

Regaining his wind, he turned on the transmitter. The video monitor came up, showing dirt and leaves on the forest floor; *'Good; one camera's not busted.'* Ted tried the rudder servo and listened for its whir. Nothing. Next, he went side-hill. Every fifty feet, he'd trigger a servo. He got lucky on the seventh pass; a metallic whirring, higher up the slope.

Climbing up another fifty yards, he waited for his pulse to stop pounding, so he could hear. The whirring was close; the fuselage hung by its tail, thirty feet up a Chinquapin, overhanging a huge poison oak bush on a cliff. The limbs were too thin to climb. He rummaged through his pack and came out with his trusty slingshot, assembled an arrow and tied his cord to it. Aiming high to compensate for the heavy cord, he let it fly, but was too low. Three tries later, his arrow struck the light balsa with a crisp crunch.

When he wrangled the plane down through the limbs he was glad; thanks to his foam packing, both cameras, radio gear and servos still worked.

The engine and tank were gone. That was odd. Ted missed several small round holes in the fabric. If only the spars were there to tell the story, he would have recognized the true cause of the crash.

Since there was no way he could get through the thick brush with the big fuselage intact, Ted broke it up, scavenged servos, radio gear, camera, and pushrods. To hobbyists a crash was a great excuse to build a new plane.

The balsa fuselage went into a cleared bare dirt spot. With one match, his beautiful six-month wintertime building project was history; soon all that remained was a pair of sooty monokote smoke curls rising through the canopy.

When the fire was dead out, he started hurrying down the treacherous ridge. The sun was low; it would be dark soon in the deep canyon; playing hopscotch with nocturnal rattlers was never much fun.

After twenty minutes of kicking, beating and crawling through the thick understory, he emerged in the middle of the creek bed right next to his little grotto, where the pencil-thin stream of water still beckoned. Ted was thirsty again, but he wanted to get back to the truck before dark. He stood up, stretched his aching back and groaned.

Just then, a rock exploded, sending shards of rock spatter everywhere. One shard stung his hand. A loud, sharp clap accompanied the fragments. Ted had never been on the business end of bullets before, so it took a second to register. Three more bullets sprayed the creek bottom in staccato fashion before his legs got moving. He sprinted down the creek bed. Bullets struck right where he'd just stood. His adrenaline kicked in; eyes wide open, legs at full speed, he flew down the creek bed.

Just before a bend in the creek, another shower of bullets threw rock fragments and bullet shrapnel against his legs. One shot grazed the right side of his head, spinning him headlong into the river bottom. He fell over some logs that marked a small tributary. The bullets kept coming, even though his unconscious brain didn't hear them.

He dreamed of fishing with his son, of shooting with Jo at an archery tournament. Then he saw Kelly, learning to shoot her first rifle. Her shots seemed far away. Then they got louder. Then Ted came to; the shots were still coming!

Ted lifted his face, spitting blood and sand; bleeding heavily, but his skull felt intact. The bullets kept colliding with the log behind him. Then there was silence.

Someone started shouting foreign words. He heard the unmistakable ratchet-like sounds of a clip being dumped. Figuring they were reloading, he gambled and sprinted uphill in the dry tributary. 'F*uck! I'm bein' hunted!'* Running uphill, blindly for another fifty yards, before he came to his senses; '*I'm the buck now... Bucks don't panic!'*

He cupped his ears and pointed both stethoscopes toward his back-trail. Sure enough, loud, confident voices; 'Mira, you heet heem! He bleed plenty; we find heem dead, up thees draw, no?'

Then gravel grinding under hard-soled boots; they were blood-trailing him. He looked down and saw why; his head wound was a geyser. He tore off both shirtsleeves and fashioned a bandana; he'd be tougher to track.

He climbed ninety more yards before he found a bedding trail. He continued past it for fifteen yards, allowing his footprints to show. Then he side-hopped into the dry oak duff, back-tracking to the bedding trail.

Bedding trails usually led to thick cover. A buck can bed there, safe from predators. Once danger is detected, a few quick bounds in the requisite direction keeps him alive. That's exactly what Ted needed.
Walking gingerly for eighty yards sidehill, he found a large Cedar thicket; nothing would get through it without making beaucoup noise.

It was a wild boar's winter nest... The pig rooted a flat spot, roughly six by ten feet, with just a slight slope for drainage. Then he arranged several dozen fresh-cut cedar boughs, needles pointing up. Even during the heaviest rains the boar enjoyed dry, soft bedding. It gave a good defensive berth while remaining totally hidden. If it was good enough for the boar, it was good enough for Ted.

He placed his pack as a bullet stop, hoping it wouldn't have to do that job. While listening for danger he deftly loaded the clip, worked the top round into the chamber and topped off the mag with another round. He didn't want to die for lack of that eleventh round. The tiny .22 felt comforting; he was outgunned for sure, but least he had some sort of a weapon.

Next order of business; information. He put his flashlight inside the pack and turned it on, instantly confirming his hunch; TWO BULLET HOLES lit up.

He found the spent bullets, which barely penetrated his folding shovel; shallow rifling, flat bases, blunted tips and limited penetration pointed to a machine pistol... an Uzi or something like that. He didn't know much about machine pistols; he was a hunter, not a fuckin' gangster. Clearly, his pursuers weren't poachers or pissed-off farmers chasing trespassers.

He might be near someone's pot patch or meth lab. He started thinking about the strange words; *"Maybe it was Portuguese or Spani..."*

Suddenly, the lethal sound of a boot snapping twigs interrupted his thoughts. His heart raced. He gripped the pistol and fought the urge to get up and run blindly away. He knew what old Black-tail bucks know; you move, you die... It's as simple as that.

The man was very good with his feet. He'd only made half the noise Ted made while climbing the same slope, and Ted did it in brighter daylight.

Ted rested the pistol on the pack; he could clip the whole magazine without moving anything but his trigger finger, but he didn't want to give his position away; he still didn't know how many men were after him.

Despite his predicament, he couldn't help but marvel at his enemy's stealth. The trail was littered with twigs, leaves and crispy pine cones. Finally the silhouette showed against the lighter sky; tall and lean. Some type of assault rifle. Moved like an upright snake, silent, smooth, feet feeling for twigs before committing weight, perfect balance. Tai chi on a deer trail.

Ted wanted to end the tension with a volley of hollow points, center mass. But when he transitioned the sights onto the silhouette his sights disappeared. Ted practiced by getting a good sight picture in the fading daylight, then swung onto the oncoming villain. The first shot would be to the head; he'd drop instantly, perhaps without returning fire.

Ted abhorred headshots on game, but this was a man, hell-bent on killing him. If he had to shoot, he didn't want a lung-shot enemy spraying slugs before he bled out. NO, a head shot it would be; after that first pop, he would pepper the falling torso.

The stalker closed to ten yards, nine, then hesitated, eight yards away; he man turned, but in the failing light, Ted couldn't tell if he turned toward or away. He watched the thug's shoulder; if it twitched, Ted would kill him. If it didn't, he was looking downslope for his buddies. Ted felt strangely calm, holding this man's life in his right fingertip. This man would drop like a stone and Ted would live.

His scent wafted to Ted; the sweet, pungent b.o. of a bar fly, mixed with a whiff of diesel. A voice rang from below. "Paco, venga aqui."
The silhouette turned and padded back down the trail. He didn't give away his location by answering. He didn't go crashing down the ridge. He simply ceased his forward

efforts. It was unnerving; *'Paco, huh?'* He's *dangerous, but the other guy; stupid and aggressive.'*

It was ten minutes before Ted eased his grip on the pistol. He got very sleepy from the head wound. In spite of trying not to, Ted fell into a deep sleep.

Awaking with a start, he looked at the sky. The moon was down. Stars were getting dim; about 4:00 AM. He was stiff and cold, since he passed out before pulling out his space blanket. Fishing it out, it helped bar the chilling downdrafts. He marveled at the toughness of the boar that lived there without blankets, fire or long johns.

Images of Ted's old chess teacher popped up; *"You always have options... maybe not good ones, but options, just the same."* After fifteen years of whipping Ted's ass, he passed on to the big chess game in the clouds. Ted recalled the old fart's image; tousled hair, red and black flannel shirt, hand-rolled cigarette and the ever-present whiskey-and-water. The next line was always delivered in the same preacher-like cadence...
*"Even a bad move creates a countermove."*
Ted never met anyone else with Joe's clarity; and his lessons were never just about chess. Ted thought options.

He pondered escape, using darkness for cover, but in rough terrain he could twist an ankle or break a leg; he'd be dead and buried by noon. Besides, any trail made in the dark would be child's play for Paco to follow in daylight.

Option two, stay put; a good plan, except they might come back with dogs. They'd sniff out his lair, then stand back and firestorm the cedars. He wouldn't stand a chance.

He considered starting a forest fire; in full-alert status of fire season, CDF would spot it almost instantly. A helo would bring firefighters within minutes. It was a tantalizing option, but the killers could show up, cut him to ribbons and be gone; the firefighting crew carried no firearms. They could end up getting shot, left to burn in the fire Ted started.

Option Four, attack; held the element of surprise. Maybe he could kill them before they woke up. But a retired deputy buddy once told him about patches that were laced with booby traps. Besides, Ted had no idea where they were or how many men there might be.

A band of coyotes burst into song from the creek bed below, hunting mice and frogs, goosing each other and having a high old time. Then their song tone changed to excitement; obviously they found a trail that would end up good. He thought of the dead Rot, perhaps a mile uphill from them. Just then, the doggies got a whiff of man scent. They got quiet. Five minutes later the songdogs opened up near the Rot carcass; it would be whistle-clean by sunrise.

Joe always said to look at his opponent's pieces... They spied a man with a pack. They shot him. Perhaps they asumed Ted was a rip-off artist, sneaking through the timber, while foolishly searching for his damned plane.

Ted's concentration broke when the distant coyotes began snarling over the choicest bites; hamstrings, thighs, and back-straps. Soon the alpha male would drive them off. The subordinates would get the Collie's scent. Sure enough, a fainter yelp came; dinnertime in Lassieville.

For all of his thinking, no option seemed right. He was a hunter, not a chess master. Finally, he decided to act like a a wounded boar; head for the steepest, nastiest cover... Only one place came to mind; Radical Ridge.

Radical was named for its topographical distinction. Nobody went there; not hunters, pot growers, not even firefighters. It was steep, brushy and devoid of human interest. A firefighter lost his life there. Administrative decisions were made. They'd rather watch an impromptu enhancement fire than lose another good man to that steep, rugged hellhole.

He felt better, just thinking about Radical, about two miles away. The first draw was a hell of a climb, about a mile long; *"If they follow me there, they'll pay for it!"* He was confident they'd never go there... but then, up until yesterday, he was confident he'd never get shot, either.

Another of Joe's timeworn lessons invaded his thoughts. *'Count your pieces; even a pawn can become a Queen'*

He upended his backpack. The first aid kit tempted him, but removing his shirtsleeves could instigate new bleeding; a dead giveaway on the dusty trail. Then, too, white gauze would make a great aiming point.

The airplane gear caught his attention. He resisted an impulse to toss the shit; *'it might be useful.'*

He turned on the camera and monitor; he'd purchased it for its alleged one-candlepower capability. He panned; surprisingly, easier to see than with the naked eye. Ted reloaded the pack and stepped onto the deer trail. Gingerly placing his feet while watching the viewfinder; *'I've invented 'instrument-only walking'*

He picked his way down the slope to where he'd been shot. It was too deep and dark for even the one-candlepower iris. Switching it off to save batteries, The hunter began his least-favored locomotion; 'poke and hope'... poke a foot somewhere, hope you don't find a rattler, scorpion, hole, cliff or pissed-off boar.

He didn't dare use his flashlight; parts of the creek were visible from above. Any half-assed rifleman could kill him. Besides, it would blow his night vision; it was shin-bruising, track-making travel, but at least he covered the open parts before any sentinel had enough light to kill him.

He got to the trail for Radical just as the first spires of light pointed upwards across the heavens. He continued down the creek for two hundred yards, making sure to leave obvious prints in sandy spots. Then he rock-hopped back on the far side, leaving no prints.

When he returned to the turnoff, he lashed an oblong rock that looked like a grinding pestle. Considering the artifact-rich area, it might have been one, save for the slightly unworn look. Ted lobbed the rock over a Bay limb; it swung back, he grabbed it. Holding both ends, he alley-ooped out of the creek bed without leaving footprints.

He hurried up the dry creek bed, hopping from one rock to the next. He made fifty yards under the Bays before the ravine got too steep for human travel. Switching to the human trail, he started to relax, thinking his backtracking trick was overkill; then he thought of Paco's stealth in the twigs and cracklies. To move so quietly amongst the cornflakes was impossibly tough. He kept hiking the steep, ball-busting trail.

The light grew with each passing minute. Soon he was high enough to be seen from a great distance; easy prey for an average rifleman. There was nothing to do but keep walking slowly, so not to draw a human eye, and hope to get away with it. All he had for confidence was the distance he'd traveled and the early hour; hopefully they were still asleep. Still, going so slow and exposed was agoninzing.

Soon his pulse redlined, forcing scalp bleeding again. It became a ritual; step, swipe, wipe, rest. Fighting nausea, blood loss and pain, he finally made Radical's highest slopes; so steep that it seemed even the sun didn't want to climb them.

In the comparative darkness of the cathedral like serpentine sheers, he felt slightly better; he was hiding above, in the dark and his enemy would come from below, in full daylight. He worked up the steep talus slopes for another hundred yards, kicking shale and logs loose, in a continuous dust-rising mini-avalanche, lungs burning, sweat pouring. On the good side, if they came, they would also be busy grasping for roots, sucking air and slipping in the loose scree; IF they came. He prayed they wouldn't.

It was a steep sonofabitch, but the extreme pitch was also a great equalizer. If they came, they'd be vulnerable to a man already dug-in like a tick on a hound. Ted resolutely placed one foot in front of the other, churning the last few yards. A movement made him flinch; a small bat, darting and among the low weeds.

The bat served as a temporary diversion from his agony. His legs were pure fire and his concentration all but gone, so he pulled up and rested his aching back against a live oak sapling and watched the late-shift bat. By that hour, most bats were hanging in rocky crags and tree trunks. A young one, no doubt. It flew close to the ground, obviously preying on mosquitoes, which meant water nearby.

He looked back down his back trail. It looked like he'd climbed it with a bulldozer. At that instant, another of Joe's lessons came home; *'Sometimes the most obvious trap works best.'*
He hoped Joe was right. In any case, there was no hiding that trail.

He'd taken several bucks on ridges this steep, where the buck thought altitude meant safety. The tactic worked great against lions, three hundred yards of altitude wouldn't mean jack shit, once bullets started flying.

Then something about the shale and buckeyes jogged his memory; twenty years ago he blood-trailed a feral sow across this same slope; everything was green and wet then, but now in the dry season, it looked very different, bone-dry and straw yellow. He spotted the black oak where he'd hung the sow to dress it. It was taller.

In spite of his predicament, memories came back to scold him; a badly placed arrow, loosed at the worst moment, resulted in a long hard blood trail in wicked terrain. Before it was over, he'd learned more than he ever wanted to know about Radical's extreme terrain and hiding places for pissed off, wounded pigs.

Then he remembered a tiny spring, just a short climb above. He half-walked, half-crawled, head throbbing. The sun was becoming a major factor. He spotted the telltale army-green wiregrass bunches. As Ted made the tiny meadow, his throat was on fire. He approached the pool lined in blue clay, mashed into a smooth rounded bowl from countless wild hogs and bears wallowing.

He resisted the urge to sink his face in the cool, clear water; it held germs, parasites and creepy crawlers. Instead, he searched higher in the near-vertical rocks behind the wallow; water seeped out of the rocks, then trickled to the wallow below. He sucked the rivulet like communion wine. Then he waited for it to refill.

He recalled a tale of a famous hunter who drank bad water; lost his hair and teeth, three weeks in the hospital, barely survived. Ted had swallowed some nasty water down through the years, but never had a problem... still, he played the percentages. As thirst gradually abated, the wallow, which first looked like Mecca, lost its appeal. Then it occurred to him; if his pursuers climbed the ridge in the scorching mid-day heat, the wallow would be fantastic bait.

The mountains started working their magic on the hunter; soon it seemed unlikely they would follow him so high and so hard, in familiar old hunting ground. He removed his bandage and soaked it in the seep. The wound quit bleeding and the cool water felt great. As Ted soaked the shirtsleeve again, he noticed a big bear track in the wallow; "What a great place for a bear. Maybe got a den nearby'...

Just then, a movement caught his eye; too far away to make out, so he fished his spotting scope out and rested it on his pack. His hopes sank. A mile and a half and two ridges away were three men hunkered over his trail. He tried to quit shaking the scope, but he couldn't. Again he was the hunted instead of the hunter. It really sucked.

Three...
TRAILS

Paco slunk into camp like an egg-sucking dog. He had an unnerving skulking way about him. His only saving grace was that he saved Sal's ass, twice. Still, he watched the bastard like his daughter's first date. There was just no trusting the slinky greaser.

Paco rested his rifle against the door jamb and oiled onto the chewed-up sofa, grabbing a cold beer and buttered tortilla on the way. He never asked, either; that always rubbed Sal the wrong way. The boss was half drunk as usual.
"So what the fuck were y'all plinkin' at?"
Nobody wanted to be the bearer of bad news. They feared Sal's flashbulb temper. Finally Wes chanced it.
"Ah, we busted some caps at a rip-off, down by Dooley crik... chill out, will ya?"
Sal's half-closed lids opened wide.
"RIP OFF? ARE YA SURE it wasn't a fuckin' COP?"
Wes knew better than to disagree, and had the scars to prove it. Clearly unflinching of Sal's power, Paco spoke up.

"Zhou ever see a cop goes alone? Zhou ever seen a policia who goes without how you say, *BACKUP?* Hees no cop, man."

They lived in fear of feds, but quaked in greater fear of Victor Saldivar; he and his muscle could do what the cops only wished they could do. Paco was a man of few words, but had to reinforce his opinion to his inebriated boss.

"No fue policia... porque there's three reasons; first, he deedn't shoot back, and cops always shoot back, no? Segundo, perdoname, second, Eeef he WAS a cop, we'd have chingado cops all over thees rock. No, thees puto ees no federale. Hee's a reep off"

Sal softened, thinking it over...
"Unless you killed the fucker... if he died before he radioed it in, he could still be a cop... *VER-FUCKIN'-DAD?*"

32

Wes chimed in, eager to placate.

"Yeah, boss, I hit him good. There was blood all over the fuckin' creek. I saw him go down, but he ran off when I switched clips; we'll find him tomorrow, dead as a wedge, FUCKIN' A!"

"You wounded him AND *DIDN'T GO AFTER HIS ASS?*"

Now they knew it; they wouldn't mention the spy plane they shot down or he'd go ballistic. Tequila always made him unpredictably twitchy.

Paco eyed his half-drunk boss; he could kill him easy and take over the deal, but he didn't want to settle for such a small piece of the American pie. He'd been in this country for four months, but had seen enough to want more.

"He deedn't go far. Heem bleed purty good. I teen we fin' heem tomorrow, with his ojos like thees..."

He flopped on his back on the shack floor, arms and legs pointing to the sky and forced his abdomen to a bloated posture. He puffed his eyes and tongue out. All three laughed deliriously. With the break in tension, they smoked some weed and hit the sack. The cabin smelled like a locker room.

The terrible trio awoke before dawn. After a quick snack from last night's leftovers, they grabbed their weapons and headed down to finish off the rip-off artist. Paco had his trusty AK-47; Wes left his machine pistol, opting to carry his man-killer Browner 12 gauge with the sear worked to fire full-auto. Meanwhile, Sal carried an AR-16, in .223.

But the most important weapon was Heidi; part pit bull, part Rot, some German Shepherd thrown in for good measure, 90 pounds of tooth and muscle. One time near another patch, she caught a large teenage boy fishing in a stream, had most of the youth reduced to living hamburger by the time the men caught up with her. After they killed and buried him, Heidi got to play with her ball. This morning, she sensed it; she might get to play with her ball again.

They picked up the trail Paco aborted the night before. But before they got to the boar's nest, Paco saw one of his footprints. Imprinted over his track was Ted's track, pointed in the opposite direction. Paco was impressed.

"Boss—thees ees no ordinary gringo; Heee's a hunter."

"Bullshit... no hunter would hunt this steep shit when he can shoot all the deer he wants over on those easy slopes. Let's go kill him, if he ain't dead already."

"Hisso'kay... whatever u say, boss."

Heidi squirmed and struggled at her leash; all she needed was freedom. An hour of tracking put them dead center in Ted's spotting scope.

Ted tried to steady the scope, but his nerves and the shimmering morning heat waves made it almost pointless. Images wavered, like they were at the bottom of a pool of rippling water. During the heat shimmer, Ted could gain no information, so he just stayed on the trio; when breezes cleared the shimmer, the trio looked as clear as a postcard.

Seeing the dog straining at its leash turned his guts to jelly. All of his backtracking effort was wasted; the dog would find him fast. His nuts climbed into his guts while he fought panic.

Suddenly he felt an overwhelming urge to defecate; then a plan popped into his head. He hurried sidehill on the game trail, past the wallow. Thirty yards further, he found the ambush site, a small grove of young oaks with a dry gulch coursing through it. In the wet-season it was a gushing torrent, roaring straight downhill. A pile of dry logs crammed against the oaks by some ancient, heavy deluge.

Ted assembled an arrow, tipped it with a broadhead, grabbed his airplane gear and headed for the logjam. He lashed the slingshot to a log, and a servo above it. He hid the receiver and battery out of sight. Then he pierced the sling to allow a push rod to thread through it. He rigged the rod to the servo, drew the slingshot and cocked the sling.

Ted dropped his pants and crapped a huge pile, three yards in front of the arrowhead. He triggered the radio. The empty slingshot fired perfectly. Then he loaded the arrow, positioned the camera and checked the monitor; wallow in left background, shit-pile center-stage. Then he scrawled a message in the wallow clay.

Finally he yielded to the strong urge to climb up, up, away from the danger. He climbed until his lungs turned to fire, toward the jagged top of Radical. He climbed like an adrenaline-charged animal, primal fear driving him like nothing else could. He made it to a little flat rock, about two feet across; a perfect sit-down on an otherwise impossibly steep slope. He plunked his ass down and sucked air.

Once his breathing normalized, Ted turned sidehill and crossed over to get to the other side of the razorback. The far slope was almost vertical, with just enough brush to stop a careless hiker from falling nine hundred feet straight down. Slipping, sliding, raising dust and grabbing brush, he struggled to stay upright.

Finally there was a small shaded flat spot under a scrub oak; pawed out by countless high country bucks, just big enough to sit in, without having to fight the slope. Ted felt glad to have such camouflage working for him; late morning sun at his back, thick cover. It couldn't have been a more perfect hiding spot, except for the approaching killers... And their strike dog.

The perch overlooked the creek bottom, some six hundred yards away, almost directly under him. He took out the transmitter and binoculars. The trio was out of sight, so they had to be close to the turn for Radical Ridge.

The dog hit the clearing below in the creek bed.
*'Oh, SHIT, they turned the dog loose!'*

Heidi caught his scent and shot up the path to Radical; out of sight, thanks to the intervening mountain ridge. Ted turned on the transmitter and waited for the video monitor to power up. Heidi came on at a trot. She stopped at the wallow long enough to lap up some water. Then she bee-lined straight down Ted's ambush, stopping to sniff the shit.

Ted triggered left rudder on his transmitter... Nothing. He triggered right rudder. He couldn't see the arrow fly, but the dog flinched and spun around twice, biting at the wound. With her tail between her legs, Heidi sprinted off downhill, hell-bent for her masters. A dust cloud rose from the steep slope.

The dog galloped sixty yards down-slope before succumbing to the scalpel-sharp blades. Her momentum and the steep slope sent the corpse tumbling another three hundred yards before it came to rest against a Black Oak. The arrow caught the dog through the hips, severing bladder, common iliac artery and vein. The running motion helped the blades to excoriate a hole the size of a man's fist. Heidi had killed her last teenager.

After making certain that the dog didn't return, he switched off the transmitter to save batteries. Ted fervently prayed they'd lose his tracks in the rocky creek bed and leave him alone. Just as he finished his prayer the men appeared in the creek side.

Sal led, right past the turn-off for Radical Ridge. Wes followed. Paco was about to, but spotted Heidi's tracks. They had been first wet, but they already looked like old, dried piss stains.
"Amigos thees way... perhaps she smell something, eh?"
Sal spoke loudly, to reinforce leadership.
"Alright boys, let's go see what she's after; we'll come back and work this trail if it don't pan out."
Wes didn't like it.
"Hey, boss... we don't ALL need to go, do we? I mean, here's his tracks, goin' right down the fuckin' creek; Heidi could be after a motherfuckin' pig... or some such."

"Mebbe so, but we're stayin' together. The sooner we kill this fucker, the sooner we get back to work."

Ted could hear their voices, but not words. They felt secure enough to speak out loud.

*'They think I'm unarmed; hide that ace 'til I can play it.'*

Ted saw old deer scat in the gravel. It boosted his morale to know his instincts were in line with the masters of evasion. An idea popped into his head; Black-tailed deer loved the old button-hook.

When the stalkers went out of sight around the sharp ridgeline, Ted began slipping, sliding and falling down the sheer slope. His precious altitude, paid for with all that pain, was shucked in a few minutes of near-vertical slippage.

Soon he arrived, scratched and bruised, right where the thugs had just stood while conspiring to kill him. While they climbed, swore and sucked air, he would be doing something else. He smiled, thinking about the pain Radical was about to administer to those assholes.

At first he thought of making a bee-line for his truck. But the dog got his thinking right; if it was still alive, it could easily outrun him. Then too, he didn't know if other men were hiding somewhere. It was a wily old hunting trick; drivers pushing deer toward standers. He wouldn't fall for it.

Then a scary thought hit him; what if they got tired, changed their minds and came back down? With just a skimpy 22 pistol, he couldn't out-shoot three riflemen... unless he had a surprise waiting.

A plan formed quickly; he found a large Bay tree overhanging the trail. He found a short, heavy rock and lashed his rope to it, then tied the other end to his waist. He climbed the Bay tree and chose a limb over the trail. Ted lifted the rope until the rock floated six inches over the trail; a crude plumb bob.

Tying it off, Ted descended the tree and placed his hunting knife under dangling rock. He kicked some dust on the knife, making it look like it fell out of his pocket while hiking.

Ted powered up the monitor and was startled to see two men already standing in the wallow meadow. They had to be on speed to climb so fast. But seeing only two men scared him; maybe somebody was coming back down the trail! After hiding his pack, he hurried up the tree and reeled up the rock. He rested it on the limb and prayed that the leaves concealed him enough.

Far up the trail, it created a stir when they found Heidi's corpse, still oozing blood from the gaping maw in the pelvis.
"Sal... eet appears our man has heemself un arco y fletcha... *a bow and arrow!*
Wes was undaunted.
"Who the fuck cares? We'll still kill him!"
Sal was more cautious.
"I thought you said he was unarmed; so... where'd this bow come from? Didja see a fuckin' weapon OR NOT?"
Wes answered defensively.
"Man, the guy *didn't have SHIT*. I clipped 'im and we're gonna rock his ass. What can he do, shoot us? He's got a bow? WE got a fuckin' arsenal!"

The trio resumed the horrible climb. Sal looked back at Heidi's corpse; that hole got there somehow. He wasn't so sure about chasing this asshole any more.

Then they smelled water. Wes got there first, sucking heavily from the cool waters of the wallow. He knew nothing of the laws of the mountain, nor would he have cared. In his rush to slake his thirst, he didn't notice the message. By the time the others got there, Wes had a lot of bad water in an empty stomach.

Meanwhile, Paco found the same tiny source Ted drank from. He filled his throat with the cool liquid, and gave thanks to the forest gods. Sal followed Paco's lead. He wanted to suck wallow water, but Wes already mucked it into a blue-gray muddy murk. After they had seconds from the seep, they went to the wallow to cool their feet. That's when they noticed the message finger-scrawled in mud. Sal had been worried ever since they spotted Heidi's carcass... and now, *this*...

*"GO BACK"*

Being the boss, it behooved him to take action, while limiting risk... specifically, *HIS.*

The other two were locked on the scrawled message. This guy was still alive, but more importantly, KNEW they were after him.
Paco was the first to recover.
"That Putah! He theenk we come here for dreenk... Heh, heh; we come to keel heem!"

Sal kept his thoughts to himself.
*'he's watching us right now'*
He came up with a quick and dirty plan, speaking loud enough that hopefully, the rip-off artist could hear him.

"Ok, you two keep workin' his trail. I'll go check if he's backtrackin' us again. If you hear me shoot, come runin'...
If not, keep workin', alright?"
The stunned pair nodded.
"Ok, break up!"

Sal retraced his steps, eager to be away from whatever the rip-off artist had in store for them. The steep slope hastened his descent, to back where Heidi's body, bloating fast in the scorching sun.

He felt better and better with each step. It wasn't that he was a coward; it was just that he knew when to hold 'em and when to fold 'em... that's why he was boss. He was a half a mile from danger and soon he'd be eating lunch in the cool shade of his patch; *'We'll never catch him; he ain't wounded bad... look at the fuckin hill he just climbed!'*

Sal spotted the beautiful hunting knife. He bent down to pick it up. On the overhanging limb, Ted's stomach knotted. The rock caught Sal's neck and head squarely amidships. He heard the telltale 'crack'. The body sprawled face down, quivering. The rifle slid downhill, coming to rest in the gully.

Urine drained downhill. Ted climbed down to the inert human. Sal's eyes still moved, even though his arms and legs couldn't. Ted knelt so the bastard could see his face.

"I *told you* to go back, didn't I?"

Sal could only blink in fear, as the mortality sank in.

Ted carried him up an opposing ridge, away from the trail. The fireman's carry gave Sal an especially odd perspective; a tilted view of the forest, rhythmically swinging obliquely from side to side, due to his head swaying on busted spine. Strangely, he felt no pain.

After carrying the stinking killer uphill for 200 yards, Ted found a five-foot deep crevice in some huge boulders. Sal's body made a reflexive visceral twitch when it struck home, jamming his neck enough to crush his trachea. Sal's last visual image was of a dark, sloping rift occupied by a loosely coiled king snake and a blue-belly lizard. His vision faded and he died.

Turning to leave, Ted heard the death sigh. A soothing feeling hit him; for the first time since he'd been shot, he felt like the hunter instead of prey. With a trap so simple that any alert hunter should have spotted it he improved his odds by thirty-three percent. His confidence soared.

He hurried to the kill site. Checking the Colby, he found six rounds, with a seventh in the chamber. He brushed away tracks and did his best to cover up the rapidly drying urine puddle. He powered up the monitor and saw that the other two assailants were still resting near the wallow. Their body language told him that the hard-ass climb did them in. As soon as Sal left, they took five.

Ted fairly flew up the ravine, taking full advantage of the adrenaline rush from killing a man. As he got near the north end of the wallow meadow, he slowed to a snail's pace..

He stalked his way up the creek until it became nearly vertical, underneath a Bay grove. The dry rock wall would be a waterfall during wet season. Ted climbed it, using the irregular rock ledges and Bay roots as ladder rungs. In the grove was a small, shaded pool.

There came a small 'plunk' when a frog plopped into the water. With his adrenaline rushing, the tiny splash sounded more like a crashing jumbo jet. He climbed in and tried to calm down while studying the layout; the small depression under the Bay trees concealed him well. Low-hanging Bay limbs gave the spot a very dark interior.

There were moss-covered boulders. Bay roots, as thick as a man's calf, interlaced the boulders at the downhill end of the pool, forming a level nest-like configuration. When the winter rains formed rushing downhill torrents, they brought gravel, leaves, limbs and dried bones, to form pools like this one; just big enough for skeeters and the leopard frog that kerplunked when Ted's silhouette spooked it.

He studied the thugs; slightly above and across the meadow, they sat and argued. Ted couldn't hear words, but caught their tone.

Apparently, Wes wanted to go sidehill. Not because it might locate the rip-off, but because it was easier. Paco wanted to go uphill for a good vantage point. They started climbing the steep wall, but Wes started sucking air and slowing down.

Paco was sick of the soft gringo's whining; he decided to let the gringo off the hook. Without him tagging along, Paco would be much stealthier.

"Bueno; you stay here... I go to the top."
Both gangsters were happy.

Paco disappeared in the buckeyes and scrub brush. Wes found a cool place in the shade. The cold rocks felt good on his feverish ass. Those last two climbs robbed his strength, and now he had inside problems. His stomach rumbled, and he felt very shaky. His guts started swelling and paining him terribly. Aftertastes of that last stale tortilla came to him; maybe he shouldn't have had it.

# Four...
## COMBAT

Ted continued to study his enemy, who was lying upright, as in a recliner, facing Ted. The terrain was so steep that the man had to be sitting with his back directly against the talus hillside; he looked sick.

The other one, Paco, was nowhere; he just vanished. He swung back to the sick-looking one. His weapon lay at his left side. Just then, the man leaned away from the gun and vomited. He got up and dropped his pants. Even at that distance, Ted could hear projectile diarrhea slapping onto the shale like water pouring from a bucket.

Ted considered using the Colby to shoot the sick one, except he couldn't trust its point of impact. He could chance it and fire all seven rounds in a half-second, but at that range, with an unfamiliar weapon, a kill was uncertain. He'd give away his position, and they would have the goods on him.

He could stalk the guy; it was a cake-walk... plenty of cover, and Ted could easily get within forty or fifty yards, where a kill would be certain. That would only leave the Mexican to deal with. It looked better and better.

He scoped out the stalk route again; several bushes were lined up with the puking man. Then he scanned the back-dropping vertical wall behind, rising almost vertically, two hundred yards; a small round object, right where Ted walked earlier. Round things meant live things. Ted's gut tightened into a knot. Due to the heat mirage, he couldn't make it out clearly. Then came the unmistakable glint of sunshine on a barrel; it was a trap!

Ted was damn glad he hadn't started his stalk or he'd be a dead man. He fought the urge to panic, bolt and run. It wasn't any easier to fight this time than before. It took all his willpower to stay still and try to think. He whispered to calm his fears; *'Do what old Blacktail bucks do; freeze, rock-still!'* Had a rifle, no scope or binocs. He's lookin' *downhill, from bright sun into total darkness at 500 yards; no way can he see me!'*

The first half-hour was easy. In the grove of Bay trees, with large slabs of moss-covered rocks, it stayed cool. Then warm breezes began to play gently through the grove. Lying on the velvety rocks; it was a waiting game Ted could win. He kept studying the round shape, waiting for the Mexican's next move.

By contrast, Paco was laying in the searing sun. Hot, sharp shale edges made his prone stay very painful. Most people would have shifted position in five minutes. Paco lasted forty-five. When Ted finally saw it, the movement awed him; deliberate, painstaking, barely perceptible.

*'No California Mexican's so good in the woods; he's from Panama, Brazil or some jungle sweatbox... Be careful!'*

Paco quit moving. His rifle barrel, the source of just the one errant flash of reflected sunshine, lay pointed downhill at the meadow. New sharp rocks dug new holes into new spots on chest, thighs and elbows. He found the rocks annoying, but a good test of his hunter's discipline.

Paco thought all Californians were soft, and after his first few months here, he'd seen nothing to change his opinion. He hated the hot California sun; it seemed unnatural, so damned dry. He started drifting away, on sun-baked tangents, thinking that maybe his impromptu trap was without prey.

Still, he sensed something earlier when standing in the meadow. He paid attention to his instincts. They'd saved him several times in his native Colombian jungle. He decided to give it two more hours.

He settled in and accepted the sharp rocks, searing sun and biting red ants. He'd seen worse. He tried to ignore the raspiness growing in his throat; he hoped it wouldn't make him cough. The rest he could master, but a cough? The hot, dry air felt like burning smoke; the more tried to stifle it, the stronger the urge grew. Paco forced himself to stop worrying; the cough urge shrank. It could be ignored, claro.

In the cool of the north-facing slope barely two hundred yards under Paco, Wes had finished his latest diarrhea bout. He had a high fever. He lay in a half-assed heap in a puddle of watery excrement. He lost the strength to stand, move or button his pants. His insides burned white-hot. Exhausted and dehydrated, he started hallucinating. The shotgun lay at his left side, covered with resting shit flies. He passed the early afternoon hours moaning, puking and shitting brown water, interspersed with short snaps of weak snoring.

Time passed. The breeze stopped. In the midafternoon doldrums, everything got eerily quiet. Bugs quit chirping. Birds stopped flying. Ted got drowsy. He lay down his head in the cool sand, for 'just a second'. He fell into blissful dreams. He dreamed of his wife and the first time they met and how beautiful she was. It was a long, sweet dream.

A sudden barrage of loud moans jolted Ted awake; he didn't know how long he slept, but the shadows were longer and slanted; an hour, maybe more.

He immediately checked the ridge top. The round object was gone! Fearing that maybe he snored or moved during the nap, he was on the verge of panicking and running. The only problem was painfully obvious; Paco could be anywhere. Ted might run right into him, and the advantage would belong to the thug. Still, he had to move, because his nap might have blown his cover.

He risked a heads-up to look down his ravine, as the sick man kept puking wretchedly in the background. He saw nothing, which unnerved him. Pulling his head down, he tried to think like the stalker. The only logical approach was the same route he had taken.

He saw the leopard frog in his favorite hiding place, back against the wall, just like Ted. He had an idea. The frog would help him. It sure sounded better than bolting for safety and taking a bullet through the head.

He readied the pistol for combat. Then he placed the AR-16 in obvious sight, on the uphill side of him, like he'd left it there when he fell asleep.

Ted rolled over on his belly, with the Rubier in his left hand, pointing backward under his right armpit... at the only spot where Paco could appear. He tested the position, clearing rocks and debris away so the pistol could cycle its action unimpeded. With just the muzzle protruding from the back of his armpit, the gun was all but invisible. The stage would be a man asleep face down, rifle out of reach; hopefully it would confuse his attacker for one fatal second. All he needed was luck and nerve... Definitely nerve.

A covey of quail flushed 200 yards down the ravine; at mid afternoon, they'd only flush when frightened, so the jungle man was coming right up the dry creek bed; the same route Ted took, hours before.

It was a good stalk route. Its steep walls would hide Paco's footfall noise, just as they'd hidden Ted's. Then there was the wall of stone, some twelve feet tall, and so steep that a shooting opportunity wouldn't present until they were practically hand-to-hand.

He figured ten minutes for Paco to get there, considering how Paco moved on the trail the night before; he would be plenty slow and plenty quiet. Paco would have to climb the roots, just like Ted did; he would have to sling the rifle for the climb.

He visualized the jungle man, blocking out the afternoon skyline, just as the bastard un-slung his rifle... That's when Ted would fire. It was a risky trap, with Ted's backside as bait. In chess parlance, Ted would offer his queen for a checkmate.

His little buddy was wary; a million generations of survivors' DNA saw to that. The little frog perched, waiting for a

careless bug to pass by. Ted lay his head down and double-checked the pistol's sight line, praying silently.
*'Lord, please guide my bullets. Give me courage to repel evil. Please, God, help me kill this bastard, and kill him fast. In Jesus' name, Amen.'*

Then he laid his head on his forearm and baited the trap; he began to snore. Ted went into sensory overdrive, ears scanning for the tiniest noises. He kept his eyes open, so they could adapt quickly when he needed them.

He rehearsed Paco's approach route; there was the flat section where the quail flushed. The thought of quail grounded his energy. The next section consisted of tall Bays and steep rock sides. Then the ravine got so narrow there was only room for one foot at a time. Paco would get confident upon seeing Ted's scuff marks, confirming that the grove held his prey.

From that spot, either man might get a half-assed head shot at the other, if he knew where to look. But Ted preferred him close and confused, as opposed to far and alert. Years of bowhunting taught him that lesson. The final few yards comprised the climb up to Ted's hideout.

Ted twitched nervously when a Flicker spooked from the creek, barely forty yards below. Flickers liked to stay in thick cover. The bird kept flying across the open meadow until distance finally obliterated its raspy wingbeats. His heart raced. He forced himself to maintain his rhythmical cadence, snoring just barely loud enough for a set of keen jungle ears to catch it.

Earlier from the hot ridge top, Paco thought he'd spotted movement; like a sleeping hand brushing a fly or a deer's flicking ear, doing the same. He wasn't looking right at it when it happened, so he couldn't be sure. But after thirty minutes of eye-watering comparison to two other groves, he noticed what wasn't there; no tree squirrels racing up and down the luscious Bay trunks. No shitbirds, rabbits or deer. Putting two and two together, he was almost sure his prey lay there in the dark shadows where no wild critters could be seen.

He was beginning to enjoy his work; this hot, dusty, miserable mountain was almost as good as his native jungle! Paco plotted his stalk, then slid down the backside of the talus ridge.

Now he was close; he heard the snoring. His guts tightened. He loved hunting and killing men. It was something he felt born to do. And now, this wounded, foolish, snoring gringo motherfucker showed his California soft spot. Cocky with advantage, he grew hot for the kill. Soon he could feed his rifle some gringo. He whispered to his riftle; *'Thees gringo... so easy... just like the last ones... soft and stupid, not like our beloved guerillas, eh, hombre?'*

Ted prayed for nerve, but his prayer was interrupted by the unmistakable sound of gravel grinding, very close. The bottom Bay tree root groaned under the stalker's weight. Paco arrested weight transfer when he heard it. Ted mixed in a chortle or two, as though the sleeper was mildly startled. It wasn't hard to fake, since it practically scared the shit out of him. Then he resumed his snoring cadence. Heart pounding wildly, Ted resisted the urge to just jump up and blaze away; he'd face a blazing muzzle if he did.

Through the top two bay roots, Paco could see the legs of his target, but there was no killing shot from that angle. It was dark in there. He took the next step up and saw the snoring gringo, face down. The next rung gave Paco a dark view of the whole man, and part of what looked to be a rifle, out of reach. Emboldened, he stood full height at the pool's edge while he UN-slung the AK-47.

At the same instant, he little frog, keeper of the pool, spooked at Paco's silhouette, croaked and plunked into the pool. Ted's body went hot with tension when he heard it, as well as Paco's words...
"Adios, amig..."
But the first tiny hollow point took out his vocal cords; the next bullet found his upper right lung. Ted spun over on his

back, clearing the pistol for more action. He got three more shots off, while the jungle man just stood and looked surprised. He fell backward, simultaneously trying to fire the rifle.

Ted's next bullets found empty air while the body crashed in the pool below. Paco jerked the trigger; the AK 47 burped off twenty rounds. One found Ted's lower right calf, just as Ted emptied the pistol into the pool, without risking a look over the edge. In two seconds, it was all over.

The leg pain hit him. He rolled over and grabbed the Colby while hearing the unmistakable wheezing gurgle coming from the pool; a sucking chest wound. Ted peeked through the same gap that Paco's bullet came through.

It was plain to see; Paco had bigger problems than killing Ted. He kept pulling the trigger, willing the empty rifle to save him. The smoking-hot rifle barrel hissed from blood spraying on the barrel and heat shield. With each inhalation came the sickening lung sputter, while each exhale forced frothy orange pulmonary blood spraying through the tiny bullet hole; hissing, burned-blood dental-drill stench filled the air.

He appeared to be fading too fast; Ted suspected he was faking it. But then Paco's face rolled to the right, showing the truth; no longer deflected by his cheek, his left vertebral artery squirted blood almost four feet up. The man's lips moved, forming two words over and over. It looked like; GOOD TRAP... GOOD TRAP...
Soon the spurt made only two feet... then one, then a few inches. His eyes rolled back. The baddest ass in the jungle; converted into eighty kilos of maggot food.

The white-hot painful calf made Ted cuss while he looked back towards the other one; the sick dude. Ted was surprised to see that even in the open meadow, it was almost dark; his trap took longer than he thought, making sense of the jungle man's apparent superhuman speed. Ted's heightened awareness had compressed his sense of time.

Wes wobbled with legs splayed wide to keep his balance. He looked weak and vulnerable, but Ted corrected his mental error.

*'He's got a fuckin' shotgun!'*

Ted's pistol was empty and the Colby unproven; he could only make ready and hope the guy didn't have a good fix on Ted's location. Sounds bounce around in the hills. His leg hurt too much to run. With Wes standing on higher ground, Ted was at a disadvantage.

Just then, Ted heard the Browner action slam home. He went numb with fear. He recalled the weapon he'd seen through his spotting scope; sawed-off, for killing people, not birds. It would have the duck plug removed and, more than likely, its sear was filed for automatic fire. It could burp all five rounds in half a second, sending God knows how many buckshot rounds, a hailstorm of 25-caliber balls, screaming through the brush at 1200 feet a second... an 800-mile-an-hour chainsaw.  One time, the hunter came upon a bear that died from buckshot. He couldn't get the image from his mind; he would lose this firefight, and he'd die, just like that old bear... Swollen, broken and alone.

Wes had awakened from a feverish sleep to thunder or a firefight or something. It was over before he came to his senses, but many years of late-shift patch guarding honed his instincts to a few primal rules; at the first sign of trouble, lock and load. At first doubt, shoot. And at first light, shovel.

His adrenaline kicked in. Temporarily at least, Wes wasn't sick. He was a born again ex-marine jarhead killer. He ran toward the fight and jacked a round into the humpback. Then, halfway across the darkening meadow, his survival senses took over.

He stopped and listened for clues to the gunfight, if that's what it had been. The woods were still. He stepped in a big pile of human shit and wondered how, since he hadn't dumped over there. And besides; this cold shit was solid; it couldn't be his. Wes suddenly felt conspicuous, so he took cover behind a big snag and awaited developments.

*'No sense bein' a fuckin' target!'*
His shoes were covered in shit. If he knew it was the shit Ted used to bait Heidi, it might have saved his life.

Ted nervously reloaded his pistol by feel; he felt a little better. He sensed an odd balance of power. He had a pistol and a rifle, both good for middle distance. His enemy had a shotgun, unbeatable at close-range.

Wes was standing by the shit trap for the dog. Ted fished in his pack for the transmitter, praying there was battery power left. The camera monitor, but the transmitter still had juice, since the servo had only fired once, when it killed the dog. Ted un-saftied the Colby, aimed at the base of the big white oak and moved the rudder stick.

Wes heard the servo whir, reflexively swung the shotgun and yanked the trigger; the muzzle flash was clearly visible when the Humpback went fully automatic.

Ted pointed two feet rear of the muzzle flash and pressed the trigger. All seven rounds felt like one, when the Colby sounded its tenor roar. He heard the last bullet slap meat, then a grunt; the telltale ka-whop gave it away, a gut-shot He dropped the smoking rifle and clutched his pistol like a long lost lover.

Weak moans came from the dark. Ted's mind started messing with him; he could wait until morning and risk the man escaping or worse yet, the guy might counter-stalk him during the night. He could stalk him right away, while he was in shock. No option sounded good.

Then it occurred to him; at that range, a man should hear him reloading, but Ted didn't hear anything. The guy didn't have a bandoleer, so maybe he'd just hopped out of the truck, shack or whatever with just the rounds in the gun. *'They thought I'd be easy'*...

He decided to stalk the man immediately, and take his chances. As he got up, calf pain changed his plan.

During the burst of adrenaline, pain didn't register. Now it made up for it. Ted got out his penlight and pulled his pant leg up. He hunkered down in the shallow nest. Shielding the tiny light, he looked at his wound; although swollen and bloody, it was pretty minor.

He squeezed the hard lump like a pimple, the projectile popped out like a Pez; front smashed flat from its impact with a rock or a root, so a ricochet got him. He got up, using the empty Colby for a crutch. Then he passed out and dropped like a stone.

Ted awoke to the still night sky. His left cheek hurt from slamming the sand. Luckily, the swelling only closed his left eye. His head cleared slowly; the moon was down and the stars faded out. It would be light soon. He listened for his enemy; nothing.

Not knowing how long it would take to make the stalk with his bad leg, he wanted to be across the wide-open meadow before the first rays of light got him killed.

While crawling across the meadow, the faintest hints of a crimson sunrise defined the eastern horizon. In the distance, the barest outline of a mountain ridge appeared. A small red fox barked its bedtime bark, trotting uphill to its rocky lair.

Ted made it halfway across the meadow when he smelled him; it wasn't hard. Downdrafts carried scent down the steep ridge to the meadow and piled up like rush hour traffic. The sick man smelled like a raunchy outhouse. Ted feared the man backtracked him. He hugged some cover and continued toward the enemy's last known location. He wanted to know more about his injuries. Twenty yards of crawling told him all he needed to know.

He took one through the guts, obviously. Quarter-sized chunks of spleen and pancreas dotted the left side of the drag marks. Weeds bent forward, marking his direction. Every ten yards or so was a small pool of vomit and bile.

Dark purple blood clots stained the dry weeds. He'd seen enough blood trails to know this dude was in serious hurt.
*'maybe he's dead, but don't take chances'*
Ted backed out to the open meadow, hugging cover, crawling slowly... looking uphill into the brush for sign. When he could smell him again, he took cover;
*'He's baitin' me, like I baited Paco!'*
As the light steadily increased, the man's head showed in clear view, barely twenty-five yards away.

He faced the trail. The eyes were open, but saw nothing. A small trickle of blood seeped. Vapor rose in the cold morning air. Ted circled uphill to see him lying in star thistle and tarweed. The shotgun, action open, rested five feet behind the dying bastard.

Wes grunted when Ted rolled him over onto his back. Sure enough, one round took him through the guts; dark bubbles out the entrance hole. His abdomen was taut and swollen, his shirt and pants soaked in a homogeneous mix of blood, food bolus and shredded organ bits. A hot, steamy vapor exited his mouth between labored, shallow breaths.

Ted got his gagging under control. He growled at the thug.
"I told you to go back, didn't I?"
"Get... doctor"
"Sure I'll get a chopper, too, but first, WHY'D YOU TRY TO KILL ME?"
Wes looked puzzled by the stupid question.
"Our dope... I shot plane... you're... ripoff..."
Speech robbed oxygen; he drew more breaths to catch up.
"So, where's your patch?"
Wes drew his penultimate breath.
"Uphill your plane... leave it..."
Ted put a bullet through his chest. Wes rolled his eyes, stiffened, and that was it. He looked relieved.

*'I did the bastard a favor; shoulda let him die slow.'*

Ted collapsed, staring at the stinking creep. He felt like an animal; he had killed three human beings. He puked again. He hobbled over to the spring. He washed down his stomach acid and residual vomit and pondered his situation; it was bad, but it could have been worse.

First he thought about telling the cops, but he'd been on three juries. He knew how distorted justice could become. Long after the primal firefight, some pasty-faced D.A. would be second-guessing his life or death, split-second decisions.

They'd peruse sterilized deposition testimony at their leisure. They'd watch cartoons created by prosecution-appointed expert witnesses, with Power Point failure analysis scenarios, instead of seeing Radical Ridge's nasty terrain, hearing whizzing bullets and feeling rock shards spattering legs. With spoon-fed evidence like that, any verdict was possible; Ted didn't want any part of that.

His scene was bad, but not impossible; three corpses on the steepest, harshest mountainside in the county. Except for a few desperate deer hunters, nobody went there. The elements would work on them for three weeks before deer season opened. Except for a few bullet holes, the bodies wouldn't tell a coroner anything to incriminate Ted.

He steeled himself to the stench and pulled out Wes' shirttails. He rolled the corpse over and was relieved to see two exit holes... one from the Colby at long range, the other exited under the Scapula. A quick look at the underlying rocks revealed the bloody pellet, dented and scratched from its short trip through the torso. Ted flicked it uphill into a poison oak thicket. No cop in his right mind would ever look there; it was too brushy for a metal detector sweep.

Next, he limped back to the Bay grove while another wave of panic wobbled him. He vomited again; a dry, yellow proof that he was out of food and practically out of nerve. Then he saw twelve jurors, passionately giving him the guilty verdict. He gained more resolve.

*'No evidence, no trial!'*

Then he climbed down to Paco's body; an early raven pecked out both eyes. The body leaned back against the ravine wall. A single mascara-like trickle from each orbit dribbled down each cheek. Paco looked like he cried himself to sleep after a date with a punk rock star.

It seemed odd that a body should look so non-human, simply due to a lack of vitreous pressure. He opened the shirt up. A tiny red hole marked an entrance point high in the right apical lung; clearly punching a rib.

He rolled the corpse over and found no exit hole. He was adept at locating spent projectiles, from years of skinning game and tracing bullet paths, first for his curiosity, then later for his kids' edification. The tiny lead lump lay barely an inch inside Paco's hide, medial to his right shoulder blade. With a flick, the damning bullet was lost forever, uphill in thick brush.

The hole in the front of the rib posed a problem; if he used a knife it would leave telltale blade marks in the bone. So Ted grabbed a big rock and crushed the upper ribs. He cut out the dangling rib fragments by fileting off the attaching flesh. He tossed the bloodshot piece of bone and meat into the tallest brush, where the first rodent would steal it.

Then he saw the fatal throat shot, which nicked the voice box and vertebral artery on an angling trajectory.

*'Thank you, Lord, for guiding that bullet!'*

He felt for lumps, until he saw the exit hole, midway up the posterior aspect of the neck.

He washed his hands until the gravel burned his fingers. He washed his knife until all visible blood, hair and fibers were gone. After a final glance, he tied a Bay bough to his waist so that he obliterated his footprints while walking; the prints probably wouldn't be seen before the elements canceled them, but he wasn't taking chances.

Limping back down the main trail, his thoughts went to the body in the boulders, two hundred yards above the main trail. It was too deep and narrow to get to it the corpse, but the blow to the head could have happened naturally.

By the time he got to Heidi's carcass, he almost felt like he could get away with it. He gave the brutish carcass a hateful kick. It slid sluggishly into the ravine below. Gasses saluted the new position with gusto. The huge gash from the broadhead spewed a disgusting burgundy colored froth. Then he thought of his custom arrow laying somewhere up the hill. Not wanting to waste time searching for the needle in the haystack, Ted made a note to toss out his three-bladed broadheads and custom shafts. From now on he would shoot factory shafts with four-bladed heads. He headed for the blue-line creek, where he'd first been shot; it seemed a lifetime ago.

When he got to the creek he made haste to find the last... or hopefully, the only incriminating thing in the woods. Most responsible r/c pilots mark the fuselage and bottom of the wing, with name phone number and insurance numbers.

An hour later, he had climbed to the spot where he'd burned his fuselage. Despite his best search, the wing was not to be found. He recalled Wes' statement; *'your plane... uphill...'* so he looked carefully for the hidden foot trail leading up to the Pot patch.

Savvy Pot growers concealed their paths, often taking different courses, concealing trails under trees, ferns, anything. But since the plants needed constant tending, habitual travel paths would always develop.

After a few minutes, Ted made it out; a slight trace of footpath. He took it up the steep ravine, watching for booby traps. After a head-pounding ten minutes, he smelled the Marijuana; its sweet, thick scent pouring off the hilltop like melting ice cream spilling down the cone. Ted placed his feet ONLY where the dopers had obviously placed theirs, which were fairly easy for an outdoorsman to spot in broad daylight.

He soon found the camouflaged tripwire leading to a testicle-high Claymore, just five feet away. As he sidestepped the trap, all senses were on overdrive for secondary wires and other traps. It was slow, nervous going, but only forty yards uphill was pay dirt.

The patch was 200 yards long and almost eighty yards wide. Hundreds, maybe thousands of huge dark greenish-purple plants formed a thick jungle. Each plant looked exactly like the sisters next to it. Long, sticky buds were everywhere.

The oily buds shimmered with resin. At normal prices, just one pound of dried buds would easily fetch over three thousand dollars... depending on how much resin concentrated in the buds and how well manicured they were. For this patch, at rough guess, it would yield four to six million tax-free dollars.

Ted envied the drip system; it was awesome, even to the eyes of a professional landscaper. They had spared no expense or effort to do it right; solar-powered timers, pumps, electric critter fences, in-line filters, dropouts and regulators adorned the mammoth site. He wondered how the sheriffs' choppers could have missed it. Viewed rom the air, it had to stand out like neon sign.

To the east stood a small shack, door ajar. No smoke or noise came from the ramshackle structure. A quick glance inside told him what he needed; three sets of dirty dishes at the table. So, it was true enough; he *had* killed them all.

Ted went back to the downhill edge of the patch on the brink of the cliff. It seemed the most obvious place from which to shoot a plane. Sure enough, his wing protruded from poison oak bushes, barely forty yards from the eight-foot high deer fence. Ted was on it in a flash. He ripped out the servos, which wouldn't burn. With one flick of his Bic, he obliterated the last incriminating evidence... assuming nobody found that fucking arrow.

Ted never looked back. He wanted the whole ugly episode behind him, and speed seemed the best way to achieve that. In only ten minutes, he was again down at the creek. Then he thought about the Claymore, which he obviously missed. He let out a sigh of relief. *'Thank you, lord!'*

Arriving at the truck, almost exhausted; strain, exposure and hunger taxed him heavily. As he unlocked the truck he noticed vultures circling over Radical, a full three miles away, as the crow flies. Eight black vees soaring on thermals, grim reminders of the grisly scene below. The humans weren't ripe yet, but buzzards can always wait.

Ted entered his truck and reached for his jug of lukewarm water; to his parched tongue, it was fine champagne. He drank with his left while his right reached in the glove box. He usually kept small snacks there, but found only empty wrappers. His daughter found his stash. It was a standing joke. He would try to hide the candy. She would find it.

The tears surprised him. Maybe it was the relief of surviving, knowing he'd be around to watch his kids grow up and marry... or maybe it was the guilt of having to take human life or just maybe, he cried for fear of being incarcerated. At any rate, he couldn't stop bawling.

After a while, he ran out of tears and came to his head. He searched under the seat and came up with a few hard candies, partially melted and stuck to the floor mats. Honey's hairs were stuck to them; Ted popped them in his mouth, wrappers, dog hair and all. His stomach writhed in painful anticipation. Firing up the truck, he dropped it into low range so he could compression-brake down the steep hills without burning up his brakes on the savage ride out. *"Easy, Ted, in two hours you'll be home. Act 'NATURAL'... Whatever that is."*

Ted drove straight home without his usual stop for a burger. He was too tired to think of alibis or explanations for his wounds. Ninety minutes and two summits later, he hit the garage door button and held his breath until the door shut out the harsh cruel world.

Soon he stood buck naked by the washing machine. He punched the button, lumbered into the kitchen, grabbed two beers and walked to the shower. The first beer tasted great, while the hot water loosened dirt, matted hair, twigs and blood.

The shower water hit the tile; brown, then dark red, light red, pink and finally clear, as the muck slaked off his cramped, wounded body. Then he studied the mirror; a few spots still betrayed his crime. In the shower again, he finished cleaning. Once satisfied, he popped the other beer. But just as he entered the bedroom, he dropped the beer; he was out before mattress and face collided.

Ted woke up to the ringing phone; the machine said she'd been calling every night, even though she'd be home in three days. He needed a clear head to form a good story. So, he let the phone keep ringing, even though he ached to hear Jo's voice.

The clock said he'd slept for five hours. He nuked some fried chicken, sipped a beer and tried to forget about the carnage. It wasn't easy. Hell, it was impossible. Ted dressed his wounds, cleaned the pistol, wiped it with an oil-soaked rag and punched the gun safe combo.

The pistol went in the safe next to the bed, like always; on his wife's side of the bed; it made Jo feel secure, on those nights when Ted was away. They used to pray they'd never have to use it. Now Ted prayed even harder that he'd never have to use it... again.

Next item was to inspect his gear. He was shocked to find two dried-blood fingerprints on the R/C transmitter.

By the time he was done, he was fairly certain that he was clean. Or as clean as he could be, for all the deaths he caused; with something like that, an honest man can never be completely clean.

The first chapter in Ted's new life came to a close.

## Six

# SALDIVAR

Victor Saldivar hated what he heard. Three of his best patch guards were dead and nobody knew who killed them. Not only that, the cops ACTUALLY SEIZED HIS PATCH. Of course, he had others, so the loss would be defrayed. But Saldivar hated to lose anything, ever; a trait which carried him to the pinnacles of his career. From his upscale L.A. home he made some calls.

Those who worked for him did so out of a unique combination of loyalty, fear and greed. Victor's plan always factored those ingredients, keeping his men hungry, obedient, and focused. Whereas other drug rings crumbled from within, Saldivar's ring thrived.

He never smoked Pot or used drugs. The only alcohol he used was good wine with a special meal and special guests. Victor abhorred drunks and drug addicts, so his top men were clean and clear-headed. This was no accident; he routinely drug-tested down to middle management. They knew his motto; 'If you're wired, you're fired.'

Predictably, at the lower levels of distribution, the ethic eroded; as one works from the treetops to the roots of any org, terminal rootlets will be infected with the humus-like fungi that infects all earthly things. So Victor's org, just like any other, was full of vice at the rootlets.

Victor, of course, knew this. That's why he'd taken pains to insulate himself from the low levels. He had flawless layers of liability buffers, just to make sure that he would never go down, even if his org sunk.

In addition, he used traditional measures for protection; bribes to the right people, donations to local community and continual conversion of criminal profits to legitimate business fronts. Thus far, he'd achieved all of his goals while having just one adversarial scrape with the law, this current one. It made him uneasy.

His projected goals included being retired in four years, solidly entrenched in the corporate world, with no paper trail. A profitable sellout to his next-in command would be his final underworld act. Just like everything else, Victor already had that plan set into motion.

Every middle management man had vesting quietly building. With their nest eggs, his staff would be happy to see him go, with no assassination plots to spoil his dream. He was confident he could shuck the underworld and no one would miss him, much less betray him. If he made the deal sweet enough, they'd be glad to see him go.

Still, he hated losing. So he found himself standing there, aching for vengeance. His first call went to his contact, 800 miles away in Humdob County, using the latest code.
"I'd like to report a missing person."
Talvez knew the drill.
"I'm sorry, sir. You'll need to call the local police for that."

His second call went to Luis Ortega, the head of Victor's security. Intelligent, loyal, and deeply committed, Chewy was the go-to-guy whenever things got weird. He always came through, even if his methods contrasted sharply with those of his boss. To Chewy, all that was needed was an order, no matter who had to die. His loyalty to Saldivar knew no bounds. He was the ultimate henchman. His meaty fist picked up on the second ring.
"Hello."
"I want to talk to you, now."
Chewy hung up. He wasn't much for small talk.

His third call never went through, even though he had the phone to his ear. He was ready to drop the gauntlet on his most likely suspect, without even awaiting confirmation that the scumbag was guilty. He was going to call the boss of the biggest methamphetamine ring in Southern California, one Arthur, AKA "Dozer", Dexter. Victor could already see the stinking gringo, dressed in sweat-stained leather, a cigar in his filthy mouth, yellow teeth spackled over with food particles from countless meals, sans toothbrush.

61

At the very thought, Saldivar could smell the man's fetid breath. The only thing that kept Victor from having him killed was an undeniable, overwhelming fear of the man. Dexter's org was a hodgepodge of truckers, bikers and mercenaries who would slit a man's throat for practically no reason at all, with no thought to the consequences.

With all of Saldivar's business experience, he still didn't know how to handle those loose canons. That was one of his reasons for retiring soon; it had been getting harder to avoid them. Something had to give.

As he held the phone, he recalled a saying of his father's, when he passed the business to Victor.
'Son, revenge is a dish best served COLD... surprise is the spice that makes it palatable. So don't let your feelings affect your dealings; it is bad business, hijo.'

That's why Victor tried to avoid hot-blooded types; crazy Colombians, rowdy Rastafarians... And bellicose bikers. They were too self-indulgent to be good business risks. Even though it resulted in less business, the offset was a lot less risk. Of course, the net profit was better; less legal fees and less public exposure.

Victor couldn't shake the thought; someone encroached on HIS territory, killed HIS people, and stole HIS dope. Another man might let that go, but not Saldivar. His Latin blood demanded satisfaction, while his suave business traits tried to temper his craving for vengeance.

So there he stood, ready to start a war. He hung up the phone. Dozer Dexter could wait. Saldivar talked himself into a glass of wine... a rarity, without guests and a meal. He uncorked a Milani Zinfandel, the best red he'd ever tasted. He'd bought two pallets, the first time his lips touched the glass. The room-temperature wine greeted his tongue like a long-favorite love affair; full of familiar promise, no twitchy surprises. He started to relax. He started seeing options.

Almost eight hundred miles to the north, Deputy Sheriff Enrique Talvez thought about what he'd say when he called Saldivar back. Saldivar's Pot patches weren't supposed to be raided. His operation in all three major Northern California Pot counties was off limits to CAMT raids, and he paid handsomely to make sure of it.

Most of the sheriffs' administrations were glad for the extra cash and they had plenty of other patches to raid, so leaving Saldivar's patches alone made great business sense.

Over the years, his pot business funneled tens of thousands into the local Police Activities League. Without his generous donations, the underprivileged youth would have no place to go. Not surprisingly, some of these youths decided to pursue law enforcement careers, just as Talvez and his mates did.

Ricky trusted him. Saldivar eschewed drug use; he never used drugs and he never dealt in anything but Pot... in the northern California communities, where one person in five smoked Pot, it seemed a comparatively innocuous transgression.

To Talvez, Pot wasn't a drug, it was an herb. It didn't fit in the same category with meth and other hard drugs. That shit ruins people. Long ago he vowed that if Saldivar ever started trafficking in crank, coke, or other drugs, the affair would be over. Talvez hated hard drugs and the kind of people they created.

Still, the last phone call had to be about the raid on Saldivar's patch west of Hidden Crest. Some anonymous caller kicked the whole thing off. By the time the local media hovered in corporate choppers, the deputies had no choice but to bust the patch near the crime scene. It was a question of preserving their reputation and protecting future profits; your typical sacrifice play.

They couldn't even salvage Victor's pot later; there was too much media heat for that. But surely, Victor was smart enough to know this already. Still, Talvez wanted someone else to be the heavy... Many an innocent messenger has been shot for bearing bad news.

Little did he know that his apprehension wasn't justified. El Jefe, Victor Saldivar, had something else in mind.

Seven...
# CONSCIENCE

The first few agonizing weeks almost killed Ted. So far, no one had discovered the bodies. Ted hadn't told anyone, including his wife; she never could keep a secret. Her heart was too big for that. Besides, it would kill her to know he'd done such a horrible thing. She had such a firm sense of right and wrong; she would have to tell the authorities; that's how she was raised.

He told her that he fell down a ravine while searching for his plane, hurt his head and leg... and it took him two days to crawl out. He was always getting banged up, so she let it go, after first getting in a few digs about 'losing that expensive plane'. He never corrected her on that point, either; he didn't exactly *LOSE it*. The convo ended with Jo giving him another lecture on why didn't he carry a cell phone.

One Saturday night, Ted almost choked on his sandwich while flipping through the channels. He fumbled with the volume control, as three deputies hauled out a skeleton. The voice faded in as the analog display reached 39 "... the second body in as many days; more, at 11. Back to you, Rita!"

However, there wasn't "more at 11"; the details then were no more substantial than the earlier teaser; two bodies, Pot patch in the woods, continuing investigation; shit like that happens all the time in Mendonesia County.

Ted didn't sleep much, after that TV spot. He dreamed of handcuffs and monsters in the woods. He dreaded sleep. He drank more. He grew more paranoid. He got short with his workers. It was Telltale Heart all over again. An honest man pays more for his sins than a crook does. Every time he saw a patrol car, his heart skipped a few beats.

One morning, a pair of famous religious missionaries knocked on his door. Ted almost came unglued at the noise. He was gruff, but not about their message. Before long, Ted was jumping at every noise and every time someone hollered his name; a friend's innocent slap on the back brought his adrenaline to red line. His concentration and personality went to hell. Ted compensated; he tried to keep his nerve by thinking about the lack of evidence, and how they'd never link the bodies to him.

Little did he know.

# Eight...
## TORTURE

All things considered, she held up pretty well to the torture. She stared them straight in the eye with proud, fierce defiance. When they struck her, she took it without a whimper. When they burned her with cigarettes, she spat at them. They looked for fear, but found only hatred.

Jetta had hated men, since age fourteen. She wouldn't tell 'em shit. Thirty years earlier, her stepfather placed a straight razor to her throat; unable to mount any defense against the stronger, larger assailant, her only survival choice was to submit. While he raped her, he held that razor to her sweet young throat. He pushed it until the sharp steel cut through her skin. Terrified, she could only lay still and hope he wouldn't kill her.

When it was over, he licked the blood from her neck and threatened her again; if anyone ever found out, he'd come back and finish the job... and then he'd kill her mother, too. Naturally, she didn't tell a soul. Two days later she got her chance to leave; she hit the road and never looked back.

She chose a remote lifestyle high up in the Coastal Mountains. Her cabin had no phone and no electricity, save for a few worn old solar panels and an old deep cycle Caterpillar battery. Her nearest neighbor was half an hour's drive down a treacherous, locked dirt road. It was as remote as she could make it.

At first the torturing seemed impersonal; business as usual. Apparently, they assumed she'd spill her guts easily. But it soon became obvious that she had more courage than they had. Naturally, things got more personal. The cowards beat and raped her, then tied her naked to a kitchen chair. Punches got harder and cigarettes remained on her skin longer. Still, she bested them.

That is, until Chewy brought out the Stiletto. He watched her irises narrow and a thin line of sweat involuntarily formed on her brow; something about the knife she didn't like.

He walked behind her. Placing it to her throat, Chewy suddenly got what he wanted. The sharp edge opened her emotional floodgate. She caved in to the childhood terror.

"All right, all right! There was a guy out here, OK? His name's Ted Morgan; he hunts here sometimes..."
Instantly feeling guilty about turning her longtime friend, she sobbed against her will.
"But you've got it all wrong! He doesn't even DO drugs. He won't even take an ASPIRIN!"
Ortega perked up at this information. Neither did El Jefe. He pressed the knife deeper.

"I've known Ted for 20 years. He's the ONLY MAN I ever met that's not a TOTAL ASSHOLE! He didn't shoot your people... Ted wouldn't hurt a fuckin' Rattler! He's the only man who's got the guts you WISH you had, you spineless mutherf..."

She couldn't finish the M word; Ortega torqued her head into fatal rotation, bringing a loud crack. She went limp and made her death sigh, sending a trickle of urine onto the wooden chair seat. It mixed with the blood spatter and foamy, torture-induced saliva on the hundred year-old unvarnished wooden floor, while the rapists sneered and jeered at the dead dyke bitch.

"Nobody takes nothing; let's go."
Experienced in the dark skills of arson, Ortega refused to use gas from the woodshed to start the fire; trained dogs would easily sniff out accelerant, and this fire must look accidental. He ordered his grunts to put her next to the bed with a Vodka bottle. After striking a small kindling fire against one inner wall near the woodstove, they drove back down the mountain.

The tiny cabin burned at first without smoke, due to extreme dryness of the seasoned timbers and the massive circulation of air. The trio had left both doors open.

The first real smoke didn't show for half an hour, giving them plenty of head start. The burning roof was a dead giveaway; the big black flume shot skyward fast. When the firewatch spotted it, the gangsters were far down the two-track. They joked and bragged all the way down.

Ortega felt hot for the next kill; he finally knew who he was after; one Ted Morgan. He couldn't wait to tell his boss, but in the steep mountain gorges, good cell phone connections were rare. He continuously studied his phone for enough signal strength to call out.

Victor left explicit orders, to be informed as soon as Ortega had information. Unfamiliar with the rugged coastal mountain passes, Ortega was frustrated. Most of his life had been in cities, first Oakland, then Los Angeles. But he wasn't in a city. He couldn't wait to be somewhere, where the fucking phones worked.

The rented SUV swayed back and forth in the tight curves. They celebrated the violence they'd performed on the courageous lesbian, trying to prove that they had more cojones than she did. Of course, they knew it was a lie. Even Ortega himself questioned if he would have been so strong, strapped naked to a chair, raped, sodomized and tortured, in the face of certain death. *'Hombre... that was some woman, alone up in the mountains... some woman, indeed!'*

He admired courage. It was a shame he had to kill her, but he couldn't take a chance by letting her live. Saldivar must be protected at all costs.

Finally, after an hour of the winding mountain passes, they reached the highest summit. The cell phone signaled four bars, so they pulled over. Victor Saldivar picked up, on the first ring.
"Did you get the information?"
"Yeah."
"Bueno! *Do NOTHING.* I want to know more, before I make a move... do you understand?"
"Yeah."

"Call me tomorrow."

The lackeys worked the streets while Ortega went to county records. Late the next afternoon, Ortega and his two grunts knew as much as they needed to know about Ted Morgan. He placed a call to Saldivar, who put him off. Victor didn't want information floating around, with government search engines, relentlessly listening for buzzwords. He got Ortega's motel room number, at their agreed-upon motel. Then he called Talvez. Using their newest codes, they set up the meeting the same way as always; soon, secret and slick.

Fourteen hours later, Saldivar sat with Ortega at a bistro in Hidden Crest. Ortega filled him in while they ate.
"Our friend's a landscaper, works out twice a week. Married, two kids; doesn't fuck around or at least he keeps it quiet. Likes to hunt and fish; a real Grizzly Adams. Owns a house in Deerwood. One year behind on taxes, drives a Chevy four wheel drive truck. No tickets, no hay ninguna record... He's almost TOO CLEAN, boss. Dope grapevine don't know him. That agrees with the..."
Just then the waitress approached.
"Will there be anything else?"
Handing the bill to Victor, she left.
Ortega lowered his voice.
"... agrees with what I got from that woman."

Earlier, the lackeys told Victor about murdering the hermit. Victor said nothing, but his face said he wasn't pleased. Seeing El Jefe's eyes darken, Ortega changed tack.

"Two scenarios are possible. First; maybe he didn't do this thing. Second; maybe he's just getting started in the rip-off business; you know, a little tax-free cash to catch up the bills, eh?"

Saldivar raised his hand like the Pope.
"There is another possibility, Chewy; perhaps he is so clean because *he is as good as me*... Recuerde, carnal;I have no record, either."

Nine...
FRAME

They headed for the rendezvous with Talvez. It was just a short twenty-minute grind up yet another washboarded, water-barred, potholed, steep as hell Coastal Mountain dirt road. The rented truck slid, hopped and bounced relentlessly, in a tooth-chipping drive to climb the damned hill. Victor hated trucks with stiff springs; they had no business being on coast roads.

Ortega settled into his post, concealed on high ground fifty yards uphill of the meet site. It was a favorite unloading point for dirt bikers and the occasional desperate hunter. It was remote and unpopulated at that hour. They used it alternately, along with several others; it paid to vary one's habits.

Ortega double-checked his gear. He stayed put and watched Victor drive off. Soon a dust column headed their way. In five minutes, Talvez's truck rolled into the clearing. Saldivar drove to within fifty yards, stopped and checked the knoll for Chewy's danger signal; nothing... so he exited the truck and strode directly to Talvez' rig.

Enrique got out. Saldivar hugged him; a ritual pat for the wire that was never there. Victor lived by the old west slogan; *'trust your neighbor, but brand your cattle.'*

"Deputy Talvez, I have information regarding the untimely deaths of those men up in the mountains..."

Laying down a thick manila packet, he stepped aside so Ortega could document the bribe. Talvez didn't notice the sidestepping; he was ogling the packet, which was four times as thick as any prior bribe. He picked it up, felt the heft and became worried. A big job comes with a big bribe. Sensing his concern, Saldivar spoke softly.

"No te preocupes, amigo...it's *not all* for you. Don't use new men, comprende? Now, what I propose is very simple. Listen very carefully..."

Saldivar filled him in about implicating someone for the Pot patch deaths. Talvez's mind drifted as Victor laid out the details. This was NOT the Victor he knew or the usual plan. In fact, it was downright chickenshit. His attention suddenly focused when he heard the mark's name; Ted Morgan! Talvez' mind ran wild. He'd known Ted since high school; a quiet, straight arrow, good family and business.

He couldn't believe it; he avoided eye contact as Saldivar droned on. For the first time since he'd met Saldivar at a PAL boxing clinic, he thought about bailing. This wasn't about salvaging some raided Pot. This was *serious* shit.

What Saldivar proposed was simple; Frame Ted. Steal his assets. Ruin his name and reputation. Basically, fuck him over as much as possible... Make an example.

Although Enrique didn't like it, he didn't have time to think it over. He took the cash and drove off. After he rounded a few curves, putting up another billowing dust cloud, he slowed and opened the packet.
"Holy Shit! Eighty grand!"

The money began to warp his thinking; the less men, the fewer lips and fewer chances for a screw-up...and a bigger payoff. He decided to start the next day. By then he'd have it completely rationalized; what had Ted ever done *for HIM?* Maybe he really DID fuck with Saldivar... Who knows?

Ortega was packing his gear when Saldivar hiked up the knoll. Panting and sweating in the Indian-Summer evening heat, Victor confided to his henchman.
"Luis, I am afraid I'm losing him; I hope we don't have to use these tapes of yours..."
"Boss, my blackmail tapes will make him eat his young!"
Saldivar sighed patiently.
"Si, compadre, pero I don't like forcing people; one always gets better results with honey than with acid."

Ortega nodded.
"Si, jefe; but once in a while you gotta love that acid, man."

They spoke no more as they drove down the mountain. Something nagged Saldivar. The seed of doubt had been planted. It was the way Talvez had dropped his eyes; that wasn't like him Ricky.

Victor regrettably formed the conclusion; Talvez just might turn on him. It was the first time he discerned any chinks in his armor. A small chink; maybe not even there, but he had seen other networks crumble from ignoring small problems. This might be the beginning of Victor's downfall.

Here he was, engaging in increasingly brutal acts, taking bigger chances which offered no payoff; these were dangerous warning signs. He decided... he would sell out, muy pronto, before it got worse.

On the trip back to LA, it was easy to arouse Ortega's interest. Saldivar had long planned for his own exit; he'd always withheld a piece of Ortega's pay.

Ortega knew about the withholding and acceded to it from the get-go. He figured he'd never see the money anyway, but he trusted his Jefe with his life. So he forgot about the pay cut... He just wrote it off.

But now that Saldivar laid it out, it sounded damned good. The henchman was eager to buy his boss out. By the time they got home it was a done deal. Ortega would very soon be "EL JEFE."

His head began to swell with power.

Ten...
## MIRANDA

Talvez had already heard the news about Jetta Hunsacker; got drunk, started a fire, burned to death. He never made the connection to Saldivar's plan, but it wouldn't have made mattered, at any rate. The ball was rolling.

Today, he'd question Ted Morgan. He didn't expect to hear much, since they hadn't yet planted the evidence. Still, it had to look like a routine investigation. He headed to Morgan's landscaping warehouse, on the east side of town.

Ted whistled idly while he loaded tools for the day's jobs. He had a crew of 8 men and three women. Together they mowed, trimmed and cleaned one-third of the business landscapes in Hidden Crest, population fourteen, plus.

The crew did most of the work, but Ted liked the smell of cut grass too much to abandon it for a desk. Besides, it kept him available to clients; any complaint was handled swiftly... if someone forgot to edge a lawn or fix a leaky faucet, one word to Ted would fix it. His clients loved him.

He just finished fueling a leaf blower when he spotted the squad car cruising slowly up the alley. It came like a black-tipped reef shark, slowly patrolling the coral's nooks and crannies for hapless Convict Tangs.

His heart sank. His legs turned to jelly. Bracing his shaking thighs against the truck, he tried to be nonchalant, while Talvez exited the cruiser on the far side of Ted's truck.
"Hey, Talvez, what's up?"
His voice cracked. He hoped Talvez missed it. Talvez got closer, stopping on the far side of the truck bed.

"Ted, I need to ask you a few questions, alright?"
Ted went numb. He could already feel the handcuffs.
"Sure; what about?"
"You been doing any *hunting*, lately, Ted?"

He fought for air, forming a quick plan; tell the truth, but not the whole truth. He played racquetball with a few defense lawyers. One of their favorite comments struck home; "Make 'em PROVE it!" Usually, the state can't. Ted was now talking to the state, not a passing friend.
"Oh, you know, here and there."
"Been up on *Radical Ridge* lately?"
Ted almost puked.
"Me? You oughta know, that country's way too steep for these knees, partner... *why?*"

"Oh, that's right... you've got yourself permission to hunt up on the LESBO'S place. Too bad about her, huh?"
Ted snapped his head up from his fake inventorying.
*"What ABOUT Jetta?"*
"Oh, you haven't heard, eh? Burned to death in her shack. I thought you knew; sorry."

Ted felt sick. He loved Jetta. They shared many a bottle of wine in that old shack. They'd grown close through the years. His trips to Jetta's woods gradually became more reunion and less hunting, with each passing year. Ted almost cried; to die in such a horrible, gruesome way was too much to imagine. For a moment, he forgot his immediate dilemma, but then his focus came back, as the deputy's interrogatory droned on.

"... whereabouts on or about, July 26, this year?"
Forcing the image of her charred body away was difficult.
*"Huh?"*
"Where were you on July 26?"

Ted knew exactly where he was. He bit his lip to keep from saying; *'In a fucking firefight with three dope-dealing assholes... THAT'S WHERE!'*

"Uh, am I a suspect or something?"
"Please, just answer the question, Mr. Morgan."
In all the years he knew Rick, he'd never been "Mr. Morgan". He got the feeling the dash camera was taping him. Before he could censor his thoughts, he blurted.

"Why should I? If you're going to arrest me, do it... or let me be!"

Talvez watched drive off to the day's jobs. Suddenly, Saldivar's 'anonymous tip' carried more weight.

*'Hmmm... touched a nerve, eh, Ted?'*

Talvez assumed that every law-abiding citizen would talk with cops, and conversely, anyone who didn't was guilty. It's a myth, but most cops actually believed that bullshit, just the same, Talvez put in a call, to start phase two.

"I'm ten-seven at the donut shop."

This told deputy Null all he needed; Ted Morgan was away from home. Ten minutes later, Null broke into Ted's house. When Talvez selected men, phase two had Null written all over it; he lived for that kind of shit.

By four pm, Ted's nerves were shot. His work failed to distract him. He knew little about the law, except that more questions would follow. When they did, they would crumble his story to shit. Hell; he didn't even have a story.

Several times during the day, he wrestled with the idea of seeking legal counsel, but didn't know if he could trust a lawyer any more than a cop. He even put in a call to one of his clients, a defense lawyer by the name of Takon, but got nervous and hung up before the secretary got the busy man on the phone. His thundercloud of fear kept rising higher.

When the unit rolled up again, he was almost relieved to see it, except this time, Talvez got out with his Glock aimed at Ted. He fast-walked and commanded loudly.

"Freeze, Morgan! Drop your weapon and get on your knees! Put your hands on your head! Lace your fingers!"

Talvez liked busting people, especially helpless, unarmed prey like this landscaper. It was much safer than busting crank dealers.

Ted's crew stood dumbfounded, watching Ted drop the 'weapon', a small cultivating hoe.
"You others, stand back!"
He forced him prone; Ted's face collided with the turned earth in the raised flowerbed. It was almost a comfort to smell the natural scents; peat, rose blend, earthworms. The cuffs bit his wrists and he cried out from unexpected pain. The Deputy seemed to be enjoying his work a little too much.

"Ted Morgan, you're under arrest for the murders of Carlos Antonio Rojas, Salvador Rodarte, and Wesley H. Richards. You have the right to remain silent. Anything you do say can and will be used..."

Talvez droned on, but Ted drifted awat on tangents.
*'How'd they get me? What evidence gave me away?'*
Talvez stood him up, in front of the dashcam.
"Do you understand these rights as I've read them to you?"
Ted was a quick study.
"I refuse to answer on the grounds that it might tend to incriminate me."
"WHAT? Nobody takes the fifth *on Miranda!* You got any needles or weapons in your pockets?"

Ted's return stare said the gloves were off. The deputy frisked him while Ted addressed his puzzled crew.
"Sandy, keep working the accounts... You guys, finish this job. Bernie, call my wife and come by the sheriff's office... *I mean JAIL,* Monday; Willie, ...."
His oration was cut short...
"The rest of you... Shut up and disperse or I'll arrest you all for obstruction!"
Oh God, Talvez did love his power. Enrique deliberately shoved Ted's head down hard while putting him in the unit.
"Sir, WATCH your head."

His neck cracked loudly; Pain ran down both arms. He stayed silent; wouldn't give the bastard the satisfaction. He didn't know much about the game, but it was obviously about intimidation and force. But compared to dodging bullets, it was a piece of cake.

The squad car wasn't out of sight when Ted's business suffered its first casualty. "That's IT! I QUIT! I always KNEW he was too good to be true."

Ted hired Leah when no one else would; she was trying to kick drugs, had a custody problem and a prison record. He helped her get into rehab. Later he paid for a lawyer so she could get her daughter back.

In time, Leah came to worship him. And now her white knight was busted, like a common scumbag. It was too much, but it sure fit with her expectations of the world in general and men in particular; men are assholes.

The crew buzzed. Bernie came to his senses.
"Let's go... We got GAS to burn!"
That was their motto. Theirs was a profit-sharing company. The rest of the crew went back to work.

Ted's head spun with shock as they led him into the sheriff's department. He kept his mouth shut while his brain hovered on the mystery; *'How did they catch me?'*

He knew most of the officers. Some were old rock-fishing partners. Others played on his Slow Pitch league. But now they looked at him differently. The new game was simpler than softball. He was the Christian; they were the lions.

They placed him in a holding cell, a wire-caged booth with a stainless steel bench bolted to the floor. Two walls were cold, brown concrete cinder-block. Multiple blotches of new brown paint covered the latest round of graffiti; some had been scratched so deeply that the words still spoke from under the new paint. The other two walls were fogged safety glass with a wire mesh sandwiched in the middle.

There was one way in or out, the locked door. In the event of fire, he'd cook unless some sympathetic deputy unlocked it. Ted spotted a video lens in an overhead air duct. Since he was handcuffed to the bench, he had no choice but to be on camera. It galvanized his attitude.

*'I ain't telling 'em SHIT!*
Then the thought hit him.
*'Geez... I'm already talkin' like a CON!'*

Soon normal business activity permeated the sheriff's office. For almost four hours Ted sat there, chained to the cold table. His ass hurt. His legs went numb. He got more nervous, like a caged Puma. He fought the urge to shout; *I'm INNOCENT*

By the fifth hour it occurred to him again.
*'It's all about intimidation... Don't sucker for it.'*

Time dragged on.

## Eleven

## COUNSEL

The holding cell was designed to dehumanize and demoralize, to strip away psychic power. He vowed to NEVER play their game. The only problem was, he didn't know what game they were playing. But whatever it was, he wasn't going to help 'em put a needle in his arm.

Ted's musing came to a halt when a familiar voice headed his way. Everybody knew Charlie Takon. He was the only lawyer in Mendonesia County to argue before the US Supreme Court; and he won that one. G. Charles Takon, Esquire was also Ted's very first landscaping client.

The cops hated Takon and he loved it. As the door opened, Ted started to say hi, but Charlie frowned.
"Shhh!"
When the deputy closed the door, Charlie sat down right in the path of the hidden video. He motioned for Ted to move into the shadow of Charlie's massive frame. He smiled and spoke quietly.
"They HATE that... You know, that fuckin' Billy Lee's a damn LIP READER! Guess what; So AM I! Heh, heh, heh!"

Ted felt better, just being in the big man's presence. He had an air of confidence and security. He brought out a small transistor radio and turned it on. It spat out country music yammer. Then the big man relaxed. He spoke in a voice that was almost a whisper.

"Ted, you're a good man... But good men can go down just as easily as bad ones. This system sucks, but I'm a fuckin' VACUUM CLEANER! First rule; don't say SHIT to anyone... *I mean, ANYONE!*"
Charlie liked the sound of his own voice...
"Next rule; I get fifty grand UP FRONT. That's NON-REFUNDABLE. If you walk in an hour, I still keep the fifty... GOT IT?"
Without waiting for Ted to nod, he continued;
"If it comes to trial, I charge five hundred an hour for court time. Time out of court in preparation, is three-fifty. You pay

all depositions, expert witness fees, and all the other bullshit... COOL? Sign here."
He pulled out a contract. The salient points were tabbed.

"Last rule; I don't give an ounce of ape shit if you're guilty or not, so don't fuckin' waste my time with that. I'll get you off like a thousand-dollar hooker!"

He paused for the simile to take effect.
"Now, every time they ask a question, I want you to count to five. If I don't object, you can answer... but ONLY answer the question they ask, so listen to the questions...
"OK"
"NOW, If I do object, SHUT UP, NO MATTER HOW BAD YOU WANT TO ANSWER! Remember; count to five, answer only what they asked... DON'T VOLUNTEER anything! Got it? Good!"

Takon shut off the radio and waved for a guard. After five hours of nerve-wracking imprisonment, Ted had to piss. The guard took him, then watched while Ted voided.

Soon they were in an interrogation room; a larger version of the holding cell, cliché in the extreme; four chairs, small table, one-way mirror. It intimidated him, even though he tried to resist the negative feng shui.

"Mr. Morgan, where were you on July twenty-six, this year?" Ted followed Takon's instructions, counted "One Mississippi, Two Mississippi" all the way to five.
"I don't know."
"What do you mean, you don't know? where were you?" Ted got to 'Two Mississippi' before Takon objected.

"My client answered your question to the best of his ability. If you attempt ANY further badgering, we're out of here!"

Takon was firmly emphatic, as a man who knows his turf always is. The officers and Ted were taken aback. The commander took another tack.
"Mr. Morgan, do you own a firearm?"
Ted counted for five seconds, then looked at his lawyer.

"Yes."

"What kind of firearm do you own?"

Ted counted mentally to three, Charlie intervened.

"Unless forensic evidence exists, which may make such information relevant, my client refuses to answer on the 4th, 5th, and possibly the 9th amendment.... Pending state's production of such evidence. "

Commander Tagliabue asked again.

"I'm sorry, Ted, you said you were, WHERE, on July 26th?"

Takon instantly took over.

"As I said; asked and Answered! You are hereby cautioned against interrogating my client, without presence of counsel. I will be filing for immediate release, unless of course you can show good cause to hold... *Can you?"*

Right on cue, the door opened. A deputy brought in Ted's pistol in a sealed evidence bag. The commander smirked.

"Is this your pistol, Mr. Morgan?"

Ted counted to five. He looked at his lawyer, who studied Ted's face like a long lost lover.

"It LOOKS LIKE a Pistol I own."

Ted had to bite off the words before they came out.

*'How the fuck did they get THAT?'*

The commander swelled like a toad with a good bug.

"IF I were to say the serial numbers match a sale to you, would you be surprised?"

Ted forgot to count to five.

"Yes, I'd be surprised."

Charlie studied his client like a painting at auction.

"When was the last time you saw this pistol, Mr. Morgan?"

"Last week, when I cleaned and locked it up in my safe."

The interrogator feigned not paying attention...

"And, why wouldn't it have any fingerprints on it?"

Ted got mad, forgetting to count.

"Like I said; *I cleaned it!"*

Tagliabue set the hook.

"Then how would you explain the fact that YOUR PISTOL was found thirty miles from here, on the side of a hill, near three DEAD MEN?"

Immediately, G. Charles Takon broke in.

"My client refuses to answer, based on his rights under the Fifth Amendment. And while we're at it, we're going to need a moment, before answering any more questions."

As the peace officers filed out of the room, their collective smirk was as demeaning as it was obvious. Cops loved to watch perps crawl under the fifth, like snakes crawling under a flat rock. It proved they were lying, as far as the sheriffs were concerned.

Charlie again interposed his body between Ted and the mirror, turned the radio up and whispered to Ted.

"Cover your mouth, like the big league pitchers; answer only in whispers... they can't pick up whispers!"

Ted was astonished to think that the sheriffs would bug a confidential communique, but then, they'd also apparently broken into his house to steal his pistol. Apparently, the letter of the law was a capital "F", for Fuck Ted Morgan.

"Where the HELL has your GUN BEEN?"

Ted looked perplexed.

"I don't know, it was locked up; I never left it ANYWHERE!"

Charlie noticed that he didn't mention innocence. He replayed the sentence; *'I never left it anywhere.'* Takon's mind hovered. He hated drawing blanks. He tried some free association...

"Well, your gun didn't just fly away. Fly away... what flies? Planes, balloons, litter, helicopters, cops 'n robbers... cops 'n choppers. Hmmm..."

He thumbed through the arrest report.

"Apparently, the only thing linking you to the killings is the pistol..."

Takon frowned.

"Ted, you're a smart man...Why would you be so smart as to wipe it clean, yet so dumb as to leave it at the scene?"

Takon hissed like a viper.

"I smell a rat... *a BIG FUCKIN' RAT!"*

He hunced forward. Drawn to the man's confidence, Ted similarly leaned forward. They were almost cheek-to-cheek when Takon drew a big breath and let it rip.

"If someone's trying to frame you, they're going to need TIME to nail your coffin shut... So far, all they've got is your gun and three bodies nobody gives a shit about. I can shoot holes through that in my sleep... But if we fuck around for six months trying to mount a thorough defense, they'll have time to nail you for shooting JFK! So, my friend, get ready for the fastest fuckin' trial you ever saw! DON'T ANSWER ANY more questions. *Got it?"*

Awed by the speed of the big man's thoughts, Ted sat there, mesmerized.
"Good... Ya got it already... I love it! Ok, don't talk to ANYBODY... they've got stoolies. Hell, they might even place one as your cellmate. Some prisoners will do anything for shorter time."
Takon motioned over his shoulder. In ten seconds the room was crawling with officers.

"Gentlemen, my client refuses to answer any more questions. I needn't remind you that no interrogation is legal in the absence of counsel... including snitches, cell stoolies or any other persons or entities acting as agents of the state."

Takon closed his attaché and left. There was a hollow silence. The surprised officers took Ted back to his cell. He spoke not a word, even though he was dying to proclaim his 'innocence'.

# Twelve...
## JAIL

When they got near a steel door, there was a loud BUZZ and clunk. They went through the door, which slammed with a harsh clank. They were locked between two doors. The room, if it could be called a room, had one feature; an overhead camera, recessed into the concrete. Should a hostile somehow manage to subdue his guards and gain passage through one door, the locked doors would trap him, giving the officers plenty of time to prepare nightsticks, tasers and teargas.

The second buzzer sounded; They walked the smooth concrete, yellow line in the center. They followed it to a cell; "Up against the wall, Morgan." The frisk was standard procedure every time he'd have contact with a lawyer, doctor or visitor.

He tried to think of something to take his mind off the dehumanizing procedure, such as the large sign in the booking area. He tried to recall the rules for visitors... they needed a government-approved I.D., valid driver license or passport. They had to be at least 18, sober, and on good behavior. They were subject to search. Ted tried to recall the bottom half of the sign, but the deputy interrupted his thoughts.

"OK, in the cell."

The door clanked shut. The sound pierced his heart. Individual freedom had always been the main theme of his life. When he survived the gunfight, his first thoughts hadn't been on his wounds or the killing, but on incarceration. He stared at the bars and wondered how long he could take being penned up.

The cell quickly began to work its black magic upon his psyche it gave him a sense of closure. Maybe he deserved it. He was being punished, even before he had a trial; so much for 'innocent 'til proven guilty.'

Really, if society believed that hollow motto, he could remain free until his trial. Ted immediately filed the motto with the rest of the busted myths; honest politicians, painless dentists and waterproof boots, third floor.

The hunter's eyes flitted around for clues; both beds had been slept in. The lower one had family photos pasted to the wall. It was too dark to tell, but they looked like they came from a magazine, not a camera.

A stainless steel shitter adorned the back wall. There were no visible bolts or other form of attachment. It grew from the wall, like a Sierra Sugar Pine growing from a crack in a granite boulder. He wondered how they hid the hardware.

Two toothbrushes and a bar of grungy soap festooned the sink. There was a stain near the cold water faucet but not the hot; *'probably no hot water, anyhow.'*

The walls were the same mud-brown cinder-block. The bars alone offered a break in the optical monotony. *'No wonder men go crazy in here; you can't help it!'*

He realized how criminals were cultivated; they were seeded first by their crime, then fertilized and watered by the jail and its evil magic.

Being a businessman, he understood the bottom line, to stuff as many inmates into the cheapest structure. He even approved of it when he lived outside. But it was different on the inside; a little splash of bright colors didn't seem like an over-budget expense, but more like first aid. A little salve for the scorching psyche.

Approaching footsteps broke his thoughts. A guard brought two inmates. Both were pat-searched, their mouths were searched, and finally the door buzzed open. Skinheads, both of 'em; their shaven heads and neck tattoos proclaimed it. Both had the same arrogant swagger. They simultaneously glared at Ted, as if they both shared the same shit brain.

*'Maybe they think I'm a spy, a plant... Hell, maybe one of them is a plant!'*

Each of them took a bed, Ted looked at the deputy, who read his mind; he sneered.

"Morgan, you're here 'til we find a cell for you."

The deputy smirked again, then walked away. Other inmates were being led back from the entertainment center. Each was perfunctorily searched before being allowed to enter his cubicle.

Ted already wanted out.

## Thirteen

## PARTIES

Most lawyers don't work on Sundays, but G. Charles Takon was anything but normal. He made calls. He saw some people. A few top judges owed him favors, and Charlie called them all in, for the Morgan case.

It wasn't that he believed in Ted's innocence. It wasn't the money, either. Takon already had a fortune from his practice and great real estate deals. He didn't even know why this case pulled his chain so much.

Even as a young boy, Charlie loved jigsaw puzzles, mysteries, word puzzles and riddles. He couldn't help it. Before law school, he'd been a free-lance journalist. His desire to solve a puzzle was far stronger than any mortal passion for doing good or the search for the "truth" or any of that childish bullshit. It stemmed purely from his huge intellectual craving; the pursuit of solutions.

For a man who could buy anything he wanted, with the means to sate any vice, it should have been enough; fine wine, fine women and haut cuisine ought to be sufficient. But for Takon, it wasn't. It was all about the puzzle.

So the man with the craving was the moth to the flame; he fluttered and flew and hovered around the puzzle. It might burn. It might tatter his wing dust. Hell, it might even kill him, but *somewhere* in that fucking flame is the answer.

The Morgan case had his attention. There was something there, something bigger than a routine multiple-murder. That was why he'd spent his Sunday calling in favors. After a full day of effort, he felt confident that he'd done all he could to ensure a fast track. He drove two hours to the coast for a fine evening meal. Dover Sole Almandine, sauteed Portabellos and Gewürztraminer.

The recently elected District Attorney Bill Onman slumped wearily, looking more like a broken man than a powerful, popular prosecutor.

His soft stance on private marijuana use was one of three political planks that anchored his victory; long tired of the abusive and costly CAMP programs, the citizenry fell behind him in a groundswell of public approval.

While his opponent flogged the dead Puritanical horse about the evils of marijuana, Onman spoke about saving resources to fight violent crime and hard drug trafficking. He made it known that if elected, *HIS OFFICE* wouldn't prosecute folks growing a few plants in their back yard.

He hadn't always thought that way, but his life had changed a great deal in the last twenty years. He went through two divorces. His kids grew up and moved out. Most of what he tried to teach them fell on the culturally deaf ears of youth. When it comes to a father's words, no child listens very much.

These were but a few of the hazards of public office, but for the District Attorney, there were others. Cheap, slick defense tactics, dumb judges and dumber verdicts eroded his belief in the system he once loved.

He came to see the law for what it really was; just another expression of power from the good old boy network... A system that was more interested in preserving the status quo than in meting out justice.

Now at age 52, Onman was wise beyond his years. He finally learned to simplify his life. He had met a good woman, whose gentle guidance and warm heart fulfilled him. And, he had learned to trust the working man. Hence, his recent landslide victory.

Once in office, he was quick to reinforce the plank about Pot. Folks could grow seven plants without any hassle from Onman's law dogs.

89

Onman's victory also hinged on another controversial plank. He had spoken long and loud about loosening the process by which citizens could legally carry concealed self-defense weapons. The CCW or 'right to carry' issue, was another political hotbed.

His opponent Barbara Boxlighter spewed forth on the evils of guns. To hear her tell it, guns caused crime. Throughout her campaign, the liberal press quoted her almost daily, in the hopes of getting her elected. Before the polls opened, most citizens could almost recite her stance verbatim...
*"There is no need for guns in a civilized community... the police will handle everything... Don't take the law into your own hands"...*

No matter that mass murderes spewed the same verbiage seventy-odd years earlier; Hitler, Stalin, Mussolini and Lenin hated private ownership of guns, which is the bane of autocrats everywhere... But Barbara Boxlighter knew that the masses had a D Minus in history. Apathy is fertile soil for corruption.

But her old-school pradigm didn't meet with much favor in a county where 40% of the populace owned guns and lived thirty or more minutes from the nearest peace officer. A lot of shit can happen in thirty minutes.

Meanwhile, Onman drove his old Ford truck around the county. On both bumpers was his favorite sticker, which summed up the 2nd Amendment in a nutshell.

*"Don't trust a government that won't trust YOU to own a gun".*

The average citizen was with him on that. Before Onman's term, it was impossible for a private citizen to obtain a CCW Permit. Sure, they were *allegedly* obtainable, but unless one was an undercover officer or jewelry wholesaler, there was no chance at all. He resented this oppressive philosophy.

After all, the average citizen can drive a car or buy diesel and fertilizer. Why should he or she not be able to carry a gun for self-defense? His position was logical; if an adult had a clean record, was of sane mind and gainfully employed, why shouldn't a permit be granted? Tough logic to shake.

Bill had kept his word, which made him the most popular DA in history. A CCW class found its way into the local college curriculum. The class quickly filled, with a huge waiting list. Students learned every phase of responsible defensive firearms use.

They had a background search, fingerprinting and registry with the sheriff's department. They learned the law, ethics, tactics and consequences of self-defense, under the careful supervision of experts. All successful applicants would need bi-yearly qualifying inspections and a blemish-free record to keep the permit to carry active.

The course was a brilliant screening tool; the type of person willing to go through the process was exactly the kind of person who should have a concealed weapon. They were responsible and respectful of the law. None of the graduates were hot heads or criminals. Those types didn't bother with classes.

The course was popular with seniors and housewives, who need an equalizer against violent criminals. Soon nearly ten percent of the general population could legally pack heat.

In the ensuing months, not one accident or shooting had marred the program's record. To top it off, three muggings and one rape had been thwarted. It was living proof of the old adage.

*Better to have a gun and not need it...*
*than to NEED a gun and not have it.*

Bill's fans loved him and his enemies hated him. He thrived in that kind of political clarity. It created pressure, but the lines couldn't be any clearer. As long as the majority wanted guns, he had a job.

That was the pressure Onman presently labored under. He knew Ted fairly well. They shot together at the range. They shot the shit afterward in the local pub, once the guns were stowed. Ted was a good guy. Bill had to prosecute him.

Skewered upon the horns of the dilemma, he wracked his brain for options. True, Morgan had never taken Onman's required CCW class. But he had owned that pistol for damned near fifteen years before the class began. Besides, there wasn't any proof that he had packed it concealed, so it was legally moot.

But his dilemma went deeper. Every plank of his political platform was involved in the Morgan case. There was the marijuana patch. It was huge... probably a cartel crop. There were firearms, drug dealers, and one whistle-clean good guy. And of course, there were dead bodies.

He reached for the Scotch and kicked his door closed. The curtains weren't drawn, but when the door slammed shut, the drapes were as good as drawn. None of his staff dared look. His three best ADA's pretended not to see. They liked him. Bill was a good boss and a real person in a paper world chock-full of paper-pushing assholes.

Onman thought of his crew and sipped some hooch. The closest desk belonged to Laura Martin. She had the least seniority, but she was a real looker; five feet two, a hundred and five, very fit. Her black hair, deep blue eyes and tanned skin was a stark contrast to most lawyers, who looked like professional bowlers. Martin looked more like a lifeguard.

He took the first chance to move her next to him, as soon as her track record appeared to justify it. If she also happened to be some damned sweet eye candy, well, he couldn't help that.

Laura didn't mind, either. She graduated lowest in her class. If her looks contributed to her success, who was she to object? Martin was ambitious. What she lacked in skill, she made up for with drive. Any error in one case would be fixed before her next one.

Bill knew it would only be a matter of time before he lost her to the better paying field of defense work or he lost to her in an election. The woman was upwardly mobile.

The next desk down belonged to Theodore Fishbein the THIRD. He always emphasized 'third,' so everyone would know he was the grandson and son of a lawyer. Give the kid a few drinks and you'd hear all about it.

But while his grandfather had been a hell of a lawyer, his father was only so-so. 'THE THIRD' was a third-generation Xerox copy; blurred and smudgy, barely representing the original.

His peers smirked about his haughty ways; they called him "ted three," behind his back. But if he lacked charisma, he had persistence. He trudged, working long after the others went home. When he wasn't working, he'd travel to watch top lawyers. He envied their flair and court-winning histrionics. He practiced in front of his mirror. Much like everything else, he trudged with that, too. Persistence pays, even for trudgers like Ted Three.

He vowed it; the NEW Theodore Fishbein the Third would arrive, a new gem at an old pawnshop. His slick-backed hair and cheap suits would be next to go. Ted Three already had the health club membership; a few months worth of bench press work and he'd have the physique. One day, jurors would look AT him instead of through him.

Furthest from Onman's door, Emily Baker's desk shone like a beacon. Hers was the only uncluttered desk. Onman sipped his whiskey and wondered how she managed that little trick, in spite of carrying the biggest caseload.

Baker lacked the raw beauty of Laura Martin, but she was too busy working to notice. Or maybe she noticed, but she didn't give a shit. That gave the woman her own type of beauty. Onman liked her; she was a breed apart.

He mused from time to time about her sexual preference. About all he could conclude was that she didn't have any. Most of the unmarried lawyers left work and met their lovers at the local lawyers' bar. Baker left alone.

As far as he could discern, she was totally about her work. He wondered what would drive a person like that, until he thought back on his younger days. Come to think of it, he had been much the same. Maybe that's what appealed.

Tall and thin, she looked like the perfect librarian or lawyer. She stood and sat proudly upright, unless she was reading; then she would straighten her straw-colored hair, squint and hunch forward like a peeping tom craning through Venetian blinds; as if the text were the most thrilling verbiage ever printed. She became a terrier; she would not let go of a motion or precedent until she could grab it by the teeth and shake it like a rat. After that, Baker owned the rat forever. If ever there was a person custom made for the law, it was Emily Baker.

When Onman looked at her, he saw a Supreme Court justice in the making. Odd, that such a person would choose a small red-necked county seat like Hidden Crest.

Bill's thoughts switched back to the political tar baby that lay growing in the Morgan case. It was a cancerous alien fetus, gestating, awaiting only birth before destroying him and his career.

He finally decided to abort it; he would throw the fetus to his dogs and let them tear it up. If they won, he could have some distance. If they lost, he could always say that at least his office tried the case. It was a no-win scenario, so he felt justified in trying to minimize the fallout. He called them in to give them his decision.

## Fourteen

## JURORS

The first few days brought a tsunami of legal wrangling. Before Ted knew it, he'd been through pre-trial hearings, arraignment, depositions, everything. At every opportunity, the DA's office tried to fight the fast tracking, but G. Charles Takon, Esquire crowed long and hard about his client's right to a speedy and public trial.

And, at each meeting, the judge acceded to his wishes. Truth be told, most of the ADA's resistance lacked teeth. Onman wanted it behind him, preferably before the ink dried. So it came to pass that in an unbelievably short time, Ted sat at the table, studying prospective jurors.

The bailiff seated the first 40 prospects. He tapped the judge's door. The judge entered and sat. They were sworn. Twelve people walked to the jury box. Ted saw the look in their eyes and his blood ran cold. He was the spider in the jar. They were the kids with the icepicks; would they poke a few air holes in the lid?

He thought back to when he sat in the same box, mentally checking out the accused. Back then it seemed such an odd term for a defendant. Now it seemed harsher.

He looked at Charlie's yellow legal pad; totally blank. Meanwhile, the ADA's scribbled furiously; yellow pages flying, noting first impressions for each potential juror. Charlie caught his gaze and whispered.

"Relax. Sit up straight, and try to look innocent. Those rookies over there are panicking! They figured this wouldn't go to trial for months! *NOW* look at 'em! Heh, heh!"

Delay seemed to benefit everyone in the system; paperwork, tactics, forensics, experts. Aside from the ubiquitous scheduling issues, the delays also served another purpose. Time heals. It isolates the crime from the passion in which it was committed. Hence judges and lawyers, indeed the entire system, protected delays. Hell, they needed them.

Charlie exploited the situation; the prosecutors not only looked unprepared, they were. He was glad he got away with it. Still, he pondered why Onman allowed it; Bill was nobody's fool.

The next year would be an election year, and the incumbent "Wild Bill" Onman, hero of the masses, had no intention of torpedoing his career by personally trying such a no-win case.

If he prosecuted and lost, his opponent would make him out to be incompetent. If he got a conviction, he'd look almost as bad; the accused was a local businessman, with strong roots in the community. If he didn't bring charges, he would be seen as soft on crime.

So, the only solution was to pass the hot potato down the food chain. His lackeys could cut their teeth in capital court; hopefully the shit wouldn't float back to the top. Personally, he hoped they'd lose it, so Ted could go back to work. Onman's personal properties were on Ted's route and those rentals were starting to look pretty shabby.

The rookie ADAs hissed and scurried. They looked green, but eager. They didn't even know Ted, but their job was to kill send him to the lethal injection gurney. Careers hinged upon cases like this. As far as Ted could see, the only difference between this trio and the three killers on Radical Ridge was that this time, Ted couldn't shoot back.

The judge asked each prospect to stand, give name, age, occupation, marital status and residence. Each juror stiffened before standing; rehearsing, some fighting off stage fright.

"Len Baxter, 47, I'm a general contractor, divorced. I live here in town."

"Bill Wall, 26, I'm single, drama student. I live in Cow Valley."

"Mary Detweiler, married, 29. I teach 5th grade and live 60 miles from here, in Long Valley."

An obvious ploy to get her mileage into the record.

"Jose Barreras, I am widow. I work winery, am 53... oh, I live at Mossywoods Winery", near Helen's Pass."

"Lupe Hildalgo, 26, I'm a housewife. ELK GROTTO. "

"Polly Cetani, I'm 82 and retired from banking. I'm a widow for 34 years. I live in Fair heights"

"Steve Clemens, 35. I make videos. I reside eight blocks from here and I'm single."

"Lisa Beckhart, 18 and I work for a day care center, in Fair Heights. I am not married."

"Timothy Tompkins, 29, artist! I live over in Bear Wallow."

The judge prodded the next one, who didn't stand up.

"Number ten, Mister Closser, would you please stand, sir?"

He stood up and shouted.

"SORRY, JUDGE; I DON'T *HEAR SO GOOD!*"

Those next to him jerked from his unexpected volume.

"GEORGE CLOSSER. I'M 79. RETIRED FROM RAILROAD. THAT'S WHY MY EARS ARE SHOT. I LIVE SOUTH OF TOWN. I AM WIDOWED. *AN' I DON'T HEAR TOO GOOD!*"

Juror 11 stood right up.

"My name's Glover Codie, and everybody here knows I'm a dentist right here in town. Oh; I'm 44 and divorced... *twice.*"

The last woman stood.

"Elaine Fouts, 36. I'm a sign painter in Fair Heights. I am married."

The tension eased in the room; the others settled back to see whether or not their lives would be put on hold, meanwhile hoping the first twelve prospects would keep the rest of them off the hook.

"Peremptory challenges?"

Laura Martin stood up first.

"Thank you, your honor, we would like to thank and excuse number 10, Mr. Closser."

The judge noticed that old man Closser heard the exclusion perfectly well.

"Your honor, defense would like to thank juror number 5, Mrs. Hildalgo."

The judge sat two more prospects in the vacant seats. Again, the prosecution scribbled furiously. Takon moved not a muscle. The new number five stood up.
"Bette Tilde, 37. I run a dry cleaning shop and live in town... oh, and I'm married, for 22 years."
Number 10 stood proudly.
"My name Inverness Caesar Tostani... I am sculptor. I have 49 years. I live in woods AND *I NEVER get married!*"

He said it with such conviction that it brought a titter from the gallery. The prosecution passed their next exclusion. Takon stood.
"Your honor, defense would thank and excuse juror number 6, Mrs. Cetani."
The young man taking her space remained standing. When cued, he was ready with the spiel.
"My name is Dante Jansen, I'm 28, right? I live on North State Street. I'm single and I sell uhm... I sell retail smoking products."

Some people in the courtroom snickered; Dante's head shop sold Pot-related paraphernalia; pipes, bongs, rolling papers and electronic scales. The best in the county.

In the same fashion, the court selected two alternate jurors, although the judge doubted that they would be needed. To Judge Lenah's eyes, it was going to be a damned short trial. As he thumbed through the personal ads in the back of the girly magazine, he wondered why they even were bothering with a trial. Still, it was a capital case, so alternates would have to be called. One never knew about the mythical slam dunk case; it could slam or dunk you.

Laura Martin stood up.
"Your honor, the prosecution is satisfied with the jurors. Thank you."
Takon leaped to his feet, refraining from smirking.
"Your honor, so is the defense!"
The judge instructed the other prospects to go back to the basement, since other courts might need them. They filed out, unhappily anticipating having to go through the same process again, in yet another courtroom.

After they left, the judge instructed the jury and the first recess was called. Takon was beside himself with glee. "I can't believe those guys let our jurors in! Most are self-employed. They'll want to get this over with, *FAST!*"
Ted frowned pensively.
"Why are we goin' so fast, again?"
"Speed makes mistakes, and the more mistakes THEY make, the better *YOU* look."
They went to a plea bargaining room. Charlie pulled two deli sandwiches from his case and outlined his strategy.

"You're not going to take the stand. We'll only have a couple of witnesses... maybe NONE. And get this; ALL THROUGH THIS TRIAL, I'm gonna look like a bump on a log, GOT IT? Don't get pissed off. I want you doing the same. MONKEY *SEE CHARLIE, MONKEY DO CHARLIE... GOT IT?* I want that jury thinking about their wasted tax dollars on a frivolous prosecution!
"Oh, I get it."
By the way, do you still owe your last year's taxes?"
Ted swallowed a mouthful. The Turkey and Cheddar was better than jail food.
"Yeah, I've been meaning to, but..."
"GOOD! We couldn't BUY better press! Every self employed juror has tax problems, huh?"

They finished eating in silence, then both parties went to chambers. The prosecution appealed for more time. Just as before, Takon crushed the fledglings' motions.

Fifteen...
## OPENER

The People opened with Fishbein. His cheap suit was
spotless. His hair plastered down with the latest new age
goo, strove to look fashionable, but it didn't work. He just
looked like any other salaried geek in an overly bloated
redneck county administration. Ted remembered punks like
him in high school, without the suit. Ted Three spoke
directly to the jury.

"Murder... It's usually done in *secret*. People *HIDE
evidence;* they try to get away with it. Well, you're not going
to see a lot of evidence, because THIS was a rare type of
murder. Now, my opponent's going to stand up soon. He'll
probably say we don't have a motive... or an eyewitness.
He might try to point the blame elsewhere. But whatever
he's about to tell you, it won't amount to a hill of beans.
We've got dead bodies. We've got a murder weapon.
We've got a motive... All this and more... will point you to
the ONLY logical conclusion; *GUILTY!"*

Fishbein looked at the jury, obviously hoping to score
points for brevity. It was his shortest opening statement.
Brevity is brilliance, especially when there's no time to
prepare a real opener. But before the young lawyer
swaggered back to the table, G. Charles Takon stood up. It
left Fishbein standing in symbolic limbo.

"Your honor, may it please the court; I'd like to reserve my
opening statement until beginning defense... Thank you."
Judge Lenah looked surprised.
"Very well, the People may begin their case."

Clearly, it was a brutally effective tactic. They had expected
Takon to take up the full afternoon with one of his
legendary openers; a litany of metaphors, parables and
favor-gaining anecdotes, to gather the jurors in his arms.

Each prosecutor wore the same look; deer staring into the
light of a speeding locomotive. Laura Martin recovered first.

"Uh, your honor... the People were not expecting this... we have no..."
Judge Lenah broke in.
"Are you saying that you're *NOT READY* to proceed?"

All eyes in the jury bored holes through the prosecution. Even the gallery stared at the squirming lawyers. Their witness list was pale enough, to begin with, but since they anticipated a slow jury selection and a lengthy opener from Takon, they'd scheduled their witnesses for the next day.

"A moment, please, your honor..."
Laura hissed at the others.
"We're SCREWED ALREADY! That bastard planned it! Who can we get, RIGHT NOW?"
Baker shrugged.
"We can get the coroner. He's just a block away."
Fishbein hated disorderly pursuit, but didn't have any option. He hissed at the ladies.
"OK, I'll do it!"
He stood for the judge.
"Your honor, the People call James Three Feathers."
The bailiff went out in the hall and promptly returned;
"Judge, Jimmy's not out there."

Judge Lenah looked amused.
"NO, I don't doubt it. Counsel, I'll give you a ten minute recess; have your case ready for trial."
With a pound of the gavel, the judge left and everyone filed out except Ted and Takon. Charlie grinned.

"Did you see the jury when they fumbled the ball?"
Charlie's eyes sparkled; he was in the zone.

Twelve minutes later, Sheriff-Coroner James Three Feathers took the oath with his usual solemn respect. He brought that respect to work every day, no matter how big or small his task. He was as honest as a peace officer could get. Emily Baker prepared to qualify the expert witness.

## Seventeen

## PROSECUTION

"Sheriff Three Feathers, where do you work?"

He leaned forward to the microphone, but accidentally hit it with his big nose. The bump was loud in the courtroom speakers; several people jerked back reflexively. Judge Lena advised his old fishing buddy.

"Jimmy, you don't need to lean forward any more; we fixed the mikes last week. They pick up better now."
He nodded, sat back and tentatively spoke.
"I work as the Sheriff/Coroner".
When he heard his voice, he relaxed; the pickup was good.
"How long have you been a Sheriff?"
"Nine years; before that I was a deputy for ten years."
"Where did you get your training?"
"Sacramento. After that, I got a job here."
"Have you any training in firearms, self defense?"
"Oh, yeah... Just like most officers have."
"Did you recently examine the bodies related to this case?"
"Yes."
"Would you tell us your findings, one body at a time?"
"Sure."
He sat up straight, checked notes and cleared his throat.

"I found a decomposed partial, evidence tag; "HB 17- 01.
This victim had a fracture of the 6th Cervical Vertebra.
Also, there was a fracture of the First Thoracic Vertebra.
This one probably transected the spinal cord, causing instant paralysis and death fairly soon after."
"Would you characterize the cause of death as violent?"
"Very likely, yes."
Baker sat down; Fishbein took over.
"Officer, could you back that statement up... in other words, be more specific?"
"Yes; the C 6 fracture in the transverse process was a gouge wound. The only thing likely to do that is a bullet. Also, the place where the body fell... it wasn't too big of a fall. The fractured T 1 would require a greater force to

break say, from a bludgeoning. Then the other bodies were..."
"OBJECTION. Your honor, the witness was asked to address one victim at a time; in the interest of clarity, perhaps we could do that?"

Takon's objection made sense, and it was formed so as not to inflame the jury. That might be needed later.

"Sustained. Let's first just deal with Seventeen. After that, defense will cross you about that one. Then we'll go to the next one, OK, Jimmy?"
"OK; sorry, judge."
Lenah smiled. He couldn't wait to fish again with Jimmy.

"Counsel, you may proceed."
"Thank you, your honor.... Was there anything else that indicated murder, and remember, we're talking ONLY about seventeen, right now?"
Three Feathers shrugged.
"No, that was it."
"Your honor, I have no further questions."
Fishbein swaggered back to his team, as though he'd done something magnanimous. Ted thought; *'He'll be a politician someday'*

Takon stood, buttoning his jacket before speaking.
"James, we've known each other a long time, haven't we?"
"Yes."
"And in all that time, our paths have crossed, both in and out of courtrooms, haven't they?"
A curious frown punctuated his answer.
"Yes, they have."
"And, in all that time, you've never jumped to conclusions, have you?"
"Objection, your honor. Counsel is grandstanding."
Judge Lenah agreed.
"Sustained. Counsel, please come to your point."
Takon never missed a beat.
"Thank you, your honor, I was just about to do that. Sheriff, *why are you jumping to conclusions NOW?"*
"What do you mean, Charlie?"

Grabbing his notes and swelling with air, Takon proceeded to dissect the sheriff's testimony.

"In your piror deposition, you stated that you returned to the scene several times, to search for more bones, right?"
"Yes."
"Sheriff, why didn't you get 'em all on the first visit?"
James relaxed at the seemingly innocent query.
"Oh. Because the bones were scattered by uh, wild animals. We couldn't find 'em all on the first trip."
Conscious of the jury's eyes, Takon refrained from smiling.
"In your expert opinion, after examining many crime scenes for many years; can you tell the court which kinds of animals drag off bones, out in the woods?

"Oh, lots; coyotes, dogs, raccoons, skunks, it depends."
"How about bears?"
"Sure; a bear can drag a whole cow away."
"Are there bears on Radical Ridge?"
"Sure... Everybody knows that!"
"How 'bout wild boar; could they drag off bones or parts?"
"Oh, yeah. Boars eat anything; everybody knows that."
"Are there any wild boar on Radical?"
"Sure... Radical's got lots of pigs."

Realizing that his earlier assessment was incomplete he began to correct the oversight.
"Sorry; I forgot 'em. They have sharp tusks, too."

Takon nodded in agreement, careful to look like a man seeking the truth, not some desperate ambulance chaser grasping at straws.
"And what kind of birds will scavenge a corpse?"
"Oh, uh, in this area, buzzards, eagles, crows, ravens and blue jays... sure."
"How about rodents; don't they gnaw on bones?"

Three Feathers waved his hand, almost dismissing the small rodents.
"OH, sure... they gnaw to get minerals."

Takon turned on his heels, facing the jury, looking pensive.

"Ok, now Sheriff, of all these animals; coyotes, dogs, wild boar, bear, mountain lions and so on; do any of them have sharp teeth?"
Jimmy snorted at the obvious question.
"Sure. They ALL have sharp teeth... Except birds."

"Isn't it possible that the gouge wound you mentioned, on the uh, sixth vertebra; could this have been made by a tooth, tusk, or a sharp fang? Maybe a rodent, even?"
"It's possible, but..."
"And isn't it possible, probable maybe, that the victim suffered the broken T1 vertebra in a fall?"

Three Feathers was losing ground.
"Possible, yes... Probable, *NO!*"
Takon went back to his table.
"Tell me, officer... How many bodies have you examined?"
"Sixty two, so far."
"Did you examine a body that died from a broken spine?"
"Yes."
"To be precise, wasn't that, uh, checking my notes 09- 92?"
"Yes, I believe it was."
Takon had him, and he wanted the jury to feel it.
"Could you tell the court please, which vertebra was fractured?"
James never hesitated; the memory flashed too brightly.
"The first Thoracic/ Sorry; I forgot about that old case."

Takon acknowledged his honesty with a simple shrug.
"That's ok, nobody expects a man to remember every old case, especially when he's sitting in the hot seat. Please tell the court; what did the woman fall from, to cause such a horrible..."
"Her daughter found her dead in the kitchen. She fell from a small stepladder. She still had a paint brush in her hand."

Some jurors murmured.
"So, in light of your earlier statement about the height of the fall, would you care to restate your opinion? Isn't it possible that a fall in the woods, in steep, uncertain terrain, could have caused the broken spine, and NOT necessarily a BLUDGEONING?"

105

"Yes, it's possible."
Takon let it sink in while he sipped some water.
"Officer, I see from your report and deposition, you didn't examine a WHOLE body, is that right?"
"Yes, that's right."
"Could you tell the court what was missing?"

"I object, your honor, relevance; the witness has already commented on those body parts in his control. I don't see the relevance of..."

Takon snorted at Laura's objection.
"Your honor, the RELEVANCE is obvious! They're saying my client caused a death, based upon the forensic exam. It's imperative that the jury be privy to precisely HOW adequate *or INADEQUATE* the evidence really is!"
Judge Lenah never even looked up from his reading.
"Overruled; witness can answer."
Takon wondered if he was looking at girly magazines.

"Can you tell us please; what was missing from the body?"
Jimmy checked his notes again.
"The right femur, the right tibia, ankle, foot, left radius, ulna, wrist and hand as well as the lower jaw and lower teeth."
"Is that all, Sheriff?"
"Yeah, that was it."
Takon appeared to be curious.
"Well then, where are the reports on the victim's stomach contents?"
"I did not examine the stomach."
"Why not?"
Three Feathers looked like he was addressing an imbecile.
"Because, the stomach was *gone, THAT'S WHY!*"

Now it was Takon's turn to look perplexed.
"But didn't you just tell the court the only things missing were some bones? Now you're saying the stomach, too, was missing?"
"Oh; I thought that was obvious. The soft tissues were gone before I examined the remains."
"I see..."

Charlie looked like a math professor who knew the answers to some esoteric equation.

"Please bear with me, while I ask some more questions, because they're not obvious to the jury... OK?
"OK"
"You did not examine the stomach, so you couldn't say if he got drunk and fell to his death or if he got low blood sugar, got dizzy and fell, is that right?"
"Correct."
"And likewise, you didn't examine his heart, correct?"
James shrugged heavily, seeing where his friend was going with the questioning.
"Correct."
"So you couldn't say if he had a heart attack while climbing that steep ridge, could you?"
"Correct."
"And you didn't examine the skin, so you couldn't say if he died from a bad cut, snakebite or bee sting, could you?"
"That, too, is correct."
Takon went gently, to avoid angering the witness or jury.
"Now, before we bore the court, recounting all of the soft tissue systems, the brain, lungs, liver, intestines, muscles and so on... that *were GONE*... is it fair to say you didn't examine these?"
"That's right."
Takon set the hook.
"And, yet, with the entire spectrum of probable causes of death that were unavailable for examination... would you care to correct your earlier opinion about the victim's cause of death?"
"Yes, I would."
"Please, do so..."
The jury focused on the expert.
"Based ONLY UPON the questions you've asked me today, the COD is uncertain."
The gallery gasped and Takon sat down.
"I have no further questions, regarding HB 17-01, Judge."

The room buzzed as Takon sat down. Up until then, he'd been unobtrusive... a fixture, almost. But, after the cross-exam, the jury saw him as a vital piece of the truth finding process, just as they saw themselves. They began to identify with him. The buzz kept up, until Judge Lenah lightly tapped the gavel.

"Order, please... proceed, counsel."

All eyes went to the prosecution, for the next bite. Fishbein looked raped. He stood, although obviously not as self-inflated as he'd been ten minutes earlier.

"Mister Three Feathers... sorry; *Sheriff* Three Feathers, plase give your findings on the body, labeled "HB 18-01?"

"Sure. This body was in basically the same condition, except the sun bleached the bones more. Most of the bones were there, except for some of the right ribs, which had been sheared off, at the level of the armpit, running from the third rib to the ninth. Also, the left 2, 3 and 4 ribs were broken off at the spine and were missing. I found small spots of metal spatter when I X- rayed the body."

The courtroom buzzed with the evidence of violence.
"It looked like the killer cut out the evidentiary holes... "
"Objection. Your honor, witness is speculating."
Lenah never looked up.
"Sustained. Please stick to the facts, until your opinion is specifically called for, OK, Jimmy?"
The big Indian nodded.
"Sure. Sorry, judge."
"Was there other evidence of murder?"

Three Feathers looked relieved to be on safe ground.
"Yes. The body wasn't dragged around as much as 17, and the sunlight tanned a piece of skin. This skin tag overlaid the spine. It appeared to have been cut with a knife and it had a round hole in it."

Fishbein sat down, looking smug again.
"Thank you. Nothing further, your honor."
The jury shifted its gaze to Takon, to see how he'd handle the bullet evidence.
"Have you ever witnessed the aftermath of a lion kill?"
"No sir."
"OK, you ever examine a body having sheared ribs?"

"OBJECTION!"
Laura Martin stood up and called out sharply.
"Your honor, defense has already stipulated the coroner as an expert, yet counsel's now questioning his credentials!"

"Your honor, I am NOT questioning his expertise... I am, however, entitled to cross his OPINIONS, based upon his expertise, or lack thereof, am I not?"
Judge Lenah shrugged.
"Witness may testify as to what he's seen, or not seen."
"No sir, I have not examined sheared ribs before."
"Have you any formal training in bone studies?"
"None, other than standard coroner's training."

"We just heard you testify that these bodies were harassed by wildlife; dogs, lions, coyotes, boar, even bears. You said that many of these sharp-toothed creatures could inflict a gouge-type wound. Couldn't these sharp-toothed animals also inflict such a skin wound?"
"Yes, but that wouldn't account for the ribs..."
Charlie interrupted.
"Please, just answer the questions as I ask them, OK?"
"Yes, sure... Sorry."

"Now, earlier, you testified that certain birds will scavenge; are birds capable of making a round hole in rotting flesh?"
The Sheriff looked like a cornered bulldog.
"Yes. A buzzard or a raven... but that wouldn't account for the RIBS bein' gone!"
Takon conceded.
"OK, OK; let's talk about the missing ribs. If I were to produce an expert in mountain lions that will state that shearing ribs are commonly seen in lion kills, would that surprise you?"
Three Feathers acted like he'd lost already.
"With wild animals, anything's possible."
Charlie Takon had one more arrow in his quiver.
"Please tell the court; what kind of bullet did you find in the body?"
"I didn't find a bullet... just spatter."
"Well, was it spatter from a .22 caliber pistol, like the one in evidence?"

Three Feathers was totally honest.
"I can't say."
"Could it have been spatter from a shotgun or assault rifle, bullet, such as the ones found at the scene?"
Three Feathers looked impotent. He shook his head.

"It was just spatter, you know... little lead flakes."

Charlie took a big breath.
"All right, Sheriff, let me summarize briefly and you speak up if I'm wrong, at any point, all right?"
"Sure."

Takon was on stage, which is what he wanted all along.

"This body was found in the sun. It had metal flakes in it from a bullet, but we can't say what kind. We can't say if the missing ribs were removed by a lion or man... Right, so far?"
He grudgingly acknowledged.
"Yeah; right so far."
"Sheriff, is there anything else you can tell us from this partial skeleton, that might help us get to the truth?"
"No, sir. That's about it."

Takon looked pleased. Then he went for the "no-shit" question that average lawyers rarely asked.
"Was there any forensic evidence at all, that says that Ted Morgan killed the man?"
Sheriff Three Feathers raised his eyebrows.
"Nope, not a shre..."
"OBJECTION!" Laura Martin stood, but the judge was way ahead of her.
"Sustained. Counsel, you are cautioned."

Takon let it slide right off his back.
"I apologize. Nothing further, regarding HB 18... however, I'd like to ask a few questions later, about ALL three bodies, your honor."
"Granted"

It was Laura Martin's turn at the helm. Petite, pretty and athletic, she cut a fine figure in the room; every male juror scrutinized her ass.

"Sheriff, could you please tell us about your findings in the third set of remains, 19-01?"

Three Feathers obviously liked this woman. A brief smile flitted across his face and he sat forward.

"Yes ma'am; this body was in almost perfect condition, almost mummified since it was covered in bay and tan oak leaves. It was also the only body that was found with me in attendance."

"Could you explain that, please?"

"It was my third trip. We were looking for more bones. We had two dogs. One of 'em went up another hill, far from the crime scene. He pointed a large crack in some big rocks. We found the body deep down in the crack."

"Ok, can you describe these photographs, please?"
She handed him pictures.
The judge looked at Takon.
"NO objections, counsel?"
Takon looked up, as if he too was looking at porn.
"Thank you, judge, no objections."
Three Feathers went at it.
"All but a few small bones were present; no big animals could get to it. It was in a shady area, as you can see."
Laura Martin showed the pictures to the judge.
"Permission to show the jury?"
"Granted."
Each juror came to full attention. They were looking at real dead people.
"Officer, what's so important about the shade?"
"OH, that dry shady crevice and the Bay and Tan Oak leaves helped preserve some of the organs and other details. It makes for better evidence. In fact, this body was the best evidence of all three."

"Did you form an opinion, as to cause of death?"
"Yes, I did."
"And what is your opinion?"

He spoke in a more authoritative tone.
"The victim died from a broken neck, at the First cervical vertebra and from a broken Occiput."
"I'm sorry, what IS an Occiput?"
He patted the back of his head.
"It's the back of the skull."

"Did you do any chemical testing?"
"Yes. We put traces of stomach tissue through the lab."
"What can you tell us, about the stomach contents?"
"Oh, the victim ate about eight hours before death; I found eggs, flour tortillas and ham."
Laura pranced back to her table like a super-model. "Thank you, Sheriff. Your Honor, I have nothing further."

Takon stood up slowly, with a confident air.
"What else did you find, that's more worthy of the jury's TIME than the poor man's last meal?"

Three Feathers cleared his throat.
"Ahem; the victim had cocaine and methamphetamine. I'll have to check the report for the specific numbers, but..."
Takon waved his hand.
"That's OK; I believe we get the picture... the man was on drugs. Now; you said this body gave the best evidence of all three bodies?"
"That's right."
Takon raised his hand, palm down and flip-flopped it.
"And by that, can we assume that the first two bodies gave you the worst evidence?"
"Yes, you're right."
Takon raised an index finger, impersonating Ben Matlock.
"Tell me, officer; did any of this BEST EVIDENCE, point to MY CLIENT as the killer?"

"OBJECTION!"
Fishbein stood.
"Your honor, that's NOT the intent of the exam, and counsel knows it!"
Judge Lenah ordered firmly.
"Chambers, counsel."
Five minutes later, they returned. The judge spoke.

"I must instruct the jury; forensic exams are performed to find evidence. However, any LACK of evidence cannot be construed as proof of guilt or innocence. You are instructed to disregard defense's last question. Defense, proceed."

"Thank you, your honor. Let me rephrase; did you find any bullets in this body, that match the pistol in evidence?"
"No."
"Did you find any traces, fibers, blood or any other thing, either on or near the body, linking that death to my client?"
"No."

The big lawyer raised a hand as if to wave howdy.
"OK, the photo you just saw shows some very large rocks, directly above the crack holding the body, is that right?"
"Yes... really big boulders."
"Let me offer two scenarios; tell me which seems more probable, based on the facts and your expert opinion, OK?"
"OK."
"Situation one; my client killed this man and left absolutely no evidence OR TWO, this guy was high on coke and meth, slipped and fell to his death? Which is more likely?"

Handcuffed by the limitations of the questioning, James looked frustrated.
"Well, it's more likely that he slipped and broke his head on the rocks when you put it that way, but... "
"Thank you, Sheriff. Your honor, I have no more questions about 19."
He sat down. The gallery murmured. Takon had shot another flaming arrow right through the People's wagon. Emily Baker stood quickly.
"Redirect, your honor?"

Lenah nodded and looked at her; slight build, modest dress, thick eyeglasses, she seemed the perfect agent of the court. Her skin had that ashen-gray undertone from two packs a day and a life spent under cheap fluorescent lighting. Her hair was short and unobtrusive. Her suit and slacks hid any hint of gender. He'd seen it before; cougar in sheep's clothing; librarian during the day, repressed sexual tigress unleashed at night. Surprisingly good fucks, those quiet cougars.

"Let's talk about the *REST OF THE EVIDENCE,* which Defense is so keen on ignoring; you were at the crime scene three times?"
"Yes ma-am."
"Part of your duty is to gather things *BESIDES bodies,* which help you to form your opinions, is that right?"
"Yes ma-am."
Now it was Baker's turn to raise a hand.
"In other words... at a drowning, you might look for live electrical wires in the pool or at a hit and run, for a license plate or busted turn signal plastic, *things like that?"*

"Yes ma-am... I use lots of clues. It all helps."
"So, you used... guns, footprints, cartridges, to help form your opinions in this case too, correct?"
"Yes ma-am."
"Well, could you tell the court about these other things*?"*

He looked relieved to finally be able to tell the whole truth.

"Yes ma-am; we found three empty shotgun hulls next to Seventeen, and six empty rifle cases relating to Eighteen. These were seven point six two by 39 mm. I found two empty cartridges slightly uphill from his body; two twenty threes. The lab matched these to the firearms found at the scene."
"And based on these, did you form your opinion?"
He was eager to finally be able to say it in plain English.
"These guys died in a helluva firefight!"
"In other words, they died from *gunshot wounds...* NOT from a few falls in the woods?"

"Yes; in my opinion, two died from gunshots and the other guy died from a severe blow to the back of the head."
Baker sat down.
"Nothing further, your honor."

When Takon stood up, he did so with exaggerated deliberation. For the first time, he failed to button his coat, subconsciously inferring that the next line of questions was too important to wait for cosmetic considerations. The jury sat forward. He had them eating out of his hand.

"Now, Sheriff, the People allege that my client shot those men with a little twenty-two caliber pistol, which we'll see in evidence later. Please tell the court how many empty .22 shells did you find at the scene?"

The Sheriff looked perplexed; anyone ought to know how difficult those tiny cases are to spot.

"I didn't find any, but..."

"Thank you, Sheriff, I just need you to answer the questions *as posed;* you didn't find ANY casings that MATCH MY CLIENT'S GUN, *correct?"*

The Sheriff reddened.

"Correct."

"Sheriff, what diameter is a twenty-two rimfire bullet?"

Three Feathers relaxed; he knew guns.

"Technically it's 'two two four' or two hundred twenty four thousandths, but everybody calls 'em twenty-two's."

Three Feathers looked around for approval of this technical bit of data, but he just got a roomful of blank stares. No one else in the room knew much about guns. He might just as well have been talking about death rays from Mars. Takon approved, but didn't show it.

"OK, tomorrow we're going to hear about a partial skin tag, with a round hole in it, will be seen on the state's video of the crime scene, correct?"

"That's correct."

Takon studied the jury; they looked confused.

"Now, before the court wonders why you didn't bring it up, could you tell us how that skin tag got destroyed?"

"Well, uh, one of the canine officers AHEM... apparently ate it, right after the video was made."

The courtroom squirmed.

"That is regrettable, as well as upsetting. Tell me, Sheriff, so everyone knows I'm not trying to dodge it; what was the caliber of that hole in the skin tag?"

James looked at his notes.

"Roughly twenty-six caliber. At the time of death, it was smaller, since as skin dries, the hole enlarges."

"Ah, so that hole could NOT HAVE BEEN MADE by a bullet BIGGER THAN twenty six caliber, right?"

"Yes, that's right; only a bullet SMALLER than twenty six."

"What is the caliber of a bullet fired by the AR 16?"

"All two-twenty-threes have the same diameter; point two two four."

The court buzzed with confusion; Takon immediately exploited it.

"But isn't that the *EXACT diameter of Ted's twenty-two?*"

"Yes.

"OK. And what is the size of buckshot from the empty hulls at the scene, please?"

"I uh, didn't bring my chart with me, but I think it's around a quarter-inch... twenty four or twenty five, I think."

Takon put him at ease with a shrug.

"Oh, that's close enough for now. If we need to, we can check the chart later... Please tell the court, what's the caliber of the AK 47?"

"Seven point six two millimeters... point three oh eight."

"AHA! NOW we're getting somewhere. The AK-47 was TOO BIG to make the hole in the skin tag, right?"

"Right."

"So, two other guns BESIDES my client's gun, could have made that hole, correct?"

Seeing what the lawyer had been driving at caused Three Feathers to look resigned.

"That's correct."

"Tell me, Sheriff; opposing counsel drew upon your expertise, in law enforcement. I'd like to do that too, OK?"

"Sure"

"Ok, bear with me now, because some of these questions are going to seem awfully obvious to you, but I assure you, they're not obvious to the court... alright?"

"Objection! Your honor, counsel is editorializing."

Judge Lenah looked bored.

"Sustained. Charlie, please just ask your questions."

Takon bowed slightly.

"Sorry, judge. Ok; what do the experts call it in combat terms, for a weapon's efficiency in killing people?"

116

"Oh, there's several terms. I learned it as *Effective Range.*"

"Fine. How does that differ from "Maximum Range?""

Jimmy was comfortable talking about guns and ballistics.

"Maximum Range means how far a bullet will go, if you fired it at a 45 degree angle."

Takon acted puzzled, for the jury's sake... but he already knew the answer to his next question.

"How does that differ from Effective Range?"

"That means the range at which your weapon is certain to kill the enemy. Lots of things affect it; the type of bullet, sights, whether a gun is reliable, easy to fire, the position of the safety, even the type of action affects it. But the simplest way to think of Effective Range is the distance at which you are almost certain to kill your enemy. Some experts also call it lethal range or killing zone, too, I think."

"In your expert opinion as a law officer, with weapons training, would you estimate the AR-16's Effective Range?"

He pursed his lips in thought.

"For an average man, two hundred yards. But for a soldier, five hundred, maybe more."

"And how about the twelve-gauge, ILLEGAL fully automatic shotgun firing buckshot, what would you estimate?"

"About a hundred yards."

"And the AK-47?"

"I'd say it's about the same as the Colby; average man, two or three hundred. Soldier, at least five hundred."

Takon wanted to lock it in the juror's minds.

"Ok, the shotgun is CERTAIN TO KILL to a hundred yards, The AK and Colby, to at least 200... and in skilled hands, maybe farther?"

"In the hands of an ex soldier or marine, definitely farther."

"How about my client's pistol; what would you estimate its Effective Range at?"

The Sheriff never hesitated.

"Under combat situations? I'd say ten yards, maybe twenty... I don't know, I wouldn't consider it for combat, really."

Takon feigned astonishment while the courtroom quietly buzzed at the gross imbalance in lethality.

"Why so little lethal range? After all, don't the ammo boxes say a twenty-two will shoot over a mile?"

Three Feathers raised his hand to stop the lawyer from completing such foolish, misleading statement. Win or lose, Jimmy was honest as hell.

"Sure, a 22 will *SHOOT* a mile, but that's a rifle. A pistol only shoots half that... maybe less. But that's not the effective range. A short, shaky pistol is NOT accurate... And it's a small bullet with little stopping power. Even a belt buckle could stop it. I wouldn't consider it for combat."

Takon lowered his voice to solemn tones. The court went stealth-mode silent.

"OK, Jimmy, my client's been charged for killing these men in a combat situation... I believe your words were; *'It was a hell of a firefight'*. Given your knowledge of firearms, would you comment on his choosing a 22 pistol to go up against those deadlier weapons?"
He wrinkled his brow, as if everyone should know this.
"Charlie, It'd be *SUICIDE!*"

Takon went back to the table, then pulled his best impersonation of Colombo. He spun and raised an arm.
"Oh, What was the time of death, please?"
"I couldn't say precisely, due to the severe state of decay."
Takon shrugged nonchalantly.
"You can't estimate which HOUR they met their demise?"
Three Feathers stifled a chortle.
"Humph; I couldn't say which WEEK they died. But, based upon my charts, I'd say they died between mid-July and the first week of August, this year."
"Your honor, I have nothing further."

The judge closed trial for the first day. Before the bailiffs came for Ted, Takon tried to cheer him up.
"Walk tall, head high... we kicked some SERIOUS ASS today! See ya tomorrow!"

"I'll try, Charlie. Thanks."
The deputies loaded Ted into the van for his return trip to the jail. He knew the routine, even though he hated it. He hated jail, too, but it wasn't so scary any more.

At first the inmates left him alone, but after a while they took him in; a serious long-term prisoner. They taught him to hot-wire cars, poach abalone and snag salmon. He was slowly learning the fine art of lock picking. While this advice was unsolicited, it was a welcome distraction; anything was better than staring at the bars or thinking about his fate.

## Eighteen

## SKINHEADS

His lawyer did a great job dissecting every bit of first day testimony; When he listened to Takon, it almost seemed like he HADN'T killed those assholes. Ted felt strangely good as he headed back to lock up. For the first time since they first cuffed him, he felt like he had a chance. However, that changed at dinner. Kirt sat and put his food tray down.

"Well, Teddy, didja figure it out yet?"
Kirt was pure trouble, so he feigned interest.
"Figure what out?"
Kirt sneered...
"Who your friends are, man. Who your friends are!"

Ted chewed for a minute, stalling for time. He'd already had a few threats, as well as a hair-raising brush with violence in the shower. Luckily, a guard broke that up before it got bloody.

"Why don't you explain it to me?"
Kirt scooted sideways, his face inches from Ted's ear.
"OK, you're white. I couldn't help noticing... AND, you're up for multiples... so unless I miss my guess, you're in need of a uh... let's call it a 'support group', shall we?"

He'd already heard the speech; you're in or you're dead. Safety in numbers. He put no stock in it, but this time, Ted became painfully aware of the harsh truth. Still, the thought of being branded for life as a Skinhead was too much to handle. He nodded, while mindful of Takon's earlier advice; *'Trust no one; the walls have ears!'*

"Let's say for the sake of argument I MIGHT be interested. What can the anti-Semitic, nigger-hating, spic-stabbing skinheads do for me?"

Kirt swept his gaze around for guards.
"Well, for openers, FREE ADVICE. Word has it the Campesinos are comin' for you. Don't know what you did

to piss 'em off, but you got some heavy shit comin' your way. Watch your back!"

He already learned by osmosis that the Campesinos were just a small group of local gangsters. They liked tagging buildings, sniffing paint, breaking windows. The cops couldn't do much to break up gangs; civil rights and all that shit, so the punks had carte blanche. Aside from that, his family and his day job always kept Ted too busy to worry about riff raff. He faked disinterest, to pump Kirt; it worked.

"Campesinos number about fifty in L.A. A few travel, doin' bizness, know what I'm sayin'? They're killer bees; you swat one, you swat the whole wetback hive. Some come this way during harvest. Maybe you popped one 'em, eh?"

Ted reflexively stated his mantra.

"I am innocent."

"And I'm Adolph Hitler! Fuckin-A, man, everybody in this fuckin' joint's fuckin' INNOCENT! But it won't matter; all that matters is the Campesinos *THINK you did it*. They'll come for you... they ALL come."

Kirt left. The gauntlet was down. If he wanted to know more, he'd have to join those Nazi loving assholes.

## Nineteen

## TESTILYING

Ted arrived at 8:30, the lawyers, 8:45. With the jury seated promptly at 9:00, the court came to order after Judge Jason Lenah solemnly entered and sat down.

This day would bring the 'meat and potatoes', as Charlie put it. He told Ted to stay cool, no matter what the testimony sounded like. Takon seemed to anticipate the day's events. Ted didn't share his enthusiasm. Kirt's words kept echoing in his ears... *'Heavy shit's comin' your way'*

In spite of his predicament, Ted couldn't help but wonder; *'What's heavier than a murder trial?'*

Three Campesinos entered the courtroom. They sat in the back; purple tee shirts, khaki pants and fishnet headbands. Each sported a close-cropped goatee. On each right arm, just visible below the sleeve, was the bottom of an identical tattoo. Ted missed their entrance, since the court was swearing in the next witness, Deputy Sheriff Guissepi Prondini. Fishbein spoke for the People.

"Would you state your full name and spell your last name, for the record?"
"Guiseppi I. Prondini, Pee ahr oh enn, dee eye enn eye."
He adjusted his tie.
"How long have you worked with the Sheriff's department?"
"Twenty two years, this December, sir."
"And how did you learn about the crime scene?"
He acted coached, answering swiftly in robotic script.
"Dispatch received a call from a trout fisherman. He chose to remain nameless, since he was trespassing... and since Trout season's closed."
The room erupted in chuckles. When the titter died, he continued.
"The call came in at zero seven hundred. He found human skeletal remains. We asked him to keep his cell phone on, so we could trace his signal."
"Did you find the three bodies when you got there?"
"No sir; we found two partials."

"Did you find anything else on your first trip?"
Prondini sat forward. Most of the jury did, too.

"We found a foreign-made AK-47, Browner humpback shotgun, modified to fire fully automatic, and a Colby AR-16, also capable of fully automatic fire."
Fishbein pointed a finger to the roof, mimicking Takon.
"During your fly-in, did you find anything else?"

Prondini knew the question was coming, obviously.
"Yes. We flew over a patch of Marijuana, approximately a mile west, as the crow flies, from the crime scene."

"Did you return that day to seize the Marijuana?"
"No, sir. We were booked for two days with other seizures. We returned three days later and seized it. While we were there, we deployed two men to the scene of the shootings, to do another search prior to releasing the scene."

"Did your last search produce any new evidence?"
"No, sir."

"Did you then release the scene?"
"No sir. When we seized the Marijuana, there was evidence of THREE suspects living in the cabin, so we suspected another body or possibly a living suspect still hiding in the area."

"What evidence made you think three people lived there?"
Prondini scowled, as though everyone should know why.

"Three dirty plates, three cots, multiple sizes of boots and jackets. Besides, it seemed unlikely that only two men could take care of such a huge Pot patch."
"So what did you do?"
"We returned the next day with canine officers, coroner and more deputies; that's when we found the body in the crevice."
As he sat down, Fishbein asked one final question.
"Did that search produce anything else?"

"Yes, sir. We located a Rubier Mark II pistol, .22 rimfire, at the original crime scene."

The lawyer stood back up, mimicking Takon's posturing. Fishbein was a fast learner.

"Did you run a make on that pistol?"

The deputy smirked; "Yes, we did."

"And who did that pistol belong to?"

"To the defend..."

"Objection; your honor, counsel is forgetting... the pistol found on the side of a hill belonged to no one or else it wouldn't have been laying there, your honor."

"Sustained. Rephrase."

"Thank you, judge; The serial numbers indicated what, please?"

"Approximately fifteen years earlier, the pistol was sold to the defendant, Ted Morgan."

The courtroom buzzed.

"Thank you. Your honor, nothing further."

"Mr. Takon, you may cross."

Takon was rummaging, for the first time.

"Thank you, your honor; Deputy Prondini, who found the pistol, *you?*"

"No. Officer Null found it, I believe."

Takon pointed at an exhibit.

"Please, where on the map was it marked as found?"

He glanced at the map and turned a slight shade of red.

"It's uh, not marked; you'd have to ask deputy Null."

Takon paused to get the jury's attention.

"Now, I'm confused; in your prior deposition, you used this fine map, indicating where every piece of vital evidence was, even though you personally didn't find them. Can you tell the court, WHY this ONE PIECE of evidence, incriminating *ONLY MY CLIENT, IS NOT MARKED?*"

Prondini stammered.

"I, uh, ahem... it's sort of embarrassing, but I think with the excitement of finding the third body, we neglected to document the pistol's location."

Takon had him skewered.

"Well, deputy, weren't the officers *EXCITED* when they found the first two bodies?"
Without waiting for an answer, he pressed.
"Weren't they *EXCITED,* when they found the OTHER WEAPONS? Are you trying to tell the court you were SO EXCITED about the last body that you photographed it, tagged, bagged and loaded it, in proper protocol, yet ONE LITTLE PISTOL caused everybody to LOSE THEIR SENSES?"

Deputy Prondini's face reddened, but he didn't answer.
Charlie looked at the judge; "Your honor..."
The judge instructed the lying cop.
"Please answer the question."
"Like I said; Null found the weapon, you'd have to ask him."

Takon lived for such moments; waved his hand ove head.
*"Oh, I WILL,* deputy, I will. You can COUNT ON IT! Your honor, I have no further questions for this, uh, WITNESS."

Judge Lenah called for a recess.
"Court will resume in ten minutes."
Ted looked around and spotted the gangsters. The purple shirts triggered Kirt's words; *'They wear purple.'*

They reminded Ted of three buzzards on fenceposts... except they were uglier than buzzards. They sneered, got up in unison and left. It made him wonder; *'What did I just see, a threat? What the hell could they possibly do to me now? I'm in fuckin' JAIL!'*

He had no time to ponder it, as the need to piss hit him hard. He waived at the deputies.

Soon court came back to order. Laura Martin stood.
"Your honor, the people call Sharon Willoughby."

A large fat woman in drab dress walked in; the prosecution team swelled with largess... it didn't go unnoticed by Charlie Takon. Willoughby was an expert in light firearms tracking; a state bureaucrat of no small stature. She was sworn in and sat down.

With a great deal of puffery, she narrated her curriculum vitae into the record; positions held, classes she'd attended, as well as an ego wall full of 8 x 5 diplomas, issued for attending government-sponsored seminars for the tediously boring.

By the time she was done with her CV, it was obvious to the jury; she was the Dalai Lama of serial numbers, and the jury was already swayed... Takon decided to steal her thunder, before it bullshitted the jurors any further.

Laura Martin started out.
"Ms. Willoughby, could you please read the serial numbers on... "

"Your honor, if it will save the court some time, defense is happy to stipulate the 22 pistol in evidence belongs to... or at least at one time, belonged to my client."

Takon robbed the shock value of her upcoming testimony; he was the drunk heckler, shouting out a punchline while the comedian was setting up the joke. Looking non-plussed, Laura Martin sat back down.

"Uhm, that's fine with the people, ahem, your honor. We *would have proved it ANYWAY!*"
A ripple of laughter broke out. She raised her chin.
"No further questions, your honor."

The jury watched Charlie; what else could he have in mind for the bloated bureaucrat? They didn't have to wait long.

He already had the fat bitch skewered; now it was time for the basting and roasting.

"Ms. Willoughby, we stipulated that at one time, the little pistol BELONGED to my client. Now, I'm curious... *WHO OWNED THE OTHER THREE WEAPONS?*"

Clearly, she hadn't anticipated this question. She shuffled papers. She donned her reading glasses.

"Ah; the shotgun was first sold to one Byron Hill, Thousand Oaks, California in 1999. The AR 16 was sold to the US Marines in 1991... and we have no record of the AK 47, except that it was made in the Czech republic."

Takon frowned pensively.
"I'm curious, Ms. Willoughby, why aren't the Marines, Byron Hill, and the Czech gun-makers on trial here?"
"OBJECTION! Your honor, counsel is mocking the witness!"

Takon shrugged shoulders and implored.
"Your honor, with all due respect, the REAL mockery is what's happened to my client. These other weapons were fired, their cartridges scattered all over the scene, and yet only my client's..."
"Sustained... no more of that, counsel."

Takon deliberately acted deflated as he sat down.
"No more questions, your honor. Thank you."

Sharon Willoughby stepped down. She waddled from the stand, nylons scrubbing together noisily, keeping time with her undersized high  heels, over-stuffed with fat ankles. It sounded laughably, self aggrandizingly foolish; Zip, pop. zip, pop. *See how important I am* ... zip, pop...

When she passed by the defense table, she sneered at both of them; a typical soft, fat, stupid bureaucrat, out of her element and unduly biased, whenever real-world facts dominated an issue.

"Do the People have a witness ready?"
Baker stood.
"Your honor, the People call Officer Jed Gregory."
After they swore him in she began.
"Deputy, what is your job?"
"I process evidence for all crimes reported in this county."
"How long have you been doing this?"
"Fourteen years."

She raised the pistol for all to see.

127

"I'm handing you this exhibit, marked People's seven... do you recognize it?"
"Yes; my initials on the tag; it's the pistol found on Radical."

"Could you tell the court, please, since defense is going to ask it anyway; was there any evidence it has been fired?"
"No; the gun had been cleaned and oiled."

She got close to the witness.
"So there weren't any fingerprints on it?"
"No. They were destroyed by the cleaning and the oil."
"Have you ever seen guns that were wiped clean, in your capacity as a crimes examiner?"
"Yes; I've examined several that were wiped clean."
"And, were any of those suspects CONVICTED?"
"All of them."

"So, suspects have been known to *conceal evidence?*"
"Yes ma'am; quite often, in fact."
Baker sat down smugly.
"Your honor, I have nothing further."

"Officer, do you carry a service weapon?"
"Yes, why?"
Takon waved a finger.
"Please... I'LL ask the questions, you answer 'em, OK?"
"Yes, sorry."
Takon pointed at the officer's hip, as if his pistol were hanging there at the moment.
"May I ask.. Do you clean, wipe it and oil it regularly?"
The deputy looked trapped.
"Yes, I clean it weekly."

He wagged his index finger, in the universal sign for "NO"
"Have you ever KILLED anyone with that weapon?"
"NO! I've never even drawn my weapon... except for the practice range!"
Takon raised his index finger to the heavens.
"Then is it fair to say that not all guns that are cleaned and wiped free of prints, are murder weapons?"
The Deputy held his temper.
"Yes. It's fair to say."

Takon took another line.

"Now, those other *clean weapons* you've examined; were ANY OF THEM left at the scene?"

"No, sir. All three were hidden far from the scene; one was in the suspect's basement. The other two were hidden in an overhead crawl space."

"Tell the court, in your expert opinion, how would you categorize a situation where a murderer shoots three people, THEN CLEANS THE GUN, THEN DROPS IT IN THE DIRT *AT THE MURDER SCENE?*"

"I would say it's, AHEM... unusual."

Takon craned his neck towards the witness.

"Unusual? Have you ever seen that before?"

"NO."

Takon got closer.

"Would you say it's unusual, maybe even *improbable?*"

The witness sat back, crossing his arms.

"I'd say... highly unusual."

Takon shook his head and walked to his table.

"Your honor, I have no more questions... Thank you."

The courtroom buzzed when Lenah recessed for lunch. Ted got permission to call home, but the line was busy. Although Takon insisted that his family stay away from the trial, Ted just had to speak to his wife, for some strange reason. He had a bad feeling in his gut. He hung up and went to eat his lunch.

He wanted his family at the trial, but had to trust counsel. Takon feared that family members might wince or squirm during trial, and juries often misconstrued it as an admission of guilt. Ted ate his sandwich while reflecting on the morning's testimony.

By the time Ted finished lunch, the Campesinos were finishing with his wife. They had simply walked up and rang the bell. When Jo Morgan innocently opened it, one punk struck her in the face, knocking her down and semiconscious.

Two of them tied her down and gagged her. The others searched the house. The whole thing had a ghastly efficiency to it. Luca dialed local weather, blocking all incoming calls. Julio found the liquor. Jose searched for safes and jewelry. That left Jorge and Mano to begin the raping.

After that, they all had plenty of liquor and the sobbing white woman. They found the gun safe, but it was too secure for cracking; cracking it would waste time and make too much noise.

As the last punk got up from the woman, the pack got bolder and more aggressive. The liquor hit them; they forgot that their original mission was to simply scare Ted into silence and leave the message that if you fuck with the Campesinos, they knew where to hurt you.

Luca was the youngest, eager to make his bones. He flipped his butterfly open and started making surface cuts on her naked abdomen; nothing deep, just enough to scare her. Watching her eyes roll back, he terrorized her; "Orale, BEETCH, now you know what eess like to have a *real man* between your legs, eh? Tell your old man... Don't fuck with Campesinos... or we ALL come back... maybe we find your keeds, too, *COMPRENDE?"*

The sight of blood was the ultimate catalyst. Pack fever overtook the rapists. Before it was over, the woman had countless surface cuts on her legs, arms, torso and back. At first, Jo's eyes bulged in terror and she choked on the gag, screaming as loud as she could.

Somewhere around the twentieth stiletto cut, however, she passed out. Blood loss paved the way for her ensuing coma. Her mind floated in the nether world, where she felt peace, warmth and bliss. It was wonderful, where she was.

Once it became apparent that the woman was comatose and incapable of showing more fear, they went into cleanup mode, wiping down everything they'd touched. Luca produced a role of purple crepe paper and decorated the room. Julio washed off their knives in the sink. They stole the rest of the booze and drove off in the low rider.

From the outside, the Morgan house looked just like all the others in the tract; orderly and peaceful, with no signs of the carnage laying inside. Three miles away, court resumed its afternoon session.

Theodore Fishbein stood up.
"Your honor, we call Officer Randy Null."

In a few moments, Null entered the courtroom, was sworn in and ready for testifying. Of course, cops didn't call it that... They had their own term; testilying.

As far as the law was concerned, the world consisted of two warring factions; peace officers versus everyone else. When the shit hit the fan, a few lies for their brethren were not only expected but downright demanded.

"Deputy Null, how long have you been a deputy?"
"Sixteen years."
"Were you involved in the Pot raid and body searches, on and near Radical Ridge?"
"Yes."
"In what capacity?"

Null faced the jury, just like the testilying coaches taught him.
"Secure the scene, seize marijuana, property, search for bodies, weapons and contraband."
"Showing you people's seventeen; do you recognize it?"

He tensed up and slightly reddened.
"Yes; it's the pistol I found, ahem... at the scene."
The court buzzed. Judge Lenah called for order.

"And what did you do with it?"
"I tagged it, bagged it and placed it in the evidence chain, same as everything else."
"Your honor, nothing further."

Takon stood without waiting for the judge to prompt him.
"Officer, how many times were you at the scene?"
Null acted like it was a dumb question. He hated lawyers.

"Twice... first time, to get the pot. The second time, we went back to try to find more evidence; that's when I found the defendant's pistol."
"Now, when you say the 'second time', you really mean the second time *for YOU*, right?"

"Yes... That's correct; I didn't go on the first trip."
Takon shrugged assent.
"OK, how many officers went with you?"
"I think twelve on the ground, four in the air."
Takon recapped for emphasis.
"Twelve ground, four air; sixteen cops, right?"
"Right."
"How many officers went, without you to search for bodies and weapons?"
Null looked hesitant; "I think six, but I'm not sure."
"OK, we'll call it six; how many officers on the *LAST trip?*"
"Four human officers, two canine officers."

Charlie zeroed in for the kill.
"Can you tell us WHEN you found the pistol?"
He shrugged and frowned, annoyed at the trivial query.
"I don't know, precisely... I mean, *I didn't check my watch.*"

"No, I mean... where were the others, when you found it?"
"Oh; they were on the opposing ridge, reclaiming the last body... the one in the boulders."

It too all of Takon's willpower to resist sneering. He walked over and tapped the scene map, which had been blown up large enough for the oldest eyes in the jury.

"Could you show the court WHERE you found the gun?"
Null exited the witness box and walked to the map.

"It was RIGHT HERE!"
 He drew in a small red "x"

"Let the record show the witness marked a red x on the main trail to Radical Ridge, which has PREVIOUSLY been traced in blue."

Takon let him get back in the box before reeling in his fish.
"Officer, I'm... CURIOUS. You just stated that TWENTY TWO human officers searched that trail, but no one else spotted the pistol; *can you explain that?*"

"Well, it was just barely sticking out of the weeds."

He raised his hand in objection to the pitiable statement.
"But we had two canine officers also searching the same trail. Can you explain HOW these two dogs WALKED RIGHT PAST THIS GUN? How do you explain THAT?"

Null's face grew a darker shade of red.
"I don't know, maybe the wind blew the scent the wrong..."

"THREE TRIPS, twenty two officers, trained in searching crime scenes, finding items as small as cartridge cases and two highly-trained search dogs within two feet of that pistol; the weeds, the wind... COME ON... *DIDN'T YOU PLANT THAT PISTOL?"*

"OBJECTION!"
All 3 ADA'S cried in unison. Baker spoke for them all.
"Your honor, the people object to this... *TACTIC!"*

"Overruled; counsel asked a reasonable question, based upon evidence presented. I want to hear the answer."
Pissed off at being correctly accused, Null yelled.
"NO! *I did NOT plant it!"*

Takon shook his head at the pathetic response.
"Officer, can you explain the behavior of a suspect who would go to all the trouble of CLEANING a murder weapon, only to leave it on a public bare-dirt trail?"

Null groped for answers.
"I don't know! Crooks do stupid things. Some of 'em want to get caught."

"AH! You forget one thing; my client's NOT A CROOK! As your boss already declared in prior deposition, Ted doesn't even have, as Commander Taglibue stated under penalty of perjury, 'a speeding ticket.' So, we can't characterize my client as a "CROOK", can we?"
"Not YET."

"Officer Nul..."
"No! *I found the pistol* just like I said; *AND THAT'S THAT!*"
Takon swooped down on the liar.
"Mister Null, you're wrong! 'That' is *ANYTHING* but THAT!"

Laura Martin bolted upright; "OBJECTION!"
"Withdrawn. No further questions from this... *witness,* Your Honor."
Takon sat down while the courtroom tittered. The testimony interested Judge Lenah so much that he forgot to call for order. Clearly, everyone knew that Null committed perjury.

"Does the Prosecution have another witness?"

Fishbein addressed the Court.
"Your honor, the People call Officer Enrique Talvez"
Talvez promptly took the hot seat and was sworn in.
"Deputy Talvez, you were the arresting officer, correct?"
"Correct, sir."
"Please tell the court; what did you base your arrest on?"
"Sir?"
"I mean, what evidence, suspicions; what cause?"

"Oh; I received a dispatch saying that Mister Morgan's weapon was found where three bodies were found. Upon contacting the suspect, I questioned him briefly. He acted very suspicious; he wouldn't answer my questions. He denied being at the scene. When I asked his whereabouts on July 26, he refused to answer me."
"Is that all? I mean, did you arrest him then?"
"No, I filed a preliminary. Later that day, when the lab confirmed the pistol belonged to the suspect I went back and arrested him."

"Did you read his rights to him?"

"Yes, I tried, however, the suspect wouldn't admit that he understood them."

"What?"

"I said; '*do you understand these rights as I've read them to you?*' At which point, he took the fifth amendment."

"Have you ever had a suspect do that before?"

"Never."

"What did you think it meant?"

"It made me more suspiciou..."

"Objection, your honor..."

"Sustained; you are not to comment upon an individual's guilt or innocence, relative to Miranda proceedings."

"I'm sorry, Judge."

"No further questions, your honor."

Takon stood up; "No questions, Judge."
The jurors looked perplexed, but he knew what he was doing. He'd save the Talvez tidbits. Knowing that at least one juror would have a problem with it, Takon decided to let it fester until later.

Laura Martin stood up.

"Your honor; if it please the court, the people call Sarah Thompkins."
After a short wait, the bailiff led the witness, swore her in, to tell the truth and nothing but the truth, under penalty of perjury. Sarah liked it better way back in the day, when the oath still included; '*so help you God.*'

"Miss Thompkins, you're a tax preparer, correct?"
Sarah was nervous; "Yes, I am."

"And you do the defendant's taxes?"

"Yes, I do."

"I'm handing you people's eighteen through twenty-one... please read the highlighted; defendant's TAX LIABILITY?"

"Ted owed eighteen thousand for last year's taxes."
The courtroom almost roared with alarm. Laura started to swagger, then quickly checked her impulse.

"Thank you. No further questions, your honor."

Takon stood casually. He buttoned all of his buttons... a nonverbal sign for small shit.

"Now, if we left it like that, the court might get the wrong idea, and I don't think anybody here wants that... Would you please read the SAME section on each of his PREVIOUS *three tax returns?*"

Sarah was a good witness.
"Yes. In 1998, he owed 26 thousand. In 1999, he owed 20 thousand, and in 2000, he owed thirty nine thousand... he paid these, including penalties and interest charges."

"So, based upon those years, was Ted's CURRENT tax liability UNUSUAL?"
"No, not unusual."
Takon raised both arms as a plea for logic.
"So his tax stress wasn't any worse than usual... OR HE'S KILLED A HECK OF A LOT OF PEOPLE!"
The courtroom, even several jurors, burst out laughing.
Judge Lenah needed the gavel to restore order. The prosecutors looked like slaughtered sheep. When order returned to the court, Charlie just smiled.
"Nothing further, your honor."
"Ok, we'll take our afternoon break, and we'll be back here in, uh, 15 minutes."

Charlie's aide came over and whispered fervently in the big lawyer's ear. Takon listened intently, while a grave look slowly overtook his face. He turned to Ted, speaking fast.

"Something's come up. I'll be back in ten."
The big man sprinted from the room like a bear after salmon. Ted had no time to dwell on it. With the shackles, guards and searches, a routine piss took the whole recess. As soon as he caught the bailiff's eye, the laborious proceeding fell into play.

When court resumed, Takon was white as a ghost. Small beads of sweat peppered his upper lip. He was clearly preoccupied. He stood and addressed the court.
"Your honor, may we sidebar?"

Lenah looked curious.

"Yes, approach."

After five-minutes of whispering, they returned.

"Are the people ready to proceed?"

Fishbein got up.

"Your honor, the people have one more witness, but we expected at least three or four days before this witness would be called. We request a recess, until we can..."

"OBJECTION, Your honor; my client's already been jailed TOO LONG for a crime he didn't commit; I don't see WHY he should be penalized, for the People's lack of preparation."

"Please approach."

Both sides started hissing at each other. The judge took over, before it got ugly.

"Laura, Charlie's got a good point; so far, your case has been shallow. Is your last witness a smoking gun?"

"Your honor, he's a forensic metallurgist, who will testify that those metal flakes, in Eighteen came from a rimfire and the ONLY rimfire was the defendant's; I'd say that's a pretty compelling reason for a recess, wouldn't you?"

She batted her eyelashes. Takon noticed.

"Oh, PLEASE! I could shoot holes through that, no pun intended, with my EYES CLOSED! Besides, they couldn't POSSIBLY prove they came from my CLIENT'S gun, which the People's EXPERT stated *'was cleaned and hadn't been fired.'* Judge, if they put him up there, I'll eat him up!"

Judge Lenah maintained his dominance.

"Based upon what I've seen so far, I am inclined to agree; request for recess is denied. Let's get this over with."

When they walked back to their tables, the prosecution looked whipped. Takon tried not to smirk.

Emily Baker remained standing.

"Your honor, the people rest."

"Thank you, counsel... is the defense is ready to proceed?"

"Thank you, Your Honor; we are."

"Your honor, I'd like to give my opening statement, as I previously requested."
"Proceed."
Takon was already walking closer to the jury.
"Thank you, your honor."
Facing the jury at a distance of only three feet, he lowered his voice. It was an intimate range, to which the jury was unaccustomed.

"I would like to thank you, and also to apologize, for making you come here to try this *INNOCENT man*. But you see, when someone accuses you, we HAVE TO HAVE a trial. So, when they arrested Ted on the thinnest of evidence, we HAD to have a trial.

"The judge HAD to be here. You HAD to be here. The People HAD to be here, too. Ladies and gentlemen... OF ALL THE PEOPLE IN THIS TRIAL, I'M THE ONLY ONE who VOLUNTEERED to be here, *got that?* I'm the ONLY ONE *who had a CHOICE!*

"I could've taken Ted's case OR take my daughter fishing! Well, I took it for two reasons... first; I believe Ted's innocent... and second, I just can't handle my daughter catching more fish than me *again!*"
The jury chuckled, but recovered quickly.

"Seriously; I took this case because Ted's innocent. I believe that you'll find him innocent, too. The evidence points so overwhelmingly to not guilty... you can't vote it any other way. I'm sure that's what you'll do...

But your job goes farther than just finding him not guilty. Your duty as jurors also REQUIRES that you OVERSEE the judicial process, so that guys like me and the prosecution don't get out of control... *After all, we're lawyers!*"

Again, the courtroom chuckled. They loved his frank, plain language, completely free of legal-speak. "It's a PRECIOUS thing, the jury, because without you, EITHER SIDE, MAYBE BOTH SIDES can get CORRUPT... it happened in other countries, where the ACCUSED has NO CHANCE for a FAIR TRIAL! God willing, it will never happen in America... THAT'S why you folks were summoned here and *THAT'S why* I'm talking to you right now."

"We work under the presumption that we're INNOCENT UNTIL PROVEN GUILTY; Got that? *PROVEN GUILTY...*"

"Remember, the accused doesn't have to prove innocence... Now, that really makes sense, doesn't it? After all, How can you prove a negative? Could you prove you didn't eat the last piece of pie in your fridge last night? You couldn't do it, could you? I mean, the pie's gone and you have no proof that you didn't eat it."

He got closer to the jury.
"The state has to PROVE you ate it. Without an eyewitness, they'd need overwhelming circumstantial evidence, like a dirty plate, crumbs on your lip, and a big old grin on your face!"

Again, the courtroom laughed with the lawyer's harmless parable.

"I posed this example to illustrate a fundamental concept of our legal system; the accused is constitutionally protected against having to prove a negative. The accused doesn't have to pose a defense at all!

"The State must PROVE TED IS GUILTY... I hope you ACTUALLY LIVE by that concept, because my client, Ted Morgan... his very LIFE depends on it."

"Your honor, the defense rests."

Twenty-one...
## CLOSERS

The courtroom buzzed, Judge Lenah banged the gavel;

"Order! Order! I instruct the jury to place no weight against the defendant, for using his constitutional right to pose no defense... this is a right that is GUARANTEED to us all."

Turning to the People's bench, the judge asked.
"Are the People ready with closing statements?"

They quickly huddled and Baker took the ball.
"Thank you, your honor, uhm, the people again, did not expect or anticipate, this turn of events. We uh, request a recess until tomorrow, so that an adequate closing argument be formula..."

"OBJECTION! Your honor, my client's already served too much time for a crime he did not commit. His business has suffered, and his FAMILY misses him. Is he to serve another DAY in jail, simply because the people want to think about what they're going to say? Or is this trial going to be decided upon the FACTS IN EVIDENCE?"

"Sustained... I see no reason for anything other than a simple closing argument. The People shall proceed or forfeit the closer."

The rookies scurried. Fishbein hissed at his colleagues.
"That asshole's been one-upping us with his fuckin' country yokel hee haw law! Let me have it!"
The women shrugged. Baker said; "Go for it!"
Fishbein stood up.
"As you wish, your honor, thank you... "
He faced the jury.

"As counsel just said, this is a simple case. Ted Morgan was on Radical Ridge. He needed over eighteen thousand dollars to pay his taxes. Close to the crime scene was almost five million dollars' worth of TAX-FREE MONEY, just waiting for a him to chop off a few branches and his tax problems would be over! How many of us wouldn't be tempted, in that situation?

"Ted tried to steal those plants; he got caught... He killed those men... Think about it; after he killed them, he started hiding evidence... He probably cleaned his gun, stuck it in his pocket and left the scene; and in his haste to flee, the gun worked its way out of his pocket... He dropped a vital piece of evidence, *HIS gun.*"

He took a sip of water while it sank in.
"He had NO ALIBI, when asked about his whereabouts. He refused to cooperate with interrogators. His family was *CONVENIENTLY* out of town at the time of the crime. He DID IT, folks. And, like defense counsel suggests, it's very simple; HE'S GUILTY!"

Fishbein sat down, hoping to score points for brevity.
Judge Lenah prompted the defense.
"Does defense wish to proceed with closing arguments?"

"Thank you, your honor I DO; however, it may take a while; perhaps we could take a short recess? I should close easily, before we adjourn today."

Lenah looked relieved; "Ten minute recess."

During the break, Charlie Takon advised Ted.
"Look; we're almost through. Sit straight and proud. Juries love that, especially this late in a trial."
But the words lacked conviction. He seemed distracted.
"Yeah, sure thing, Charlie."

He felt weak. His life was in the hands of twelve strangers. Takon's dilute pep talk didn't help him. His knees knocked. He started second-guessing himself; He'd killed those three men, when maybe he could have run away. After all, they weren't as woods-wise as Ted. He thought he'd eliminated all traces of his presence, and yet somehow his pistol got back to the crime scene.

141

That scared Ted the most; if the sheriff's office WAS framing him, he had bigger problems. A conviction would put him in law enforcement custody for years. He got paranoid. He even started suspecting his own lawyer... after all, he didn't know much about Charlie. Before the arrest, their only communications had been about how often he should fertilize Charlie's north-facing Camellias. Now his lawyer posed no defense at all. Ted was way beyond worried; he was scared shitless.

Charlie was reading some notes; the first time for that since the trial started. The words were neatly hand-printed in Latin. Before Ted deciphered one word, the court came to order.

"Defense may proceed with closing statements."

"Thank you, Judge. Ladies and gentlemen, I wish all of my cases were this easy... I'd never lose! Ted is as innocent as the driven snow. He's as innocent as anyone in this courtroom, and... he is far more innocent than some."

Takon looked straight at Deputy Null. So did the jury.

"Now, the law says we didn't have to mount a costly defense. That's good, because Ted's already in the hole for eighteen grand to the IRS. Worse yet, he's losing income every day he sits in jail, and he has lost a lot of business from the bad publicity surrounding this case."

"A minute ago, I said we wouldn't waste your time trying to defend... But let me tell you WHY I believe that, OK?"
Several jurors nodded involuntarily.

"The State must prove beyond a 'REASONABLE DOUBT' that Ted killed those three men. So, let's look at the state's case, then you decide if they proved it or not."

"First, they said the motive was FINANCIAL... So *IF Ted was up there,* why didn't he chop down a few plants after killing those men; nobody was alive to stop him, *right?"*
He sipped for pause and effect.

"While he was AT IT, he could have taken enough dope *for next year's taxes!* But according to the Sheriff's deposition, no plants were taken and Ted still owes the I.R.S.!"

"Next, the state has the, uh... excuse me, I can't even say it without a chuckle; the 'murder weapon'.

"Radical Ridge was LITTERED with murder weapons!" There were two automatic assault-style weapons and an illegally modified automatic shotgun, all of which were owned by hardened, professional drug dealers."

"Remember the effective range of those weapons? The People's EXPERT TESTIFIED they were TEN TIMES more lethal than my client's puny little pistol. Would you take a pocketknife to a sword fight? Of course not; that would be stupid... does my client SEEM STUPID?"

"I don't know about you, but if I were going to kill somebody and take their dope, I'd want the BEST TOOLS for the job... *wouldn't you?"*

He let that sink in, too.

"I sure wouldn't pick a little pistol, to go up against THAT KIND of firepower. Does that sound 'REASONABLE?'" Several jurors shook their heads.

"The State found NO FINGERPRINTS on my client's pistol... *NONE!* They also testified that it hadn't been fired! When you deliberate this case, remember this, because it is a "FACT IN EVIDENCE"... *Ted's gun wasn't fired!"*

And speaking of my client's weapon... After ALL THAT searching, by 22 officers and two trained search dogs going over the area with a fine-toothed comb, they failed to locate ANYTHING incriminating MY CLIENT... And then Deputy Null just *HAPPENS to find Ted's pistol,* right on Madison Avenue. *It REEKS,* folks."

Takon took off his coat and sipped a bit more water.

"Now, I don't really know what type of scam is going on, but I know this; SOMEONE'S TRYING TO FRAME MY CLIENT! You might want to address that issue... You have that kind of power, you know."

"Next, let's look at the bodies; one fell from a boulder into a crevice. The expert said he was on Coke and Crank. I want you to see this picture with me; Steep country, craggy rocks, and a doper, HIGH on drugs. Either my client sneaked up on him and broke his neck, then stuffed the body in a crack or the man simply fell and broke his neck...

"I don't know if you've ever been around someone who's high on methamphetamine, but they're pretty paranoid; would it be easy to sneak up on him? In dry weather? Walking over cracking twigs and dry leaves? *No way!*"

"They tried to imply that Ted killed the other two men with his little pistol. Meanwhile, they're hauling this arsenal of illegal automatic weapons. Doesn't sound REASONABLE, does it? Well, it's not. Remember; two of the bad guys' weapons fired projectiles of the exact same caliber as my client's tiny pistol."

"The People have 'bullet gouge'. Yet their expert said it *could have been* from an animal; many wild animals, even mice, can gouge bone... *remember?"*

"It's not a pleasant topic, but neither is sending an innocent man to prison, so let's look at Sheriff Three Feathers' testimony; wild animals had two months to scavenge the bodies. That's plenty of time for a bear, lion or a wild boar to locate the remains and, as much as we'd like to pretend otherwise, EAT AND SCATTER them. It's a hard, cruel world, high up in the woods, folks."

He took more water while he watched the jury intensely.

"The truth is, after all that time, it's a wonder that there aren't MORE gouge wounds."

144

"Next, let's study the People's insinuation that Ted REFUSED to cooperate with interrogators, so he must be "suspicious". According to Talvez' deposition, the initial interrogation went like; *'HI, Ted... do you know your close friend burned to death last night? Oh, by the way, where were you uh, July 26, sixteen weeks ago?'*

"Now, imagine if an officer came knocking on *your door,* first shocking you and then DEMANDING to know your EXACT WHEREABOUTS, several months earlier... I can't speak for you, but I can barely recall what I had for lunch yesterday!"
Tapping his rotund belly;
"Does it look like I forget lunches?"
The court tittered again.
"Does my bad memory make me a homicide suspect? Apparently, the people think it DOES! Who among us can say where we were, on a specific day, sixteen weeks ago? If we can't, then we must all be killers!"

"Next problem; Sheriff-Coroner James Three Feathers... one of the most highly respected and decorated sheriffs we've ever elected, said that he couldn't tell the time of death other than 'mid July to first part of August'... Would you convict a man on that kind of nebulous information?

"I sure couldn't! I would want the information to be accurate beyond a reasonable doubt. Besides, the state offered no proof my client was absent from work or home at the estimated time of death. All they said was; *'Well, he can't prove he wasn't, so he must be guilty.'*

"Well, Ted can't prove that he didn't eat that last piece of pie last night, either... so he must be guilty."

The jury looked like they'd already made up their minds. Nevertheless, from past surprise verdicts, Charlie vowed to continue.
"Deputy Talvez suspected Ted because he REFUSED to answer questions. Do we live in such HITLERIAN times that you're a suspect because you won't talk to a cop? What's next... *Thought Crimes?*

"Why should we be 'SUSPECTS', if we won't answer a cop's questions? The Fifth Amendment isn't a right that some COP grants you when you're arrested... it's a constitutional right, granted to us ALL, all the time, whether or not you're under arrest."

"Let's say your daughter's driving home from a late shift job; a sex-starved young cop pulls her over. She didn't do ANYTHING WRONG; he wants to see her driver's license, so he knows where to stalk her. Is your DAUGHTER a suspect because she won't talk to him? The People would have you believe she is!"

"Let's look at the state's ANONYMOUS TIPSTER. We didn't get to see this guy, did we? We didn't get to cross-examine him, either. We're asked to believe Officer Null that such a person exists! Where have we seen THIS before?"

"Now, I could ramble on, believe me. And with some of my old cases, I have done just that. As a defense lawyer, I'm supposed to do whatever I can to protect my client. But in this case, I don't need to pull any slick shenanigans. I'd just like to re-direct your attention to the facts in evidence; after that you'll have ONLY ONE possible verdict.

"The People found a hillside full of fired weapons. Ted's gun hadn't been fired! Ted's gun turned up mysteriously, after 22 human and two expert canine officers swept the entire scene. They have no accurate time of death. They have no motive, unless you believe that malarkey about Ted's tax bill."

Takon changed tactics suddenly.

"YOU KNOW WHAT? Forget everything I just said. I love Colombo; he always looked for  murder weapon, motive, and opportunity. When you go into that jury room, play Colombo. Ask yourselves; "Where's the motive, weapon, opportunity? You won't be able to answer those, based upon the facts in evidence."

Takon took another slow sip of water.

"You know, I've been lawyering for many years. I got out of law school and thought I knew everything. Well, now, I'll settle for knowing just ONE THING. AND, in THIS CASE, I DO know ONE THING. All of you know it, too. Ted's NOT GUILTY. Ladies and gentlemen of the jury, Thanks."

Baker took the People's rebuttal, but she didn't look enthused. After all, Takon was right... And everyone in the courtroom knew it. Still, she had to try. Emily pushed her glasses up on her nose and scanned her notes.

"Ladies and gentlemen, once again, defense counsel has oversimplified the case; he wants you to act like Colombo, a fictional character on TV. But this case isn't fiction, it's reality. Unfortunately, REALITY doesn't come as neatly packaged as a TV show.

"He said we've got NO WEAPON, but we DO... and it belongs to the defendant. He said we've got no motive, but we DO... and it serves ONLY the defendant."

Now it was Baker's turn to sip some water and stall.

"Counsel also said it's OK if you don't answer police questions, and he's right, but WHY WOULDN'T an innocent person answer questions? If I were wrongly accused of a crime, I'd tell the cops everything, *wouldn't YOU?*"

Several jurors squirmed in disagreement with the prosecutor's naive statement and sat back in their chairs, but Baker missed the body language tell.

"Defense also implied some type of cover-up, but did they *present any evidence to show it?* Ladies and gentlemen, *that*'s a typical defense tactic; when all else fails, blame somebody else. Well, they tried to blame the sheriff's department... But what would the department possibly gain by framing the defendant? *NOTHING!*"

"Ok, so the pistol didn't get marked on the map... *so what?* The officers still found it, didn't they? That sounds like a murder weapon to me. And what if the gun was cleaned? How much does it take to carry a cleaning kit in your pack?

For all we know, the defendant could have *deliberately* left it behind... essentially paving his way for an acquittal.
"Defense also said some highly insulting things to deputy Null, purely in the interest of getting his client off. But did we see any evidence that Null did anything wrong? NO."

"In fact, we didn't see any defense posed at all, did we? And, of course while you can't let that SWAY you, you can use it to help you decide about the fairytale scam involving the sheriff's department... because IF there were evidence, Defense most certainly would have produced it!

"We must ask ourselves if the entire department suddenly went berserk, just to convict this one man. I think not. So there you have it, ladies and gentlemen of the jury. Like Mr. Takon said; It's a simple case; the defendant is simply guilty on all counts."

"Your honor, the people rest."

The jury headed for deliberations, after the judge instructed them. The judge left after that. So did most of the gallery. For most defendants, the waiting would  be bad, but for Ted, it would be far worse. Takon broke the news, as soon as the courtroom emptied.

"Ted, I found out at the last break that your wife's been hurt real bad. I didn't tell you then, because the doctors said there's nothing you can do... But I got permission from the judge to take you to see her... *LET'S GO!*"

"Huh?"
Ted's mind went blank. His legs turned to jelly. He would've fainted if he were standing. Two bailiffs drove him to the hospital. Charlie Takon followed.

When he saw Jo, a bailiff had to hold him until he got his feet under him again. He gawked at a big ball of cotton and gauze, hooked up to tubes and monitors. Only her right cheek and mouth protruded from gauze;  swollen and bruised, her lips as big as oranges.

Ted saw the chart name; Jo Morgan! He wanted to touch her, but no place was free of bandages. A nurse came in.

"Your wife's in a coma, due to hemorrhagic shock. We're doing all we can. We can't say if she'll make it or not. Excuse me."

She left for another room where she might offer another patient a better prognosis. Nobody likes to bear bad news.

It didn't take a doctor to read the feeble signs on the monitors; most gauges have the normal range in the middle. Hers were practically falling off the left sides. Ted couldn't see her chest rise or fall. He lost his visual focus. His legs buckled, and he grayed out. The bailiff grabbed him again and kept him from collapsing.

Regaining consciousness, Ted heard Takon speaking in hushed tones with his best investigator. The bailiff's hand now rested on Ted's shoulder, in heartfelt sympathy. They took him back to jail. Ted felt like a coward because he couldn't wait to get away from the horrible carnage.

Two hours later the private investigator visited him. Dan Cabral was a big burly man. His lineage was an equal mixture of Scottish and Portuguese. His neck was heavily muscled, and was as wide as his head. At five feet ten and 265, his dimensions were almost square. With a close-cropped, naturally tight curl, he was more two-legged Red Angus bull than man.

Ted wondered how such an imposing physique could be unobtrusive enough to be a sleuth. Little did he know, Cabral was a master of his craft.

"It's bad... your wife was cut up, real bad. Doc said lots of cuts, all shallow. Still, any time you lose that much blood you can die. Worse yet, Doc Grady says she might not come out of it; it happens."

He found the matter-of-fact format strangely comforting, in spite of the grave information. It was better than some mealy-mouthed doctor's fake pep talk, full of half-truths and optimistic bullshit. Ted looked straight into the man's eyes, to probe deeper.
"Is that it?"
His penetrating stare unnerved Dan.
"No; Doc says she was gang-raped... said there were traces of at least three different types of sem..."
"I get it! I get it!"
That was too much to bear.
Leaning toward Cabral, Ted whispered, hoping it was low enough that the eavesdropping mikes couldn't catch it.
"I want to know who did this. I'll pay you double your..."
Cabral interrupted softly, getting up to go.
"Not a dime... *This one's on me!*"

Cabral had never worked for free before, but this case stirred his heart, which hadn't happened in a long time.

Then Bernie took the still-warm seat after the bull left.

"I just came back; she's unchanged... what do you need?"
"Call Dave Semple; I need him in the courtroom tomorrow. Find two people who will take my calls. The hospital staff just hangs up when they hear the fuckin' jailhouse scambuster beeps. Next, keep track of your hours and find a bookkeeper to take Jo's workload. And PRAY for us."

Bernie stood; "Already done; all of it... I'm gone."

Ted left for chow.

As soon as his food tray was loaded, Ted carried it toward a table where Kirt sat. He set it down.
"I'm ready to deal with my problem."
Kirt smiled a tight, lipless sneer.
"After chow, brah... *not here.*"

After dinner, three top skinheads appeared. Ted opened the negotiation.
"First, I don't want to be a skinhead but I have an offer. You get out of jail, you got jobs with me; fair enough?"

Viktor Schnoel was a tall, bony young man with a sickly complexion and pockmarked face. His abdomen sank inward, probably from parasites. Ted wondered how such a sickly person could control so many others, but jail taught him that appearances were deceiving. Besides, it didn't take much strength to jab a knife, pull a trigger or detonate a bomb. Schnoel's raspy, weak voice crackled through the air like static.
"Yeah? In exchange for what?"
Ted twitched from the poor, but shameless impersonation of Dirty Harry's voice.
"For information... *Deal?*"
"Deal."
Truth be told, Schnoel would have done it for free, just to fuck with the Campesinos. The trio left as one. Later, a visit from Karl Schroeder, Schnoel's right hand man gave Ted his orientation.
"Da Fuckin' Campesinos hit your lady. We oughta kill them all."
"Are you sure?"
"Yeah, kill 'em all, startin' with..."
"NO, I mean, are you *sure it was Campesinos?*"

"Oh, yeah. They draped the place; I mean, your house, in purple. Those wannabe light-nigger wetbacks got a little tatt, a Madonna, for chrissake, with 'Soledad' for the first Camp killed in lockup. It's the Campesinos; bank on it.

They attacked her four or five to one... good thing your kids weren't there or they'd be just as fucked up, bec... "
TED throttled him; *"How you know about my kids?"*
Schroeder jerked in surprise at the sudden change.
"Take it EASY, bro! I seen pictures on your bunk. Besides, ya got bigger problems than a few skinheads ogling your daughter's photo, right?"
Ted conceded, sorry he'd shown weakness to this trash.
"Go on."
"We'll hook up with our people outside... I get out in three days. We'll go after those motherfuckers; we'll bang 'em up so bad they won't fuck with pure blooded white folk again!"

"Maybe, but I got a better idea. Thanks for the scoop."

Feuds never accomplished anything but escalation. He kept thinking, deep into the night. Whenever fatigue overcame him, visions of his wife's ordeal snapped him back. He outlined many plans. Most were pipe dreams, but he found them comforting on some level. Others looked promising at first glance, until he scrutinized them.

But by dawn, one plan held a high percentage for success. Ted worked over the materials list while deputies drove him to court. The voice in his head kept saying; *'They'll pay... They'll fuckin pay!'*
It soon morphed into a mantra, choking out rational thoughts like crabgrass killing young flowers.

He was relieved to see his buddy sitting in court. Ted grabbed a pen and Charlie's legal pad. Meanwhile, the courtroom filled. Ted gave Dave the eye, looking for a way to get him the list. Ted and Dave hit if off, many years ago. They spurred each other to greater marksmanship. Dave usually shot better... just enough to hold the edge. Nobody in the county came as close to beating Semple. Dave approached when the bailiffs backed off. They knew Dave.
"I'm sorry about Jo! What do ya need?"

Ted shook his hand. The bailiff allowed it. A break in protocol, but he felt sympathy after seeing Ted's battered wife the night before. Besides, it was obvious; Morgan

would probably walk, so one little handshake wouldn't mean shit in twenty minutes.
Semple felt the folded paper Ted palmed him, while choking back tears of gratitude and pain.
"Thanks; I hear the jury's 11-1, but I'm scared as hell."

Semple usually knew how to cheer him up, but was at a loss, so he said the first thing that came to mind.
"Well, ya WOULDN'T be, if ya weren't such a big PUSSY!" It got a nervous chuckle and jarred Ted back to toughness as no other statement might have. Just then, Judge Lenah came in, sat down and called court to order.

"I've been informed that the jury is at an impasse... Apparently, they feel it might be resolved if they can visit the crime scene; I will grant them this unusual request. We'll RECONVENE here, day after. Court's adjourned until Friday at 9:00."

The gavel sounded hollow to Ted. Everybody got up and bustled out, but Ted stayed seated next to his lawyer.
"What does that mean?"
"Honestly? I don't know... Maybe somebody wants to see where the pistol was, but it could be anything. Hell, maybe they just want a ride in a chopper. Don't put stock in it. Try to get some sleep; you look like a fuckin' hamburger patty!"

Dave walked to a nearby restaurant. He sat in the rear and ordered an omelet. When the waitress left, he opened Ted's note. There were two columns. He read the left one first; " 1 bx .243 80 gr BTHP. .284 130 gr. coppers. New barrels & bolts. 12 gauge components"

The other column had different items; "call Ziggy, 555-2318; 12 bags fertilizer 10-20-20. 12 rockets, igniters, wire, 12-v m/c battery. Pay Cash. *HURRY.*"

Dave dove into his meal while contemplating Ted's list; the rifle gear meant long range shooting. He'd never known Ted to be a shotgun fan, so the reloading components puzzled him. Dave finished his omelet as the thought finally hit home. His buddy was going to get even! It made sense; Ted took the horrible news just a bit too well.

Semple placed the orders, overnight delivery. Most of the shooting goods suppliers knew Dave by voice, since he ordered so much from them. It didn't raise any questions. When Ziggy started to ask about the rocket stuff, he told him to *shut up and do it.* He could be intimidating, when he wanted to.

Back in the can, Ted learned that his wife slipped deeper into coma. He thought about the worst-case outcome; life without his soul mate. He shamelessly let his tears drop to the floor. The callused riff raff remained silent... a high honor for any cellmate.

By evening, his plan was almost perfected. He rehearsed it over and over, correcting errors. He was going through it for the hundredth time, when a guard appeared.
"Morgan... visitor."
When he got to the visiting room, he saw Dan Cabral hunched over the table.
"I found out; five or six of 'em... from a gang call..."
"Don't say it; the walls have ears."
Ted's eyes pointed to the partially hidden video camera in its characteristic hiding spot behind a ventilation screen.
"It's better if you whisper."
Cabral obliged.
"Yeah? Well, I bet you don't know this... they're hooked into a DRUG RING... which is what *you're mixed up in.*"
Cabral nodded toward the hidden camera.
"As they say on the news; more, later."
The guy was a real professional. He got up to leave, then turned back and sat down. This time, no whisper.

"Oh; I called my brother-in-law, in Boston. He's a neurosurgeon... says a temporary sink deeper into coma, isn't always BAD; if she's going to recover, she'll probably turn the corner in 72-96 hours... thought I'd end this meet on a good note, huh?"

Coming from anyone else, it might have sounded like optimistic bullshit, but from the straight talker with no neck, it was reassuring.

Ted's son was next, sitting down before Ted even got up. He'd disregarded Ted's orders and came to jail anyhow.
"Hey Dad... how's it goin'?"
Ted almost cried with relief.
"I'm OK, son; How's Kelly?"
AJ shook his head solemnly.
"Broken up about Mom, holding her hand... or the gauze."
The boy tried to fight off the mental image of his battered mother, mummified in gauze, but his voice cracked.
"Dad... If I'd have been home I ... "
"NO, son! It's not your fault! Just be glad Kelly wasn't home or we'd be worrying about both of them! Just pray for your mom. Hell; *pray for us ALL!*"
A scratchy intercom proclaimed; "Visiting hours are over."
"I'll see you tomorrow, Pops. Hang in there!"

Later, Schnoel came by Ted's cell... Same sick grin.
"More advice; Heavy shit's comin'. Protect your kids, man!"

He learned to put value in the jailhouse grapevine; it was faster than the media and more accurate. He bummed a dollar and hit the phone.
"AJ? Listen CAREFULLY... Your lives depend on it. You and Kelly move in with buddies. Don't say which ones. Don't leave numbers on the answering machine, notes on the fridge, e-mails or texts. Tell Kelly to leave Mom alone; she'll be safe in the hospital."
AJ was dumbfounded.
"Sure, Dad, but what's the..."
"I can't explain now. Just DO IT NOW! I know where you'll both be. I love you."
He walked back to his cell, slightly relieved.
*'This time the bastards will find an empty house.'*

The realization finally hit him; clearly the Campesinos wouldn't go away. Ted re-hashed his plan with deeper determination. Around 3 A.M. it looked excellent. Finally his fatigued body committed treason against his will and it

157

forced Ted to sleep. His last thoughts centered on the small feeling of closure that having a good plan gave him.

After breakfast, he located the skinheads lifting weights together. He addressed Schnoel.

"How much you know 'bout the purple motherfuckers?"

"Happy to tell you, man, but it ain't much... Got a brother comin' out of Quentin next week; needs a job, cool?"

Ted nodded halfway through the question.

"Yeah, sure; he's got a job. I'll call it in tomorrow."

"Right; the Campesinos are chickenshit LA barrio cowards... typical of all non-whites. They'll come, five to one or they won't come at all. There's forty or fifty, with maybe a dozen jailed at any point... figure forty on the street. They'll drive miles to rumble, especially if they think the fight's gonna be easy."

Ted nodded vacantly.

"THAT'S *IT?*"

He got on the bench press.

"Just about... Remember; one comes, they ALL COME. Like a swarm of bees... you're gonna need a lot of dudes, man!"

Ted waggled a finger in the negative.

"I didn't say anything about going after them, DID I?"

"No man, you didn't say shit... an' I din't hear it!"

Twenty-five...
## REVELATIONS

That night, Ted was surprised to hear that his lawyer was waiting to see him. He had a chance for a private face-to-face. It would be just the three of them; Ted, Takon and the hidden spy camera. The door slammed closed. Charlie whipped out his trusty little radio.

"Cabral found out the whole deal. Those gangsters that cut your wife are grunts; probably snuffed your friend Jetta, too. They work for a drug dealer named Saldivar; he's in bed with half the sheriffs in Humdob, Mendonesia and Del Norway counties!"
Takon let it soak in for five seconds.

"He's hooked up with the law! *got that? The fuckin' law!"*

Takon turned his palms up in feigned supplication.
"No wonder they framed you! You're in a REAL bucket of shit here, Ted, and I don't just mean the legal end of it!"
"Charlie, I need your help; I want to give you temporary power of attorney over my busine... "

"No, think this through Ted. First of all, you're NOT going to lose this trial! You'll probably be free in a week, maybe less. Besides, I don't do businesses... and lastly; I fear you're about to engage in actions that could get me disbarred, were I to know about them. So don't tell me... *GOT IT?"*
"Yeah"
The burly litigator hunched closer and spoke quieter.
"However, based upon what Cabral told me; Hypothetically speaking, if I were swatting bees, I'd not swat just one or two... I'd nuke the whole fuckin' HIVE... And I'd DAMN SURE kill the QUEEN."

He got up and took his radio.
"I'll see you when the jury's in. I still can't figure why they wanted to see the crime scene, unless they just wanted a chopper ride... who knows? Stay strong, Ted!"

That night, Ted recalled a piece of land that would suit his needs. It was out of state, so Saldivar's stooge sheriffs couldn't meddle in an official capacity. It was remote and rugged. Having hunted the eastern Sierras before, he had an edge; familiarity with the terrain.

By two in the morning, he'd spit-polished the plan, then managed a few hours' sleep before chow. For the first time since his wife had been raped, cut and bludgeoned, he noticed a cold, steely churning in his gut; it felt good.

Ted ate breakfast, thinking about the gangsters; he felt her pain and fear, their butterfly knives slashing her skin. With each passing hour, he was going increasingly nuts. Soon all he could see was rage, death, and destruction.

By lights out, Ted's former identity was all but gone, replaced by a cold, calculating killing machine. His only goal was to kill the assholes that ravaged his sweetheart.

Hopefully, the verdict would be not guilty... although Ted no longer really cared. His wife was already paying his sentence. If he got sentenced to hard time, he'd just have to wait longer to kill them. It was only a question of killing them now or later. Either way, he would kill them... *ALL of them.* The thought gave him a moment of ease. He was out when his head hit the mattress.

Ten AM found Ted in shackles, a bailiff on each side. They walked into the courtroom; Dave caught Ted's eye. He nodded and mouthed; *I got it.*

A switch snapped inside Ted's mind; his guts got hot, just thinking of it. His mind phased out of the trial proceedings and he thought only of revenge. He couldn't wait to stick it to those cocksuckers.


The judge entered, brought the court to order and asked the jury.
"Have you reached a verdict?"

But instead of just the foreman standing, the entire jury stood up. The bailiff took the forms to the judge, who read and returned them to Len Baxter, the 47 year-old divorced contractor; his melodious baritone resonated throughout the courtroom.
"Yes, Your Honor, we HAVE, but first, I have been asked to read a short statement. Is that OK?"
Judge Lenah looked interested.
"Well, it is UNUSUAL, but it's ok... you may proceed."

Len took a big breath and got into it.

"We the jury, having heard the facts in the People Versus Theodore Morgan, find that there is sufficient evidence to suggest corruption inside the Sheriff's Department. We hereby request that the Grand Jury investigate it. We request these court transcripts be available to the Grand Jury."

The court went crazy with affirmation; six gavel bangs brought it again to silence.

"As to the charges in this case... We find the defendant, Ted Morgan, NOT GUILTY on all charges!"
The crowd went nuts. The courtroom emptied fast. Lenah didn't even get enough control to thank the jury.

The media pointed microphones at the exiting ADA's. Questions came too fast to be heard, but the buzz was on; collusion, corruption, drugs, perfect fodder for ravenous reporters. They barely noticed Ted; he was old news. Dave drove him to the hospital, talking excitedly.

"No shit, Ted, you're a free man! Jo's going to need your support, so don't do anything crazy, ya know? Pick up where ya left off, eh?"

For Dave, buying all the gear for Ted seemed surreal, almost harmless, when he thought his buddy would be locked up for years. But now *he was out*... it started feeling awful fucking real.

Ted looked straight ahead, sounding rehearsed and empty.
"Yeah, right... Did my stuff get here?"

"All except the barrels, they'll take a week. The rest is in my spare room. Zig's order is in your warehouse. Ya owe me two grand, by the way."

Ted didn't need the barrels right away, so that wasn't a problem. They bounded up the hospital steps, two at a time, side by side. Soon he stood over his wife. It was obvious to everyone; she was much closer to death. Her body looked deflated, a half-filled air mattress with a slow leak. Her yellow, pale skin portended serious liver troubles. A doctor came in.
"Can I see you outside, please?"
Once in the hallway, the doctor laid it out.
"It's not good, it's bad. I give her ten-percent. Comas are very unpredictable... I'm sorry."
"Would it help if I stayed with her?"
"No. All that crap you see on TV about talking to coma patients is Hollywood bullshit. It's better if you go home, get some rest; you look like shit. No charge for that diagnosis, by the way."

They left. Dave suggested to the robot.
"You know, my spare room's already got your toys... may as well have YOU in it, too."

Dave took Ted's guns and gear, to avoid losing it to another gangster raid.

Ted agreed; it would keep the press off his ass and he could do faster work with Semple's upscale reloading gear. After a short stop at his warehouse to check on the other order, he moved in.

Ted exited the truck with the doctor's prognosis ringing in his ears; ten percent... ten percent... "

## Twenty-six

## EXPLANATION

Before the courthouse was completely empty, the ADA's charged into Onman's office, looking like they'd just been mugged. Truth be told, *they had been.*

Onman watched with pride and empathy as they stormed his cubicle. They were young, eager, and so naive. So far, they only knew the law. But to be good prosecutors, that wasn't enough. Baker started before they got his door shut.

"Boss, I've never seen such a trial! We're going to file a..."
"OK, OK... but hear me out first, alright?"

He motioned for them to close the blinds and sit down.

"First of all, I want to tell you all how proud I am."
That set them back in their chairs.

"There's NO WAY you were going to win; I knew it, the judge and jury knew... and you can damn sure bet that Charlie Takon knew it!"

Bill reached for his hooch and paper cups from the water cooler. A shot went into each. He passed them around. He rolled scotch on his tongue.

"The only one who didn't know was Ted Morgan; that poor asshole sat there with his hat in his hands, sweating it out. Imagine what that's like... being arrested, bullied, cuffed and tried; everyone around you's speaking in tongues."

Onman looked up, surprised to see astonishment in their eyes. They'd never heard this from him before.

"Hell, forget that; Imagine the strings Charlie pulled to get the case FAST-TRACKED! I bet he pulled in a lot of markers; I'll bet that sonofabitch has his tentacles in the judges' offices."
His crew grew even more astonished; they were sipping hooch. It was time to educate them further.

"You guys think the law is enough, but it's just a starting point... just the tool, to be used best by whoever holds the most clout. In this county, and I suspect in others too, that means the good old boy network.

"With respect to People V. Morgan, I was sure you were going to lose before I gave it to you. It's a hot potato. First, take another sip of scotch and kindly remove your lawyer's hats for ten minutes, so I can explain it!"
They did.

"Let's just look through the eyes of a normal citizen; the accused is a taxpaying businessman without priors. The deceased are dope dealing scum, with long criminal records... You KNOW SOMETHING? Jurors need ONLY those two facts to come to a verdict... And *the law be damned!*"

"We scour the jury pool, we hire consultants, looking for advantage. The judge instructs them to keep open minds, we make flowery oratories. But the jury's probably convinced before the first witness testifies.... Scum on one side, good guy on the other. That's enough for most jurors. That's just how it is."

Bill raised the bottle and looked around; Baker and Fishbein nodded. Laura Martin passed on the second shot.

"The deck was really stacked against you. You faced the finest lawyer north of the Golden Gate, pullin' God knows how many markers in. You had scum for victims and a hero for a defendant... and you had something else against you."

Onman's eyes and voice lowered, his mood darkened.

"Now, I've suspected some kind of corruption in the sheriff's department for a while now, but until now I didn't have anything to go on. But now this jury really put the crab in the pot. They read it into the record, for Chrissake, for the Grand Jury to indict! Man, that's career-making stuff!"
He drained his cup and capped the bottle.

"So forget the Morgan minnow. We've got BIGGER fish to fry. Besides, Ted has suffered enough... "

He stood up and grabbed his hat off the hook.
"By the way, did you know his wife was raped and beaten almost to death? Oh, of course you knew, during chambers... anyhow, hell... Even if he did kill those bastards, they ought to give him a fuckin' medal! That's off the record, by the way."

Onman locked his desk, a sign of the workday closing.
"Now, *as for the bigger fish...* I'll say this; if the grand jury does order an investigation into the sheriff's department, shit's gonna hit the fan, so break out your best slickers. We're sure as hell gonna need 'em. IF and when we do this investigation, heads will roll. Hell, some of 'em might even be ours, but if you've always wanted a good fight, we're sure as hell gonna have one! Now let's take the rest of the day off, you raging alcoholics! First round's on me at Chambers!"

The intended levity didn't work; the trio was dizzy from the coming Titanic task, not the scotch. They left the office together, with Fishbein spouting off.
"Hey, fuck this job!"

Even Onman laughed; Ted Three was feeling the whiskey. Chambers made great drinks, and Onman had a tab. Before long, the state's most popular DA and staff grew numb to their recent loss. Or win. Or whatever it was.

Theodore Fishbein the Third sipped his Third drink as he thought about Ted Morgan; poor bastard got off, only to find his wife beaten, butchered and raped. They didn't make enough whiskey to numb THAT kind of pain.

## PREPARATIONS

Semple slipped his buddy a Mickey; three crushed sleeping pills in a cold beer. Ted hated drugs, but there are times when one must help a friend, regardless.

Ted awoke around 2:00 to a dark house. He went through his supplies. His hit the pot full of cold coffee, nuked a cup and reworked his plan again. By daylight it was detailed as well as it needed to be.

After Semple left for work, Morgan booted Dave's ballistics program, calling up optimum loads for the .243 and his STW. The Shooting Tricks Western was fairly new to Ted. Dave had purchased the first 7mm STW in the county. Soon he owned three, so he sold the oldest to Ted. Soon he had the screen plastered with powder charges, projected velocities and external ballistics tables.

While the "Seven" shot best with full-throat loads, Ted was careful to keep his .243 loads in the middle of the tables, where accuracy lived. He could still hear Dave's ancient admonition; "Dammit, Ted, it don't do any good to send a sizzling bullet into the rocks... better to send a slower bullet into the ROCK...*CHUCK!*"

He primed the empty shotgun hulls and charged them, then fitted the shot cups. He cut spreaders from twelve-pack paperboard. At thirty yards, a spreader pattern could hit several men standing shoulder to shoulder.

The spreaders each formed a vertical X. Into each section, Ted placed one buckshot and several number Five shot. Finally, he topped the hull with eights. Crimping finished it off; a box full of man killers. If the muzzle pointed toward it, the enemy would taste lead. To the casual observer, they looked like normal shotgun shells.

Each shot size had a purpose; the buckshot would spread the smaller shot quickly, and penetrate vitals. The number Fives would be lethal inside thirty yards, while causing devastating injuries out to fifty. The size Eights were too light to kill beyond twenty yards, but would cause paralyzing pain out to fifty or more. Ted felt hot inside, thinking of the pain and destruction they would inflict on the scumsuckers. He cased the weapons and headed to the range.

Although he'd been there a few months earlier, it seemed like years; a lot had happened. The sign looked like an old friend, with its sun-faded, hand painted message.

*Hidden Crest Skeet and Rifle Range*
*new members welcome; call 555 0404.*
*Responsible citizens only*

He worked the combination, drove through the gate and Locked it again. Then he drove up the dusty road to the sign-in station. Ted hoped Darrell wouldn't come out. The old groundskeeper lived on premises. He was retired. He was also stone-deaf, a side effect of being first a gunners' mate on the Missouri, then a Winchester factory shooter for three decades, long before they thought of hearing protection. What the Missouri's behemoth guns hadn't done to his ears, a few million rounds of unprotected trap and skeet loads had.

Ted liked him, but the old salt's conversations burned big chunks of daylight. He quickly logged his name and member number, but not quick enough. The old man was only twenty yards away, but was yelling.

"HEY, TED! WHATCHYA *BEEN UP TO?*"

So Darrell hadn't been reading the paper. He shook hands.

"Same old same ol', amigo; tryin' out some new loads, and I don't have much time, so I'll talk to ya when I'm finished."

Ted didn't notice the hurt look in the old man's eyes, but it wouldn't have mattered. He drove over to the shade structure and parked under the familiar old painted plywood sign.

Red letters on white turned sun-faded yellow spelled out the unimpeachable rules...

RANGE RULES
All guns must be cased and
empty until ready to shoot.
Actions open unless firing.
One rifle per shooter at bench.
All weapons must point downrange,
Actions open when empty.
When finished shooting, step back from bench
until all shooters are finished.
No alcohol.
Unnecessary talking is prohibited.
Distracting shooters prohibited.
Respect others.
Aggressive behavior, rapid fire or profanity
will result in immediate expulsion.
NO EXCEPTIONS

It was a fairly sacred place, and the rules worked. In the sixty-eight years since its inception, not a single gun-related accident marred its record.

It took three trips to carry his gear to the bench and gun racks. He tested his rangefinder on the large steel elk, at 500 yards; "497", the precise reading. Next, he walked down range to the two-hundred and five-hundred yard backstops. He stapled up his targets. Returning to the firing line, he set up his ammo trays, spotting scope and sandbags while his heart rate steadily normalized, after the thousand-yard hike.

He uncased the .243 Browner. Setting the parallax to 200, the target looked crisp and clear. Loading the clip, Ted checked his ballistics table; "200 +1".

He put on his hearing protection, then snuggled into his best technique; left forearm relaxed on bench. Left hand touching forearm sandbag. Right palm lightly touching the stock... Finger out of trigger guard.

168

He nestled in, until he and the rifle became one. Just then, the earmuffs slowly sealed, the foam gradually obliterating the outside world. He could hear his pulse and the seashell hum of extra-cranial blood flow.

The world shrank slowly, to just what he saw in the scope and the cardio rhythm in his ears. The cross hairs rested steadily on the X. Save for the heartbeat wobble, the sight picture was solid.

He carefully took up what little trigger slack there was and exhaled half his breath. A split second later, the rifle fired and a hole appeared an inch above the X. He followed it up with two more rounds. Three holes touched each other. He unloaded the rifle, policed his brass and placed them back in the reloading block. He cased it.

Then he shifted his attention to the bigger rifle, the Seven. He turned the magnification up to 24 power and looked; the dot reticule swayed rhythmically back and forth across the X, eighty times a minute. What had seemed like a minor tremor in the little rifle's low-power scope now looked like Stevie Wonder pounding a piano; waggling back and forth like crazy. He knew enough to try not to hold it still. Nobody can hold the pulse. Then he nestled in.

Ted timed the shot, taking Semple's relentless advice for shooting on a slack heart. When it looked right, Ted pressed the trigger. There was no slack to take up, for this was a custom trigger. Recovering from the recoil, Ted saw a hole six inches left and six high of the bull. He fired two more rounds, holding the same sight picture. All three holes would easily fit under a quarter.

The new loads caused the barrel to vibrate differently. He was glad to see the tight group; the rifle liked the load. Tightening the Seven in his gun vise, he aimed the reticule exactly on the bull. He turned the elevation knob while watching the reticule climb level with the group. Then he did the same with the windage adjustment, until the reticule centered the group.

His next three bullets hit dead center in the X. Dialing in ten clicks of "UP", the next three shots hit five inches high. Four holes touched, with one flier two inches low. That would put the bullets two inches high at 300 yards. At four hundred yards, they'd print four inches low, and at five hundred yards, they'd print sixteen inches low.

The computer generated holdovers out to a thousand yards. They were theoretically perfect, assuming several bits of information to be true; air density, temperature, elevation, wind and shot angle will affect it. Next, estimating ranges in excess of three hundred yards is fraught with error. A lot happens to a bullet during a half-mile flight. Ted would save the long range testing for the locale where he'd be shooting. It's one thing to be close; it is another to be a perfect killer.

Swinging toward the 500-yard target, he fired a group of three, surprisingly close to the calculated impact. Then he put the second dot on the 600 yard target; an Elk silhouette, cold steel, freshly painted black. When the recoil subsided, a gleaming white splotch glowed dead center in the chest. Simultaneously, the resounding KAWHUMP reached his ears. The projectile excoriated a four-inch crater, one inch deep in the steel, like an ice cream scoop leaving a butter-smooth crater. He cased it.

Since the shotgun was a close range weapon, there was great need for reliability and firepower; he stapled two paper silhouettes to sticks, thirty yards from the bench.

He fired one from the shoulder, at the left target... Four of the buckshot found the silhouette; one groin, two chest, one in the nose. A Fifty-inch circle of number fives peppered the bad guy. The Eights' holes were too small to be seen at thirty yards.

Firing from the hip, Ted cranked the other four spreader rounds at the right silhouette. Before the fourth empty hit the ground, the shot sawed through the sticks; the paper target fell. Eighty percent of the shot found its mark. Ted took the telltale targets with him.

He loaded up and started to drive off, when Darrell's screen door swung open. The old man hobbled down the front steps of his double-wide.

"Ho, Ted!"

Expecting Ted to stop, he looked hurt when Ted kept going and simply hollered back. But then Ted figured it would look suspicious. He backed up, clouds of dust swirling into the cab. He killed the engine.

"How's the missus, Darrell?"

The old man grinned; he was a lifelong bachelor. They could always spot the newest members; invariably they'd ask about his nonexistent wife.

"Oh, she's the same as always, eh? You surprised me with that shotgun; never took you for a smoothbore fan."

Ted was glad he pulled the targets; if anybody could spot a triplex load on paper, it would be the old wingshooter.

"Oh yeah, my friend in Winnemucca asked me to come shoot some quail, so I thought I'd warm up. Trouble is, that shotgun kicked me too hard to enjoy it... Listen, Darrell, I'd love to chew the fat, but I'm in a bit of a rush."

"Ok, but next time, ya owe me a sit-down and a beer."

"You got it, pardner. See ya."

Ted drove to his warehouse.

Selecting his biggest trailer, he loaded his four-wheeler. Next went fertilizer, fuel tanks, backpack spray rig, tarps, leaf blower, first aid kit, chain saw and hand tools. The last thing was his small tractor with bucket and box scraper; small enough to work in a suburban back yard.

When it was fully loaded, it looked like Ted was going off to do some work. In a way, he was. He drove to a gas station. While the various tanks filled he did a thorough inspection; oil, brake fluid, tire pressure, belts, hoses. It wouldn't do, to have his plan fail because of an avoidable mechanical glitch.

Ted fueled the four-wheeler and a spare can with gas. Diesel went into the yellow cans. He tightened the caps hard; he didn't want any diesel leaking into the fertilizer... until the time was right.

He paid cash before driving back to Semple's, choosing to wait until dark to load his shooting gear; it would be hard to explain why rifles were going into a landscaping rig.

The evening meal was tense and strained. Dave and Anna tried small talk to pull Ted from his black mood, but their friend was in a zone of his own. After dinner, Ted abruptly retired to his room. He went through his gear one last time.

After dark, Ted started loading, when Dave halted him.
"You haven't said much, but it looks like you're going huntin'. Now, I don't want to tell you your business, but you've gotta know, taking off this late is sure to cause questions. Why don't ya get some sleep first?"

Ted barely heard his friend; "Yeah... whatever, I gotta..."
Dave grabbed his shoulder, spinning him around.
"Hey! This is your FRIEND, REMEMBER? Now, either you get some sleep, or we're gonna hold ya down and slip ya another MICKEY!"

For a second, Ted looked like his old self. He smiled.
"SO THAT'S why I slept so good last night... You sneaky bastard!"
He chuckled; Dave cared enough to violate Ted's anti drug ethic. Ted choked up; good friends are rare.

"OK, but this time, you won't have to lace it... let's just have a cool one, huh?"
Dave didn't expect such a fast switcharoo, but they had a few beers and Ted seemed to loosen appreciably. They hit the sack at midnight.

Ted awoke to the smell of bacon. Dressing swiftly, he wasn't surprised to find Dave cooking their traditional hunting breakfast; smoking crisp bacon, fried eggs, coffee and buttered sourdough toast. He even laid out paper towels to blot up the grease.

Ted knew what his buddy was up to. If he didn't, one glance at the living room door would have solved it; Dave's backpack, duffel and saddle-worn 7 mag were ready.
"Damn, this smells too good for a kitchen."
"Yeah; wouldn't it taste better, up in the Rubies?"
Ted's mind involuntarily filled with the naked beauty of Nevada's Ruby Mountains.
"Damn, it'd be nice to be at base camp right now."

Dave forked an egg into his maw.
"So what are we hunting this time?"

Ted wolfed his eggs while he considered the offer. It would be tempting to take Dave; there wouldn't be a better man to have at his side in a firefight. But he couldn't put such a life-changing task on his buddy, no matter what.

"*WE* ain't huntin'; and if anyone asks, I'm going for some landscaping rocks. And once I'm in the desert, I figured I might do a little long-distance target practice'."
"Rocks?"
"Yeah, *rocks*... and while I'm gone, I need a big strong man, right here, to protect my wife 'n kids... How 'bout it?"

"You got it! Just make sure you hit those fuckin' rocks hard." We don't want any un-shot rocks left, *DO we?"*

Ted loaded the last of his gear. He turned and saw his buddy's eyes, tears welling. He hugged him and choked out 'Thanks.' At least he knew his kids would survive, with a bodyguard like Dave Semple. That was a huge burden lifted. Ted lit out.

## Twenty-eight

# HIGHWAYMAN

The hard-breathing Chevy hauled the heavily loaded trailer in the slow lane. Every car sped by in the faster left lanes. He was careful to obey the 55 mph speed limit for trailers, since a speeding ticket would document his whereabouts.

His recent incarceration had taught him plenty about evading suspicion; no detail could be ignored. So, in spite of his urge to hurry up and kill them all, He steeled himself to the agonizing snail's pace.

Three hours later, he arrived at Interstate 5, the largest freeway in California. He pulled into a McDonald's. Ted blended with normal morning customers, mostly tourists and truckers; each one wore the look that said; *'I'd RATHER be somewhere else.'*

Of course, Ted would rather be mixing it up with the Campesinos, but first things first. Reviewing the local paper, he found the news as bland as his meal. That breakfast meal might just as well have been pulp, for all he cared. Eating was just a means to an end. He needed to keep his strength, so he could kill the cocksuckers that did his wife and burned his friend to death.

He headed south on I-5, there was little to do but set the cruise and hold the wheel still; the freeway was mostly straight sections, some twenty miles long and monotonously flat. The miles rolled away while he passed almond and cashew orchards, canola and safflower fields and the ubiquitous rice fields. The heavy scents saturated the air.

By the time Ted hit eastbound I-80, he achieved a strange, psychotic clarity. Each detail of his plan clicking into place, Ted barely sensed he was climbing the Sierras, in the slowest lane, among trucks and Winnebago-types. Average speed was around forty, but not by choice; the steep climb and thin air forced this limit upon every driver hauling a heavy load.

The middle lane averaged around sixty, the left seventy, until someone saw a squad car; then a Christmas tree of brake lights, the fast lane braking to 50, with chaotic lane switching; hi-speed musical chairs.

Ted avoided the fender-bending, cop-drawing melee by settling in behind a big rig hauling lodgepole, doing a steady 39 up the grade. With the heavy trailer, Ted couldn't make much more than forty anyway. Besides, the extra time allowed him to rehearse his trap. When he reached Donner Summit, each facet lay in perfect place, like feathers on a hawk's breast.

He drove past Donner Lake, named for the settlers that perished there. People have a long history of being stupid with Nature's laws. Arriving too late, they ignored warnings from the locals. Not wishing to stay in Nevada territory for a whole winter, they pushed on. Soon they were stranded in deep snow. They ran out of supplies. They ate their mules, horses, dogs and everything else. Burning their wagons for heat, they soon ran out of everything. Before it was over, most of the Donner Party had fallen to cannibalism and hypothermia. The Sierras have no sympathy for ignorance.

The next hour was downhill. He stayed in the middle lane, to avoid disciplined truckers in the slow lane, all of whom left their rigs in the same gear they'd climbed the pass with. Anyone shifting to tall gears would meet a fate that was only slightly better than what the Donners met.

The awesome beauty of the Sierra Nevada Mountains belies their sinister nature. They are steep, high, and unforgiving. So the truckers kept their rigs under control, engine brakes blasting every five seconds to retard their descent; a moving symphony, pounding out a rhythmical bass.

Ted's truck wanted to roll faster, but he kept it to fifty in the center lane in the unenviable position of blocking faster drivers, who switched lanes and swooshed by him doing eighty. It worked.

He pulled into Boomville, famous as the first or last chance to gamble in Nevada, depending on which way the tourist was going. Cars with out of state plates were everywhere, buying gas and parked in the casino lot.

Ted blended with the hustle and bustle, filling both tanks, checking fluid levels and tires. He went into the casino for lunch. Any buffet was good; high turnover dulled waitresses' eyes. Soon a cute little waitress smiled her plastic smile.
"One? That will be twelve fifty, please."

She led him to a booth, underneath a miner's sluice box. It looked old, heavy and authentic. He idly wondered if the giant gold-prospecting trough would remain on the wall or if it would fall and kill him before he finished. Ted noticed very little flavor, but it was better than jail food; that shit was bad.

Turning south at the junction, he set the cruise and settled in for the next leg. Traffic on 395 was interested only in getting somewhere else. The scenery was spectacular, but most travelers weren't interested in boundless expanses of junipers, sage and cedars, monotonously rolling hills and quaint, desolate valleys.

To a typical hunter, however, Highwway 395 was a wonderland. It coursed through some of the finest wild game habitat in the western states. It was also some of the most under-hunted country in America. Ted hunted it before, and never saw another hunter there.

He set his cruise control for 60, well below the average speed of eighty, for those with Nevada plates. Those with California plates were held to a different standard. Given the weirdos from the Bay Area, the double standard made perfect sense. Folks from California just didn't pay attention while driving in the desert.

So, the troopers were justifiably biased; they'd write them a ticket with a hefty fine, while the locals got a pass, unless they were doing something really outlandish. He entered the Washorn valley, where harsh winds from the Sierras blew down across the interstate like a gigantic wind tunnel. The blacktop was scarred from prior stupid people who disobeyed the high wind advisory signs, the blinking warning lights and the unwritten law of the desert. Several dozen shrines and crosses along the shoulder highlighted the lethality of the horizontal shears, which easily exceeded 80 mph, often tipping tourists and big rigs with great dispatch.

As Ted drove the 'Gauntlet', he saw the lake... incredibly out of place in the dry desert, its gunmetal water chock full of wild geese, seagulls, ducks, hell divers, mergansers and wind surfers. The whitecaps betrayed the presence of the extreme wind. He saw several hang gliders high up in the air, dangling like mobiles in a huge baby blue sky nursery, soaring in the very currents that would soon overturn some hapless Winnebago, twelve thousand feet below.

Ted made the climb into the greater Carbon area, his truck gaining speed during the descent. He blew right past Carbon City. The fewer stops, the better.

The traffic thinned considerably after Ted drove past Granderville. Most tourists pulled off to see Virginia City, Carbon City or drive up to Lake Tarhoe. There was the occasional trucker, a biker here, a wayward tourist there.

The vastness of the country began to reassure him; his plan had a chance, and the chance lay in just such a feature... geographic isolation.

Soon he found it; a fairly small bowl, three or four miles across. A faint two-track headed west towards the Sierras. After waiting for one lone truck to pass, he shifted into low range and idled toward the mountains. When he came to the first dry creek crossing, Ted spotted a flaw in his plan; his prey wouldn't be driving four wheel drive rigs.

When he finally found a spot to turn around without breaking an axle or sticking a cedar branch through his grill, Ted turned around and got back on 395, southbound. It made him nervous; if he could miss such a big detail, how many others had he overlooked?

A few miles south, he found another possible site. This felt right, for no apparent reason. He shifted into low range and idled into the desert, appraising the two-track's accessibility for city cars. It was dry, firm and blown smooth from the nearly constant wind.

He idled for a mile before hitting the first gully, deep enough to scrape the frame on his trailer. He crossed, then it hit him; 'My leetle friends can't cross that!'

Soon his tractor filled in the rut. He walked the tractor several times to pack the soil; any low-rider could cross it. Ted drove the little tractor back onto the trailer and continued up the two-track.

Soon he hit another gully, deeper, because he was approaching the base of the mountains. This time he off-loaded the tractor first and filled the gully bed before driving over it.

Ted knew the right setup when he saw it; almost ten miles as the crow flies from the interstate, far enough to obliterate noise and isolate his victims. There was a small knob overlooking the back-trail. He could see the interstate, its chalk-white line, smooth, straight and silent. Its whiteness stood out against the bluish-green background. It looked like a game trail, carved by the hooves of a million deer, over a million years.

To the east, behind the knoll, ran a ridge of tall mountains. Ted estimated them at around 12,000 feet. The eastern part of the knoll swept slightly down, then back up to greet the base of the mountains. The western slope panned out below, in the gullies that Ted had just fixed.

Anyone driving the two-track would be easy pickings. If Ted had to retreat, he could slip down the back and high-tail it up one of the brush-choked draws.

He couldn't help hoping his opponents would show at sunrise, when the sun would be in their eyes... but that was too much to hope for.

He set up base camp in a thick grove of junipers, two hundred yards due east and uphill from the knob. The trees were short, but they provided dense cover. A man could walk within ten yards and miss his camp.

He hurriedly cooked up some instant rice, coffee, and a pair of quail that failed to flush with their buddies. The spreader rounds worked great. The meal would be cause for acclaim under normal circumstances. Nothing tastes better than wild game, eaten at altitude. Yet there was no joy in the meal, just as there had been none in taking the quail. He simply needed to order to fulfill his plan.

Ted walked from camp to the ambush site, to rehearse his escape routes. On the way back, he took the other route, to eliminate any nasty surprises. He got one; the white flash of the viper's mouth popped like a strobe, as the Diamondback's rattling hit his ears. His reflex jump carried him five feet sideways. Adrenaline surged through his body and kept him on razor edge all the way back to camp; buzzing, striking rattlers will do that to a man.

He opened up his ice chest and poured a tall glass of Calistolada Cabernet. Back when Ted used to hunt with his brother, Dave always packed a bottle of cheap screw-cap, the 'celebratory vintage.' When either of them made a kill, that night would see the wine opened; when it came out, there was reason to be jubilant.

Now, years after his brother took another path, Ted found himself participating in the hollow ritual; lonely for his family, hungry for revenge, but... damned glad to find such a great place to extract it. He sipped and prayed for his wife's recovery. Soon he was in his sleeping bag and snoring. Maybe it was the desert air, wine or his soon to blossom plan, but it was his first good night of sleep since killing those three assholes on Radical Ridge.

The piercing sun quickly burned him awake. He lit his stove, heated coffee water and listened to the weather radio. Aware that high altitude boils water fast, but cool, Ted tossed coffee into it and set himself for the long wait. The weather radio finally coughed up the local forecast; balmy and mild for the next five days.

He loaded his tractor bucket with plastic tarps, fertilizer and diesel fuel, after packing the small items in his backpack. He grabbed his note pad and rangefinder and drove to the two-track.

After excavating all loose sand and logs from the nearest gulch crossing, he laid plastic sheeting, poured a bag of ammonium nitrate fertilizer and diesel into it. He rigged a rocket igniter, battery and receiver, trailing the antenna out for good reception.

Folding the plastic back over the top, he dozed sand over the crude bomb. A few passes with the tractor compacted it. Then he drove side hill, fifty yards to a large stand of junipers; the closest available cover. Another bomb went there. Ted did the same at each place where survivors would probably run after the gulch bomb went off.

He built a test bomb approximately three hundred yards from the two-track. This was set on channel one, normally reserved for elevator function in his model aircraft transmitter. Hurrying back to the knoll, Ted couldn't wait to see if the bomb would work; they seemed to work on TV, but this wasn't Hollywood... it was reality.

Turning on the transmitter, he gave the transmitter some 'up stick'. Ted didn't need a scope to see the huge cloud of dust, flying tree trunks and rocks. It took three seconds for the sound to hit him, but it hurt his ears. The noise was awesome; the dust cloud mushroomed, echoes rang from the mountaintops.

He mixed water and powdered watercolors in his backpack-spraying rig. Using the rangefinder, each bush or tree that was one thousand yards from the knoll received a big blast of blue paint on the uphill side. At eight hundred yards, the brush and trees got a blast of orange. At six hundred, yellow, four black. The final radius was set at lethal range for buckshot; fifty yards. This was sprayed in purple, for the color of crepe that those pricks draped in his home.

By then the dust cloud quit rising. He was glad it topped out at three hundred feet, where a crosswind shear skimmed it off flatly, like foam skimmed from a beer stein. The surrounding mountains screened the cloud from all but the most distant eyes, far out on the interstate. Hopefully, distance would camouflage the off-white telltale.

He drove down to check out the explosion site, amazed to see a trench almost ten feet deep, clean to the bedrock. The gash spanned thirty feet; *'Good grave for the fuckers.'*

Next, he tied giant balloons at each of the colored ranges, drove back to the knoll and brought out the rifles. He cranked the scope to 24 on the STW and settled it into the rest. The crosshairs started settling down. He located a balloon on the BLUE radius and put the lowest dot on it. His shot was right on the money, but kicked sand a foot to the right. Then he noticed the slight sideways breeze. He held on the left side of the balloon and burst it.

He gapped between the lowest and middle dots for the 800-yard range, breaking a balloon with the same windage, one dot left. For the 600-yard holdover, he gapped the upper dots, bursting both balloons in four shots.

By then, the barrel on the 7MM was hot, so he picked up the .243, the scope set to 12 for the black range. He pressed the factory trigger and the balloon popped. His guts tightened; soon heads would pop like balloons.

Finally, he set up the rockets; after dark, he test fired one. It hissed, clearing 400 feet before its parachute popped, carrying the rocket a half-mile south in the horizontal shear. With everything set, he went back to camp.

He tried to force away the images of those punk bastards raping and carving his wife like some writhing, screaming turkey. Ted drank while wine praying she'd survive her ordeal, that her pain and degradation would subside, perhaps, at some point down the road.

For the first time, he cried, letting it all out. His pain and sorrow were stolen away by the cold desert wind, heard only by a few owls, coyotes and God.

Morning broke, warm and dry. He unhitched the trailer, loaded the four-wheeler into the truck and drove down to the blue line. Offloading the quad, Ted drove it back to camp. He started the leaf blower, pointed it at the trail and drove the quad down the two-rack... his tracks vanished in the man-made wind. He hid the quad in the cedars and hiked back to the truck.

Twenty-nine...
SOUTH

He wanted to floor it, but willpower prevailed; he couldn't risk getting busted for speeding. He was so obsessed that he almost missed the cutoff. Taking it, he ended up back in California, almost before he was ready. The hours over the pass whizzed by like minutes, due to intense concentration on his plan.

Brutish hunger finally pulled him out of his psychotic thoughts. Ted pulled in to a busy truck stop. The waitress kept giving him the eye, but he didn't notice. That was his first mistake. Hell hath no fury like a truckstop waitress scorned. And this fine looking 28 year-old was definitely feeling scorned; she wasn't accustomed to having guys miss her signals.

Even with a full house of horny truckers, she couldn't let Ted go. Something about his eyes; so dangerous. As she carried out orders and wriggled away from the regulars, she cast a glance or two Ted's way.

He seemed wrapped up in his own little world, like nothing else mattered. Mattie brought his order around to his side of the counter. Her right breast 'accidentally' touched his left elbow. The man jumped like he stuck his dick in a blender. She whispered huskily, in mock alarm.
"Oh, excuse me, sir, I didn't mean ta startle ya... I just wanted your lunch to be *hot 'n good.*"
She emphas
"Huh? That's ok, forget it"
The worst thing you could say to Mattie was to forget her. Her eyes blazed with fury.
"HEY, MISTER! What exactly should I forget... you pawin' my tits or your rude attitude? I think old Buster oughta teach you some manners... whattyathink 'o that?"

The last thing he needed was attention.
"Oh, no... I apologize. Here; take this... as a tip."

Ted handed her a twenty, got up and dropped a second twenty on the register to cover his order. The swinging door hit his heel on the way out. Old Buster, in the corner booth, never got up; he continued to examine Mattie's ample young cleavage, while she played for the crowd.
"How come the good ones *always* get away?"
They laughed and went on with lunch.

He took the truck to normal speed for that part of the valley and set the cruise, seventy per; anyone going LESS was a suspect. After a while he saw a small dot on the roadside. Soon he saw it was a tiny woman sitting on her backpack, holding out her right thumb.

Normally, he would never pick up a hitchhiker, but something about the woman registered. Her backpack looked almost identical to his... before it got riddled with bullets and stained with his blood.

Her hair color, eyes and features were identical to his, as if he was picking up a female version of himself. She climbed in the without checking out the driver. The truck built speed while she settled in.

"Hey, man, thanks for the ride. I been waitin' on that piece o' shit road for two hours... ya think anyone would pick me up? *Fuck...* One guy stopped but his ole lady got huffy so he drove off... Do I look like the kinda woman to steal her man? *Do I look like that?*"
"HUH?"
"What do ya mean, *'HUH'?* Do I look like a woman who'd fuck a man so fine he'd leave his wife on the spot? Bitch coulda give me a ride an' make her own call, ya know?"

She didn't wait for an answer.
"I don't screw guys who are married... Y'aint married, are ya, mister? Anyway, I gotta get to Mexico tonight. I don't care whose cock I gotta suck, but I NEED to get to Tijuana tonight... *got it?"*
Ted flashed on Charlie Takon, and his favorite expression.

He felt an odd kinship, for some reason; took a chance.

"How much do you know about gangs?"
"A little... *why?*"
I need to know about a gang... How's fifty bucks sound?"
She eyed him suspiciously.
"Whaddyawanna know?"
"Campesinos; Purples in L.A... can you help me?"
She sensed his pain and began to open up to him.
"Well, I know that's their color, but ya knew that already or else ya wouldn't of drove so far south already, right?"
"*Drove South? What do you mean?*"

"Sorry, I didn't mean nuthin', but your license brackets say Humdob county... I had an ol' man up there 'til last week. I waited tables... it's a ways north, shore 'nuff!"
Ted relaxed.
"What else do you know about the purples?"
Brittanie relaxed, too.
"Well, I know they're in LA... And some of those little pricks came to my restaurant and stiffed me; then they trashed the bathroom... I had to stay 'nother hour without overtime to clean it up... why?"

His heart leaped; it's a small world after all. Brittanie, with an "ie", probably saw the same bastards that attacked Jo. He tried to hide his interest.

"How many did you see? Did you hear any names?"
Brittanie liked him more all the time.
"I saw six of 'em, about a week ago, shore 'nuff... they all had the same tattoos, limp-dick hairnets and baggy pants. And butt-ugly tank tops; acted like they were on a mission from God, or sumthin'... that's about it."

"You know where they stay?"
Brittany acted like TV was interviewing her.
"Well I heard the middle of the Barrios... but I ain't sure. I don't get into LA much; are YOU goin' ta LA, mister?"

Ted slipped her the fifty and slowed, to pull over to the gravel shoulder; she knew what they were stopping for. She started loosening her bra.

Only instead of a hump, Ted let her out. She was alone again. Brittanie felt a loss, but only until the next big rig pulled over. She'd make it to Mexico, shore 'nuff.

Ted decided to stay the night, closer to LA but not in it...to glean more facts before he spooked his quarry. Besides, he still had some things to do. He went to a clothing store and a costume shop.

He emerged with a blue suit, fake moustache, black cowboy hat, bolo tie, cowboy boots and other incgonito odds and ends. He drove to a print shop, donned the western disguise and went inside.

He recalled that during the Oklahoma bombings, some fifteen years earlier, the feds searched invisible electronic fingerprints, from copiers and faxes, to chase down the scumbags that made the bomb. Whether or not it was true, he wasn't about to chance it.

He entered the office supply store and bought a ream of purple paper, then created his message on the store's workstation computers and copiers. After he'd copied fifty fliers, he made a dozen with large solid black directional arrows, paid cash and drove away.

Ted spent the rest of the afternoon seeing the local tourist traps, the only way to blend in such a town. After that, he was ready for food. A local Danny's looked good enough. The constant exchange of customers practically guaranteed he'd never be picked from a lineup.

He sat down and opened a map. He'd only been to L.A. only once, twenty years earlier; not sure how long it might take to get into the bowels of the beast and its legendary eight-lane traffic snarls.

The more he studied, the more he realized he needed to stall for about eight hours. It was either that or 8 hours plus a day. Ted's booth afforded him a view of the freeway, frontage road curio shops and struggling businesses. Of them all, the Buckhorn Saloon caught his eye.

186

A lot of business and under the table shit went on in bars. Ted fired up his truck and loped the mile to the honky-tonk. He elected to wait for the clientele to get lubricated. While he waited, Ted focused on his upcoming task... find and kill everyone responsible for the attack on his wife. Then, if time and opportunity permitted, he would take G. Charles Takon's advice...

*'I'd DAMN SURE kill the QUEEN BEE.'*

He took a nap.

When he woke up it was totally dark. A half-dozen or more pickups, two greasy hogs and six cars littered the nearly flat half-acre gravel-and-busted-glass parking lot. A red neon sign glared at road-weary eyes; "Buckeye Sa_oon"... the "L" was burned out. A cloud of moths swirled around the crackling, buzzing neon. Ted put on his cowboy hat, mustache and Caterpillar bolo.

It was a local crowd; cowboys, oil rig workers and their girls, all trying to convince themselves that this was a good time. The jukebox hammered out 'Oakie from Muskogee'. Three guys sang, off-key. Ted pulled his brim low. A few heads turned to greet the newcomer. Seeing no familiar face, the heads went back to their beer business.

He walked to the dark end of the bar and ordered a Coors. Merle finished up and Willie Nelson took over with 'My heroes have always been cowboys.' Ted scanned the joint; three guys and a gal played eight ball at one table. Four at the bar, ten or twelve others alternately drank and danced on the floor littered with peanut shells. Everybody knew each other, obviously... except for Ted. It worried him, but he corrected the thought; *'It's a highway bar... the occasional tourist's expected.'*

A burly young cowboy pulled up a stool.
"Howdy; name's Lon... where ya from, buddy?"
Ted shook a hand almost as big as Ted's head.
"Lodi... YOU?"
The young stud repeated himself.

"Born right here. Name's Lon... What's YOURS?"
Ted chose a familiar name.
"David... friends call me Dave. Want a cool one, Lon?"

After three cool ones, Lon disgorged more information than the yellow pages. Yeah, there were gangs driving through. Some were purple. The good old boys kept them from settling in this berg, but couldn't stop them from buying gas and such, on their way north and south. What they did in LA was no business of his, but try it here and by God, there'd be bodies to bury.

Ted soon grew bored with Lon's typically redneck rhetoric; it seemed tame, compared to what Ted had in mind. He knew Lon's type; young stud, full of piss and vinegar, big heart, small brain. All he wanted was a sympathetic ear, a few brews and pussy; not necessarily in that order.

Ted drifted to the pool tables, where a woman was beating everybody. The others now shot whiskey, not pool. He nodded. She didn't nod; she stared instead. He didn't know that she'd been giving him the eye already. Ted put his quarter on the felt and went for another beer. Returning, he saw the woman motioning for him to rack.

"I was third, no?"
The slender brunette shook her head, whispering huskily.
"The first quarter's mine, so that sleaze ball in the booth stays away. The other belongs to the Floyd brothers..."
Ted followed her gaze to a dim booth. The mouth-breathing duo slouched over a table covered with empty pitchers, oblivious to all but the last half-empty pitcher.

"So... you wanna play or what?"
Ted dropped a quarter in the slot and waited for all the balls to drop. He racked. She broke, a solid, two stripes.
"I like the BIG ones."
The choice for stripes was questionable, since two were married to the rail. 'Becky' ran three balls, then missed and easy bank shot.
"Your shot"...

He chalked the cue, circling the table, studying his options. When he completed the loop, he unknowingly backed into his opponent. Her body felt firm; he knew that he'd bumped into her right breast.

"What looks GOOD to you?"
Ted missed the double meaning.
"I'll shoot the three, then go for the one. After that, I suppose I'll improvise... Is that OK with my opponent?"
"Well, I like the "improvise" part... Let's see how it goes."

Ted missed. He hadn't shot pool for years.
"Say, mister, you're not much for pool, are you? I'll bet you're not here for the scenery, either... What gives?"

Ted took a slow sip while his mind raced. He hand't expected her to be so forthright. His story had better be good; she was obviously not a common barfly. She was muscular, lean, curious and intelligent. He stalled for time.
"Why do you say that?"

She got close. He felt her hot breath in his ear.
"Well, for openers, most guys wouldn't be caught DEAD saying; 'I SUPPOSE I'll...' anything. And unless I miss my guess, you just bought the hat... and that bolo? Bullshit! You've never been ON a Dozer; your hands are too pretty to be a dirt mover. Name's Becky."
She didn't back up when finished.

Ted found her directness disarming. Maybe it was the beer or the cumulative stress of being shot, arrested, tried and acquitted, but he was attracted to this brunette, five hundred miles from home. He started spilling his guts.

"I'm no pool hustler. I'm no sex hound, either."
Becky giggled in relief. She was accustomed to being manhandled; the stranger was getting to her in an unexpected way. Hoping for a sexual interlude that might last more than three minutes, she prompted him again.

"So, what ARE you good at?"
Her blinking lashes and wide smile got to him; she saw him blush.

He found the scenario highly intoxicating. He opened up to the stranger in the strange town, where likely no one would ever find his plan out.

"Don't get me wrong... I've had plenty beers; I'd be crazy NOT to want to sleep with you... hell, I might even WANT to stay afterward"

"But...?"

"But I'm on a mission. After I finish, I just might come back here and whip your ass at pool. Fair enough? Call me Dave".

She noticed the phrasing; 'call me Dave'... not; "My name's Dave" or "I'm Dave... most intriguing.

Ted looked into her clear blue eyes, surprised to see total concentration. It unnerved him to the cellular level. She took a peek at the Floyds, who failed to recognize their turn again. Becky racked, he broke. The three went down. Then he noticed a fresh beer at his table.

He made four balls, then missed. As he backed away from the table, he again backed into Becky's body. This time, he stood for it, enjoying the firm physique, aptly applied.

"So, Dave, I see that white band on your ring finger; I see that far away look in your eyes. I usually avoid trouble in my men... but you are NOT my average man. Maybe we can help each other. What do you say, DAVE?"

He stood stock-still, enjoying the physical sensation. The firm breasts pressing harder into his back with every word overwhelmed him. Her cool reasoning and succinct awareness was equally attractive. After all, it had been thirty years since a strange woman had offered herself. His response sounded lame, even to him.

"Maybe when I come this way again. But if not, at least we did tonight proper; now let's finish this game, OK?"

Becky didn't appear mad. In fact, she looked happy. She was testing to see if he was as big a sleaze as most men got, after a few drinks. He passed. She ran the balls and sank the eight.

Ted went to piss. Once clear of her pheromones, his head began to clear. He left through the rear door and strode to his truck, eager to get out of Dodge. Fumbling with his keys to unlock the cab, he caught the soft metallic outline of a patrol car in the shadow of the billboard. Were it not for the weak neon reflection playing off the emergency lights, Ted would never have spotted it.

Although a seedy hotel sign proclaimed VACANCY' a half-mile away, Ted knew the trap; local sheriff, can't wait to bust out of town tourists. He climbed into the back of his camper, after hiding his keys behind the left rear tire. His jail time taught him a thing or two about wrongful convictions for DUI suspects... One Asian dude got three years because he fell asleep in his car, with the keys in his pocket. Quite a stretch from 'driving while under the Influence' but the cops do love to stretch. The last thing he wanted was a run-in with the law.

He settled into his sleeping bag and blankets; then the truck jiggled. Sitting bolt upright, he saw lip-gloss reflecting weak neon.
"We can do this the easy way or the hard way, *DAVE.*"
A thin, cougar smile crossed her lips.
"The hard way's for me to holler. Then Byron will come squealing in here, with his nightstick out... he's had the hots for me for years. Or we can do the easy way; invite me in... And nobody gets hurt."

His thoughts flashed back to the truckstop hubbub... He couldn't afford any attention. Although he doubted that she'd really yell, he nodded. Besides, there was another reason to let her in; he was horny as hell.

In a surprisingly short time, Becky was buck-naked. It had been a long time since he'd been in bed with a firm, hungry woman. Her body was hot. She smelled like musty cigarette smoke. She climbed onto him and cooed huskily as she slid onto his shaft.

Ted made the psychological adjustment to fuck her. After all, his wife was in a coma and the doctors said she

191

probably wouldn't come out of it. Besides, Ted was afraid that if he shunned her, she'd make a fuss and the squad car would come. But the biggest reason was obvious; it was already happening.

She rolled over, tossing the covers off. She wanted him to see her in the half-light. She gasped and pulled him to her, glad he didn't object. He seemed dispassionate. She vowed to change that. He was the first smart, hard man she'd met in three years; wasn't going to waste him.

Her lips found his testicles. Ted moved not a muscle; his thighs were rock-hard. Encouraged, she worked up his shaft. Her lips formed a channel that fit perfectly under his pole, and she worked slowly to its tip. She looked at his face; a blank, upturned open-mouthed grimace. She'd seen it before, and took it as a sign of intensity. Her lips slowly worked to the tip, fingers probing his buttocks and abdomen. Still; the man lay perfectly still. Oddly, this turned her on more.

This "Dave," if that was his real name, was clearly not the average honky-tonk fuck. Ever since she got in bed, he'd become increasingly quiet, his cock increasingly hard. She needed him to break his threshold.

Sensing that he required more trigger, she placed her vulva against his right shin, noting involuntary throbbing in his abdomen. She started false fucking his shin. He climaxed instantly, while she swallowed, taking over half of him into her throat, working it and pumping her vulva against his shin. She vowed to give him another chance. Maybe he hadn't fucked for so long that he forgot the etiquette. After all, she was young and he wasn't.

Whatever... she was determined to get what she wanted. She giggled with delight when she felt instantaneous re-hardening. Clearly, he had some unresolved issues and she intended to resolve them.Her clit was hot from rubbing his shin. Her body trembled for release. She slid up and surrounded his brass-like member. Her lips explored the man's lips, tentatively at first.

He tasted sexy. After his first climax, he relaxed, apparently forgetting his taboos... maybe even his wife? The first orgasm was a threshold, but there was no going back. He got back on page one of proper sexual etiquette.

While she took full advantage, she started wondering about his wife... What kind of situation would cause such a good man to stray so far? Her question evaporated as she unexpectedly climaxed; her first orgasm in years.

He climaxed, too. It surprised them both for a moment. Then he started nibbling on her neck and massaging both nipples. Her second orgasm was hers alone. He never noticed. It pushed her on, eager to fulfill every fantasy with this strange lover. She forced away all thoughts of his wife; after all, every woman has her needs.

Ted couldn't resist the lust, either. This woman fit him perfectly. When he swelled, she tightened. When he climaxed, so did she. When he rested, she seemed to want rest. It was impossibly perfect. They fucked all night long.

Regrettably, with the first strengthening rays of dawn, she saw that distant look in his eyes again. Her night of fantasy was yesterday's newspaper; only important to those on the front page.

Still, as she dressed, she couldn't help but wonder why she was quitting. It had been a long time since she'd felt so complete. Without a word, she pored her blue eyes all over the man one last time; her last drink at the oasis before returning to the desert. Then she nimbly climbed out of the camper slipped into her beat-up old Camaro.

Ted cried himself to sleep. The sunrise brought the full measure of solar intensity. The heat probed deep into the camper shell. He felt deep remorse. Still, the situation called for drastic measures. Fucking Becky was definitely drastic. He walked to the Denny's, to loosen up his legs and work off the partial hangover. He wondered; would SHE feel as bad as he did? Would she feel anything?

The food had no taste, just like last night's beer had little taste. The only thing with any taste was the sex. He hated to admit, but that was a reawakening; sexual CPR.

The images were so intense that Ted hoped he'd never see her again. He headed south. Maybe the miles would help. It took fifty or 'em before the psychotic thoughts returned, slowly settling over Becky's hot body like snowflakes, at first melting from the heat... then finally, accumulating and covering. May God bless the miles.

## Thirty

## BAIL

Double-checking his disguise, Ted studied the mirror for obvious flaws; Becky's sharp eyes taught him that. The cheap suit and loafers worked; a lawyer was spawned.

Morris Fishbein strode crisply into La Raza Bail Bonds, a converted pawnshop; its main room was narrow and deep. Boxes and files strewn all over. Halfway back, Ted spied a defunct wall-mounted air conditioner; flaking drywall, black mold testified as to time of death, maybe ten years earlier.

He saw the substitute form of coping with LA's relentless heat; a fan pivoting to and fro, silently paddling stale air around the dank room.

There was a small serpentine path of bare hardwood weaving between overstuffed banker's boxes. It looked more like a dry creek bed than the floor of a business office. He walked deeper into the dirty office, picking his steps carefully to avoid disturbing piles of files, Ted felt nervous; that is, until he spied the owner, in the rear.

Julian Barrera sat at his desk, dispassionately wolfing a cheeseburger. Blotches of grease soaked through the wrapper; some of it escaped to land on his shirt. There was fresh ketchup on his dirty white tee shirt, overlying stiff marinara stains from last night's feeding frenzy.

"Good morning, sir. My name is Morris Fishbein... uhm, perhaps you've heard of my work?"
Barrera grunted in the negative without looking up; just another salesman, messing with his lunchtime tranquility.

"NO? Well, I work with underprivileged youth."
Still no answer. Morris held out his bogus card.

"Well sir, My group, 'Youthful Urban Potential', is on a mission to eradicate violence; by using alternatives and positive social affirmation, we want to restore PEACE in the Barrio... *don't YOU?"*

195

Barrera grunted, but still didn't look up. Ted wondered why he even bothered with a disguise for such an apathetic chump.

"And, to that end I have been authorized to post bail for the young Campesinos boys that might be incarcerated at the present time."

Fishbein drew a bundle from his attaché and dropped it smack in the middle of the desk. Against the backdrop of grease-stained taco wrappers, limp French fries and sweating can of diet soda, the crisp two thousand dollar package had its intended effect. Barrera sat bolt upright in his chair.

Ted dropped the second pack nonchalantly, deliberately tip-rolling the double r's;
"Now, Mr. Barrera... Is that how to say your name? You ARE familiar with the Campesinos?"
Barrera's attitude resuscitated. He dropped the burger.
"Si, Si, senor; Yes, I know them well. I think that there's three... (His eyes shifted to the cash) maybe four in jail right now. You want me to *bail them ALL?"*

"Yes, please. Here's a good faith payment, to get the ball rolling; my assistants have ascertained that in fact, only two Campesinos were in jail last night, but if there are others, please bail them, too. My assistants will arrive tomorrow with more cash. We need to have all the Campesinos out by tomorrow for the self-empowerment retreat that we have planned."

Barrerra nodded while Fishbein turned to leave, then spun around to punctuate his point.
"One other thing, sir; our group is funded by anonymous donors, who request absolute secrecy, because some people are CULTURALLY biased against helping these young Hispanic men. We don't need receipts... feel free to keep any cash left over after bailing these poor boys."

Barrera grinned, nodding as Fishbein rambled on.

"We insist on your silence, if we are to do any more business in the future."

Barrera eyed the cash greedily.

"Yes, yes... I understand; You want me to bail other gangs, too?"

"Not right now. And, by the way, we don't care for the term, 'gang'. We prefer 'group'... But yes, later we'll do another group... Would you like that, Mr. Barrera?"

The money was already in his pocket.

"Si, si, love to help these gangst... I mean groups."

"Good... it has been a pleasure meeting you. Good day, Mr. Barrera."

He whirled and left, feeling the man's eyes all the way out. He was glad he used the disguise. Cash affects vision. Ted drove to the county jail, just three blocks from Barrera's joint. He hoped his ploy would work like he'd planned back in jail. The promise of future cash, with so many gangs in LA, Barrera would see a huge cash cow. Hopefully it would keep him silent long enough to kill the purples.

A little after five o'clock, Ted's investment paid off. Three purple-shirted punks exited the side door of the jail. Ted scrunched low, but the chance of being detected was slim; he was parked two hundred yards away. He focused his binoculars; the trio swaggered, acting tough.

They flashed gang signs. A black and gold Impala low-rider cruised up. They got in. The low-rider drove past Ted, so close that he heard their music and laughter. The low rider was fairly beautiful, as far as low riders go. Its overall theme of gold and black carried to the visors and upholstery. Gold-plated spoke wheels finished it off in typically gaudy fashion. It was easy to follow.

He fought the urge to drive up and shoot them like trapped rats. He parked a block away and steadied the spotting scope; seven others came out to greet the bailed trio with their special handshake; clenched fist, forearm to forearm. They all dressed just like in court; khaki pants, purple tees. Cookie cutter pussies, all.

They swaggered and postured all over the street; a territorial display, perhaps. He decided to check it out. Ted cruised the whole Barrio. With an hour of study he had a workmanlike opinion of their behavior.

He noticed the similarities between gang behavior and the White-tailed Buck's. Both had core turf, surrounded by a buffer zone, where one could encounter rivals without confrontation, allowing for feeding, fleeing danger and meeting new sexual partners; interactions which were mutually beneficial to all. Adjacent to the buffer zones were rivals' turf. Crossing those posed great risk.

Stalking a big buck was hard, but getting the stag to stalk him was as easy as 1,2,3... Drop a challenging scent. Run away and hide. When the buck answers the challenge, shoot. It should work for gangsters, too.

He drove off and found a really cheap hotel, perfect for his plan. The joint had seen its best days, back when Liquor was king; it once welcomed senators, champion boxers and the finest hookers in Southern California. Those were the days; huge marble floors, gourmet cuisine, brass spittoons, spit-polished limos and uniformed bellboys.

But now the Dempsey slouched in old age. Where once the marble floor had its own attendant constantly mopping and buffing it to a high sheen, it now sported horizontal skid row bums.

The floor hadn't seen a mop since Hoover wore skirts. The lobby, once proud, smelling of vogue cologne, Cuban cigars and lobster, now reeked of dry rot, screwcap wine and piss stains. Even the Dempsey's cockroaches were slow and old.

It was the kind of place where nobody saw nothing, heard nothing or did nothing. It was perfect. He paid the crusty old clerk 20 dollars and went up. The clerk stuffed the bill in his pants and went back to his racing forms. He'd take another shot at the trifecta tomorrow. He gave out the key without looking at Ted.

Once inside, he double checked his weapons and laid out his sleeping bag, to serve as a barrier against the creepy crawlers that had to be thriving in the mattress. His head felt heavy as he hit the sack; the strain of the last few weeks got the best of him. He was out before he knew it.

Twice during the night, he awoke with nightmares. The first was of purple knife blades cutting his kids up, purple blood running down the steps, purple prison bars.

The second terror, later, was a gigantic pair of handcuffs and brown cinderblock walls. One handcuff pierced his chest, exiting his lumbar spine and testicles. The other ring ran through a squad car roof. It didn't take a shrink to decipher it.

After the nightmare woke him, he found further sleep impossible. Soon his rig found a local Danny's like a horse finds its stall. He ate until 5:30, then sandbagged the booth, sipping coffee and scanning the paper. At six, it was time to lay down the challenging scent.

Ted was relieved to find the barrio quiet. This wasn't like deer hunting, where deer would already be up and moving. Gangsters were lazy and slothful. He drove to the Purple borders. Each corner got a flier. Then he drove to the core area and put a flier under the wiper of each low rider. The text was simple and direct.

*"To the cowardly Campesino Putahs who attacked a defenseless woman... I am one man, alone. 14 north. 395 to Bridgeport. Follow signs; Come or others will know this; every Purple is a woman-cutting maricon."*

With the fliers posted, Ted felt the need for a 'kicker', a catalyst. If he were bass fishing, he might use a rattle. If he were turkey hunting, a rival tom's call would simulate competition. However, he was hunting people; a different catalyst was needed.

The psycho gringo went to the closest low riders. The metal bat rang out and the windshield caved with a sickening crunch. He'd never hit a windshield before, but was surprised at how easily it collapsed. Several swings brought the grill onto the street. The second car got the same treatment. Each got an additional flier when he finished, smack on the driver's seat.

Walking toward his truck, he was surprised at the quick response; running half-dressed from their cribs, yelling and swearing, they looked like purple killer bees coming from the hive. Bees with guns! Hot leaden emissaries whizzed past him, clattering metal and ricocheting off pavement.

Bolting for his truck, he felt a rush of adrenaline just like on Radical Ridge. Back then, it terrified him, but this time, Ted found it erotic. His guts turned to fire and his dick got hard. He reached for his shotgun. He hit the ignition, with gangsters quickly closing.

Most of the Campesinos stopped a safe distance away, content to generally hail bullets at an unknown, potentially dangerous target, which could be a rival gang's trap.

But one young gangster kept coming fast, pistol at arm's length, palm down. Ted fumbled to start the truck; '*shoulda left it running; might die right here, from one fuck-up!*'

He kept trying to start the truck, but the clock in his head said it was too late. He looked at the youth, sixty yards, closing fast; the first 9mm bullets rattled against the grille. Ted poked the shotgun out the driver window; the blast caught the punk's gun hand and right side of his chest, flipping him to the asphalt, soles of his feet facing Ted.

Before the empty hull stopped rattling in the cab, the second blast caught the punk on the soles of his feet and the underside of his outstretched arm and pit. His writhing and screaming, as well as the loud blasts, served as effective repellent. The rest of the gang stood fast and listened to the anguished cries. The punk spun in circles, wailing in agony. Ted's tires squealed down the street.

Before he realized it, Ted was doing ninety on the Grapevine. He came out of his adrenaline high, only to notice the temperature gauge; almost pegged. A quick glance at the other gauges told him that except for the high temperature, the engine was OK. He took the next off-ramp, shut off the engine and coasted to a station.

Copious steam vapors rose from the grill. He opened the hood, careful to avoid the steam cloud. The radiator was intact, but somehow a bullet managed to pierce his top radiator hose.

Once again, Ted's luck held. The hose would be a quick fix, whereas a radiator leak would be a deal breaker. He went in the gas station and bought all he needed; replacement hose, screwdriver, antifreeze and sealant. Ten minutes later, the temp was back in mid-range.

While he drove, minor distractions surfaced and nagged him. For example, that gutless little nine-millimeter bullet; how the hell did it penetrate good old American steel? Why didn't it just glance off the hood, pierce the windshield and fuck Ted up? It was fortuitous, surely.

He began to have doubts; he doubted that his challenge would actually cause a bunch of gangsters to give chase. And, if they did chase, would he be able to kill them all? Finally, Ted thought of his sweetheart, in a coma, alone in a hospital bed, shrinking into a netherworld, with tubes in her veins and nose; he doubted she would live. That did it; he hit the gas pedal... fuck doubt; it would work. It HAD TO.

The tiny pellets felt like charcoal embers burning his body. They dragged him in the crib and found that Felipe's wounds were minor. Only six number Fives had penetrated skin, even though dozens of small shot caused welts before bouncing off his vest.

The leather vest stopped most of the tiniest birdshot. Instead of a pink hole, with a tiny ball an inch deep in his skin, he only received a huge welt; fair trade for his arrogance.

The bulk of the pattern, including the lethal buckshot, flew a foot and a half left. He was one lucky little gangbanger. As Esmiralda probed each hole with tweezers and extracted a tiny pellet, Felipe grimaced silently.

He knew he was lucky. He'd once seen a drive-by shotgun hit; buckshot ripped through the car door and tore a hole in the man's chest. All the guy could do was whine weakly. From start to finish, the dying took less than fifteen seconds. Felipe recalled the shotgun barrel sticking out of the truck; it looked like a battleship cannon. The buckshot clattering into parked cars still rang in his ears.

Soon a lively conversation grew as they worked gradually from stark fear to a building bravado. Felipe kept quiet; silence would improve his status. He'd worked very hard to be accepted as a Campesino. He vowed to stay silent, no matter how painful it might get.

Miguelito, just entering the crib, spoke up, stealing Felipe's thunder. He held up three fliers.
"MIRA! Look at thees! Some Bendejo put these ALL OVER OUR TURF, MAN! What are we gonna do, essays?"
Esteban answered immediately, lest he lose face.
"WE gonna fuck his ass! Thees gringo will pay! LOOK what he deed to FELIPE!"
Esmiralda spoke next, amid murmurs.

"Verdad, pero we must go to Manolito, you know? Get the whole gang... is this not the way?"
The mini gang reflexively nodded. Lito was boss; thirty-four purple shirts did his bidding. Esteban kept control.
"Si, si, we'll get together, but right now, I want every fuckin' one of these picked up! We can't let others see! GO GET EVERY DAMN ONE OF 'EM! Start at the edges of our turf; WORK BACKWARDS. Bring 'em to me *AHORITA!*"

Engines started, tires squealed; astonishing efficiency. In ten minutes, the barrio was clean of Ted's challenging scent... and all before the other gangs got out of bed.

At high noon, the Manolito Rodarte called for silence.
"Bueno; I have spoken to ORTEGA about this matter."
He said that as if it were a simple thing, like he'd just come from Mars. Nothing special really, just a little jaunt.
The room gasped. If they were quiet before, they were living dead upon hearing it. Ortega was their god. Rodarte let the impact slowly settle into their drug-soaked brains.
"As you might know, Luis Ortega is now "El Jefe..."

A few looks of disbelief surfaced; Rodarte addressed the issue, so he wouldn't lose their attention.

"Si, Si, as of last week, Victor Saldivar sold out to Luis Ortega. HE is now in charge of the whole operation! He says what I say; we can't let this bitch run around alive. It's bad for business! We will go and kill this gringo!"

When the roar died down, Manolito again spoke.
"Tex Mex, Rico, Jaime and I will stay to work out the details. The rest of you, go home, get ready to rumble. We meet here tonight, 'sta bien?"

All heads nodded as one.
"Good... Nobody gets drunk or wasted. Lots of time for that later when we CELEBRATE, no?"

But Rodarte left out one tiny fact; he hadn't spoken to Ortega. He just used the propaganda for extra kick. True,

Ortega probably would approve, but Rodarte could handle this without running to Papa, like some sick little bitch girl.

When the squad leaders were alone with Manolito, he spoke in a serious tone.

"Hermanos, we go norte to kill this man... It must be done well. Ortega will be lookin' for new middle management... it could be us, eh?"

Heads nodded.

"Bueno... we can score points and have some fun!"

He mimicked a rednecks' beer commercial; his voice went high and whiny.

"AH tellsya WHAT... It jes don't get no better 'n this!"

They laughed, but Tico interrupted the mirth.

"Perdon, 'Lito... What if thees gringo has *COMPANY?*"

Manolito detested Tico... it was always what-if with Tico.

"Then we kill them ALL. Pero, this man is alone... Did he not come here alone? Even his leetle posters taunt as ONE man alone. And, he wants to fight ONLY those who did hees ole lady, so he won't expect Campesino solidarity, VERDAD?"

Tico nodded dubiously, which pissed 'Lito off even more.

"Besides, even *IF* the motherfucker HAS friends, ARE we not THIRTY-FOUR, against one or two or three? Soon everyone will see; the PURPLES are not to be hassled!"

The leaders went to their cribs to prepare for business. Nobody paid attention to the small youth quietly sitting on the porch, soaking up every word.

## Thirty-two

## MACHO

Luis Ortega heard about it through the grapevine, shortly after his crew hauled ass. This was unacceptable, for a man who'd only been in the top seat for two weeks. His logical brain told him to shift their work load to another of his gangs.

Meanwhile, his Latino brain told him to get control of his rogues and finish Grizzly Adams gringo once and for all... Cut the head off the snake. Get some respect. Finish what he SHOULD'VE finished up north. The Latino brain won.

Ortega started packing. The phone rang; Victor's voice seemed eerily strange.
"Chewy? Word's out; our man has come down here. Old friend, DO NOT GO after thees man, comprende?"
Luis hated the condescending tone.
"Boss... I mean, Victor, don't get me wrong... but you're out of this business now, verdad?"
"SI, si, I am out... but you're more than business; you saved my Baja ass many times. Now I wish to return the favor, carnal... I should never have started this thing with him. That was my mistake. So let it go, amigo... let it go... Esta bien?"

Feeling conflicted about losing his grunts and now this condescending chat, Ortega went a little power-crazy.
"No, no esta bien, Victor... CHUPA LA PENGA! Yo tengo todo el mundo..."
Victor could only wish his ex-henchman well.
"Claro que si; the whole world is yours! *BUENA SUERTE!*"

He had relinquished command to a blossoming egomaniac and not a moment to soon. As Ortega made haste to extinguish un pequeno peon, Victor scurried to further insulate himself from the chaos that inevitably follows such brash action. He called his lawyers. He left messages.
He recycled Ortega's stinging remarks.
Yes, Chewy, we shall see who sucks it, believe me!"

He uncorked a Cabernet and turned on his favorite thinking music. This would require some serious thinking.
CH 32. STOWAWAY

His long slender fingers deftly stole the candy. His arms were so thin and flexible that he could easily reach up into most vending machines. Perhaps in a better environment, he might have become an obstetrician or veterinarian with those small, nimble hands. However in the harsh reality of the Barrio, his skills were utilized in pursuits less lofty.

The candy was for his friend, the newest Campesino. If he could impress Mano, then his chances of getting into the gang would improve. Amelio was almost thirteen... well, technically, he'd just passed his twelfth, but he was in a rush to grow up.

He'd been born in L.A. to a single mom he never knew. A year after his birth, she took a stray drive-by bullet while leaving a supermarket with him in her arms. It was never determined who his father was.

The rearing fell upon his abuela, who appeared, just two days after the death of his mother; Tina had seen the shooting in a vision. She immediately left her ancient pueblo near Ratonita Pass, New Mexico. Considering how fast she got there, no one disputed her... as if anyone cared about an old Navajo woman's inconceivable story.

Later, at age nine, he asked how she knew his mom died. The answer made no sense to the young city boy.
*'Sometimes, a thing is just seen.'*
To a street-wise boy, Tina's story seemed crazy. He put it off as mere chance and disregarded it.

But as a very young boy, he'd patterned after his only role model, spending hours on her couch, absorbing the old woman's ancient tales like a dry sponge taking water. The river of rural parables and anecdotes had a trance-like affect. Melio soon knew all her stories by heart.

Originally, Tina had planned to take him back to the old village, but her plans changed when she got to LA. she was astonished to learn of subsidized rent, food stamps and welfare. It made it easy for her to stay.

She found his attention addicting. Back home, she was just another old woman with a bunch of threadbare anecdotes that everyone had heard too many times. But in LA she found a new audience; Amelio and his friends thrived on her tales. So, the days turned into years. Life was good.

That is, until the boy turned nine. He'd already seen two murders and other dehumanizing acts; people being mugged, raped and stabbed right in the street. Grandma's stories paled in comparison to the drama on the street. He began running with a loose crowd. It got worse from there. This brought him to stealing things for the gang.

He eagerly awaited his chance to become a Campesino. It was his only rite of passage, in a society that sorely lacks them. The gang offered a sense of family, protection and solidarity. That this behavior was one of necessity escaped the youth's observation. The "Purples" hung tight or they died. It was that simple. In spite of his youth, they let him hang close. They could always use replacements for those lost in shootings and prison.

He loitered near the crib with pockets full of candy. He saw excitement in their faces. Members crowded in until no more could fit; the rest leaned through open windows. Finally, Julio spilled it to him; "Melio'... we're gonna go north to fuck some gringo up. We'll make points, uh?

To Amelio, 'north' was an abstract, like the tall tales his grandma told about the desert. His whole world was east LA. He was still young enough that his identity hinged upon his physical environment. He was what he'd assimilated in the barrio and nothing more.

So the gangsters loaded up their guns and gear; he waited until the older members were entering the cars. With Mano standing by to close the trunk, Amelio hopped into the car trunk holding the least status.

Any berth in a leader's car would surely result in a bus ticket home if he got caught. Yet, if the lowliest passengers detected him, he might have a chance to stay and maybe make his bones at some future heroic fantasy moment. He hoped to avoid detection until he was far enough 'north' to prevent rejection; a poor plan, but he was young and desperate.

After three hours in the trunk the plan changed itself. He'd already moved the bulky pointed firearms so that most of them weren't digging into his skinny frame. But when the convoy slowed for the mountain road, the swaying made him carsick. The slower speed allowed exhaust fumes to collect in the rusty old trunk; he began to vomit.

It took only a few seconds for the passengers to smell it. Manny signaled the others. At the next pullout, the convoy pulled over. He opened the trunk.
"Hijola!... we have a STOWAWAY! MIRA! Amelio esta en coche!"

He clawed frantically up, out and away from the puke-riddled coffin. He made it to the shoulder before the next wave of nausea hit. Meanwhile, everybody got out, pissed and stretched. Some gathered round the sick boy. Then they realized the gravity of their mission when the Mercedes came squealing around the corner.

## Thirty-three

# SUMMITS

Louis Ortega wasted little time second-guessing his first executive decision; if he let them go, he'd lose control... On the other hand, if he called back the Campesinos, they would question every subsequent command... He would lose macho. He finally crystallized his thoughts.
*'killing that gringo is best left to the expert... ME!'*

This would save macho, reinforce leadership among those most in need of it and possibly provide a chance to spot rising stars for his org.

Luis already knew that steel is best tempered by the flames of combat. Granted, 'combat' was a strong word for one measly white man against thirty-odd gangsters, but it would have to do. He sped to intercept the group with his lightning-fast Mercedes.

He brought his Colby AR-16 with three full mags. Inside his jacket, overlying his tailor-made kevlar vest, Ortega kept his favorite pistol; A custom 1911. He loved the stopping power and reliability of the old war-horse. It saved his life on many an occasion. With the pistol came two spare full leather-sheathed mags of forty-five caliber man killers.

After three hours of high speed driving, Ortega began the tortuous mountain climb. His Mercedes liked the twisty road more than the low riders did. He gained ground rapidly.

Halfway up the pass he squealed 'round a tight corner and spotted the Purples lining the roadside, gathered round a single thing. Figuring that they'd found the gringo and killed him, he pulled over and stomped the brakes, tossing gravel all over. He took charge.
"Que pasa?"
Shocked ed at El Jefe's appearance, they divided; a parting of the seas, bracketing a puking boy of ten or twelve. He walked to the boy. The retching eased and he

stood up. Ortega's eyes met his. He vaguely recalled the youth.

Luis had heard of this boy; not that Ortega was a caring person, of course. He barely knew the Campesinos, aside from a few of the older leaders. But there was something familiar about the kid's story that struck a chord in the merciless henchman's heart.

His history was a lot like Ortega's. Neither had known their parents, who died young. Both had Mestizo blood in their veins, fire in their eyes and an innate drive to achieve great things. In the boy before him, he saw pride; it registered before the group's apologies hit Ortega's ears.

"Senor Ortega, we deedn't know... thees leetle manzanita, he sneek in the trunk, you know?"

Other excuses were quickly ladled over this one; Ortega put his hand up for silence. Soon the only sound was the air whistling through pine boughs, a hundred feet above.

"So, the fox wants to run with the wolves now, eh?"
Amelio, unsure of his punishment, looked straight into the smoky brown eyes. He'd heard grisly stories about Ortega, just like everyone else. Still, the boy's pride was on display. He would not wince! He returned the look.
"Si, Senor; Yo quiero mucho!"

Ortega's suddenly outstretched his arm startled, startling him. But no strike smote the youth's cheek. Instead, Ortega flashed the Campesino's sign. The crowd gasped; not only did Ortega know their sign, he admitted the boy with it! Always a quick study, Manny shouted support.

"Orale! Somebody get thees new gangster a SHIRT, EH?"

Before he could grasp the idea, 'Melio was admitted into the gang. One member tossed him an oversize shirt, another drew an ink tatt on his right arm. The real one would come later. The indoctrination was over; *he was... a CAMPESINO!*

210

Then Chewy Ortega made the longest speech of his life.
"Ok, listen up. I saw the flier from this... this gringo... putah motherfucker. HE ees only one man, VERDAD?"
The crowd timidly answered; "Verdad."
"And we are, what... THIRTY OR SO, VERDAD?"
This time, the answer came more assured.
"VERDAD!"
"So we shall find this gringo, and fuck his shit up, VERDAD?"
The crowd was hot now.
"VERDAD!"
"And when it's done, NO ONE will mess with the CAMPESINOS... IS THAT NOT ALSO VERDAD?"
They took up the chant.
"VERDAD! VERDAD! VERDAD!"

Knowing when to quit, Ortega cut it short.
"ALRIGHT! Now let's load up and kill this asshole!"

They poured into their cars, sounds of slamming doors and starting engines echoing through the mountains. The convoy took to the mountain pass with Ortega leading. Due to the steep winding road, their progress was restricted to twenty-five on straight sections, and half that in the countless switchbacks. The slow speed afforded some of the city punks their first close look at the mountains.

First-timers like Amelio gazed slack-jawed at the stark, brutal majesty of the Sierra Nevadas. He gazed at the tall sugar pines, or what he could see of their trunks. They grew so high above his field of view that he could only guess their true height. He stared at the brushy understory scrolling past his window. Now and then he'd spot a chipmunk munching pine cones. Once he saw a gray animal with a bushy tail; could've been an Ewok, for all he knew of wildlife. Almost to the top of the first pass, 'Melio saw a deer's head in thick brush. The head pivoted to watch the cars while they made the switchback. He said nothing, sensing that little gangsters are better seen than heard.

At the top of the pass a fork in the road appeared. The convoy stopped and they all got out. Some stretched their legs. Everybody found a place to piss again. Then the leaders converged on Ortega. He was afraid to admit it, but he didn't know which fork to take. He began to feel the sweat of command, when command runs out of intelligence. Just then a voice came to his ears, saving Ortega from disclosing his ignorance.

"Senor, I teen... a la derecha, por favor."
All eyes went to the newest member; the upstart. Ortega turned to see who said it.

"Oh yeah, *the right?* Why so, Little Fox?"

Amelio pointed... tacked to a tree was a purple sheet of paper, with a large black arrow pointing to the right. The crowd buzzed with excitement. Everyone was glad for the sign, except Ortega and Amelio.

The boy hid his fear because he was determined to prove his manhood. Any hesitation might cost him severely. Ortega kept his misgivings to himself, for the same reasons. He puffed up to hide it.

*"ORALE!* He makes it EASY FOR US, NO? Without the sign, we could not find and kill this gringo!"
The gang piled into cars to resume the lethal voyage. Ortega's Mercedes now held passengers.

Taking the right fork brought them to another climb, then to another summit. After that it would take them down and up and down again, over several more summits.

The road steadily degraded in quality. The asphalt became broken and littered with potholes caused by seepage, storms and run-off. Practically everywhere were landslides and dead-falls caused by storms and heavy snowpack. Most of the road was bare dirt, pine needles, punctuated by small patches of cold patch.

The convoy slowed to snail's pace to thread its way around dead-falls, precarious washouts and slides. They were accustomed to good pavement down in the cities. But up in the passes, no paving machines could survive. The air was too thin, the elements too elemental; so the only repaving came from county crews shoveling cold patch at any spots likely to be in need of supplementary traction. Budget restraints meant that few repairs occurred on high passes. Once the snows came, the pass was simply gated closed.

The cars labored, gasping for rarefied air. Ultimately, the gang made the tallest summit, high above timberline. The change in scenery astonished even hard-core gangsters like Chewy Ortega.

They got out and gaped at the rugged panorama... As far as they could see to the west was nothing but snow and ridge after ridge of unending mountains. There was not another car or person in sight.

Nothing spoke but the wind, whistling and echoing. After a brief wordless pause, they got back in their cars. They were unused to such cold, harsh elements. They slammed doors and started down the eastern side of the Sierras.

Soon the scenery changed. Trees, so plentiful on the California side, were suddenly scarce. Gone was the copious snow pack. The air became dry and intensely laden with a scent that reminded Amelio of bitter artichokes. It gave some of the punks nasty headaches. If they'd known it was called Mountain Misery, it might have helped. Then again, maybe not.

As they lost altitude, the road got slightly better. Its descent became more gradual. Finally a marker said; "elev; 6,000", they came to a tiny sign; 'Welcome to Nevada'. The roads abruptly got worse. It was as if the Nevadans didn't give a damn if they slid off the road or not. By then everyone was breathing thicker air... so no one really cared much about road quality.

However, it was still a lot harder to breathe this air than LA's smoggy, sea-level gasses. It put Amelio on edge; up until then, he'd only breathed the LA chowder. This thin, clear stuff was a whole new thing.

After a long while, they came to Highway 266. Again they saw a purple sheet of paper, discretely tacked to a bush ten yards back from the road, signaling another right turn.

Ortega again had a bad feeling, but he kept it to himself; something about the positions of the fliers... deep enough in the bushes that most men would miss them or dismiss them. Only the Campesinos would be attracted to the color enough to stop and read.

Amelio also thought about the fliers he'd seen in LA; the message bothered him, since it sounded like one man against the guys who did his wife. As a little guy, he couldn't understand why a man would VOLUNTEER for such a mismatch. Surely he must know that a gang moves as one unit, so the bigger question was; what lay in store for the Campesinos? Was it just a stupid man or was it a trap?

Ortega vacillated between thoughts like Amelio's and the firm young breasts he fondled. Carmelita's job was to make the big chief happy. He smelled nice and had a firm, solid body. She hoped he'd like her enough to take her up to the big house. She could do fine by a man like Ortega.

On her right was a backup whore, Rita, standing ready to please if Carmelita somehow fell short of the task. Ortega loved competition; it motivated people. He needed the distraction from the gnawing feeling in his gut.

An hour up the road, Ortega was busy with the young whore's lips on his cock, so he missed the next flier... And so did the rest of the convoy, but in the last car, Amelio saw it. After ten miles of lights flashing, horns blowing, they finally got every car stopped. Circling back, it took fifteen minutes to find the flier, which simply said; "AQUI." A black arrow pointed east to a very faint two-track.

## Thirty-four

## TURNABOUT

With Ortega leading the way, the low riders crept cautiously onto the sandy trail. Old habits die hard, especially successful ones; after idling along for about a mile, he got out. He stood on the hood of the next car and watched his backtrail for cops.

He waited for all engines to die and all ears to hear him. "I want a man on top of each car. If this Putah tries to get the drop on us, we'll show HEEM, EH? OK, LOAD UP!"

Amid cheers, trunks popped open. Magazines clicked into actions as the Purple's arsenal flashed its deadly teeth. Mano handed the boy a cheap Italian pistol with seven rounds in the clip. It had cheap plastic grips, simulating pearl. The action and barrel was likewise a cheap attempt at chrome plating. Its sights were nothing but stamp-forged rear groove and front blade, silver-soldered on the barrel. This allowed no sight adjustment, but it made people feel like they were buying a gun. People want sights, even on cheap guns.

The tiny .25 was a purse gun, designed for rudimentary self-defense at purse-snatching distances. All that is asked of such a gun is to come out of a purse or and go bang. But of this, the boy knew nothing. He had a gun and he was a Campesino. A small gun and a small gangster, but he was better off than yesterday, when he was a candy-stealing nobody. He put the pistol in his right rear pocket.

Armed to the teeth, barrels pointing out of open windows. Each car sported a sentry sitting on the roof, feet on the hood, ready for whatever the gringo might bring. The convoy proceeded slowly across the desert. Amelio felt the cold steel in his rear pocket, rubbing his ass with each bump in the trail. It felt wonderful, but small, when he thought of all the firepower he'd just seen. Just the same, it was *HIS gun.*

Straining for a clear view, Ted's eyes watered; he made out several dark objects, which could only be vehicles headed his way. His gut turned into a knot. His plan appeared to be working.

He turned on his transmitter, loaded the .243, laid out three full clips, and put his earplugs in. That first test-bomb taught him all about earplugs; he didn't want his ears ringing during the gunfight. He double-checked holdovers.

All that was left was to watch the low riders crawl across the irregular terrain. It was agony; they took over an hour to cover what Ted covered in twenty minutes with his truck.

Soon he could make out the cars; a man rode shotgun on each roof, except for the lead car. The tension hit him and suddenly, he started to lose his nerve. His plan now seemed so brutal, so savage and oh, so... chickenshit.

Then he re-ran the mental tapes of his comatose wife, raped and sliced beyond belief, her life force flickering dimmer each day, tubes stuck everywhere. For all he knew, she could be dead already. That erased his doubt. Just then, the lead car came to the final bait, the last flier.

Luis Ortega ripped the paper from the cedar branch. He read it with contempt.
*'I only want the pussies who hurt my wife... the rest of you can turn around, leave and live.'*

It was Ted's final kicker, to get them past any second thoughts they might be having, so far out in the desert. Ortega waited for everybody to stop so he could read it aloud to the group. Then he mimicked the gringo.

"Oh, poor me... look at all those barrio bastards coming at me... and I am all alone!"
He waited for the laughter to die.
"ARRIBA HERMANOS! Let's get this over with!"

They cheered. Nothing thrilled the Campesinos like holding unquestionable advantage. They followed their leader. There's a fine line between devotion and stupidity. Ortega's followers would soon learn it.

The convoy crawled slowly, with tumbleweed and alkali brush scraping and scratching undercarriages. At the snail's pace, they had one last chance to reconsider. Several of them wanted to chicken out, while the rest boldly trampled over the dissent. They talked loudly, swore and made jokes to cover up the fear of the unknown.

Ted watched, overwhelmed with emotion, but pleasure topped the list. Actually, it wasn't real pleasure, but it would do. He was about to break the law, after living by it his whole life. He thought about the first men he'd killed. Back then, he had no choice, it was kill or be killed.

Now it was different. He lured dozens of people to this remote spot, while only five or six actually raped and lacerated his soul mate. The rest were innocent... then he corrected his thought.
*"Innocent of THIS crime, maybe, but they probably raped and cut other women!"*

The thought of gangsters ransacking, raping and pillaging innocent people got his thinking right for the task. He would kill the whole hive; or at least, he would try with all his might. If his bombs worked and if he shot straight, there wouldn't be any Purples left.

The cars stopped. A dozen men stood in front of the lead car, obviously listening to the boss man. Ted put the scope on the car and dialed the lens up to 24 power. His dots aligned on one man pointing and giving orders; he had to be the boss. Obviously, he was reading the last flier.

Ted watched them get back in their rigs for the final step in their quest. Slowly the convoy came on.

After what seemed an eternity, the convoy finally crossed Ted's bomb in the gully. He had them! Images started overlapping; his sweetheart, lying in the hospital, bruised and battered, bullets blasting rocks, stinging shards, a cell door slamming shut... and the last one, just a red-orange blur; REVENGE! He was surprised to hear spoken words come from his mouth.

*'TURNABOUT'S FAIR PLAY, YOU BASTARDS!'*

His thoughts refocused as Ortega's car bogged down, barely inside of the 1000-yard range. A few gangsters got out and went to assist. The stopped abreast of Chewy's window for instructions. Ortega stroked the whore's thigh with his right hand while his left waved at the trio to push his car out of the sand.

From decades of hunting instinct, Ted's sight picture automatically took over. He put the lowest dot on the right edge of the driver's chest and touched it off. He jacked another round in while the rifle recoiled. Ted swung onto the closest man next to the driver and pressed the trigger. He worked the action while swinging onto the next stander. Three shots, three seconds.

Inside Ortega's car, no one knew what happened. A hole snapped the windshield; the copper bullet entered Ortega's mouth, driving his incisors through the base of his brain. Ortega's head jerked forward from the exiting shock wave. The mushroomed projectile flew through the headrest, turned sideways and slammed into the rear seat. Ortega's squeeze, brain spatter all over her, started screaming.

Geraldo, standing outside the car, dropped like a stone. He never twitched. The third bullet the hit Chico low, taking out his balls and rectum. The hydrostatic shock exploded his common iliac artery, turning his lower abdomen into jellied ooze. He made three steps before he ran out of chi.

The rest of the gangsters thought it was a game at first, until a far-away boom betrayed the evil. Then a second and third boom drifted to their ears. Lupe got the message first.

"Haysoo Christo!!! Someone's shooting!" *It's a TRAP!"*
Ten men tried to get back in their cars; eight made it. Ted could see the dust from the spinning tires, followed three seconds later by the squeals heralding their chaos. The last car line became the lead car when retreating. Ted grabbed the transmitter; he flipped the rudder stick. But the bomb delayed a few seconds, so the lead car passed. The second car wasn't so lucky.

He saw the front half of the car fly straight up; three major body parts ejected from the spinning cage. The first car, past the bomb already, panicked from concussion and spun off the two-track and got stuck. Its occupants sprinted for cover in the junipers. Ted let them get into the trees and ran the throttle stick up and down. Juniper trees, rocks, and body parts erupted on both sides.

The explosion and screams came through his earplugs barely three seconds later. Meanwhile, the main group hid behind the only safety they knew; their cars. Five frightened gangsters just lay in the desert, arms over their heads. Ted barked two of them off before the others wised up. He triggered two more bombs. It was impossible to see if they killed anybody; dust clouded the view. Arturo shouted excitedly, from the safety of the junipers.

"Stay the fuck down! Don't run! He's up on that hill! Find out how many of us are still alive, Hernando!... *'NANDO!!!"*
Although 'Nando killed three unarmed innocent people before, he had never been the other side of a muzzle. It put a bad spin on it.
"Oye, hermanos!... Quien vive?"
Within earshot there were nine with Arturo and six below... not counting the constantly screaming whores in Ortega's front seat, still too paralyzed with fear to move.

Jorge had clout, ever since he assaulted the gringo bitch up north. He shouted above the screaming and gunfire;

"Ok, we stay in the trees. We surround him. Arturo's got guys over there."
He indicated the north side of the road, but nobody could see him through the bushes.
"He goes up that side, we go this side, we get the drop and fuck his ass up."
He brandished his pair of Mac 10's to embolden the grupo. Somebody hollered support.
"ORALE, CARNAL!"
Just then another high-speed bullet crack-snapped the Mercedes windshield, then another, silencing the screams in time for the group to hear the big rifle's second report. So... the gringo would shoot helpless women; it blew their minds. Dissent began to rip the group apart.

"I say we give up those who hurt his squeeze... cut our losses. Who's with me?"
These were the last words from Antonio before Jorge's machine pistols cut him basically in half.
"Anyone else think we should split up? We are one! Let's get up there and flank his ass! AHORITA!"

He stood for effect, momentarily making him a target.
"Benny, take those guys below and keep close to the street... I mean trail... whatever. I'll take the rest up this way. Stay the fuck down and watch out for fuckin' bombs... stay clear of *fresh-dug ground!*"

The bombs formed a smokescreen, but he saw at least a dozen people running like hell. His high-power scope provided only a narrow field of view, so he could only see one or two at a time. Worse yet, they broke into doubles and singles, like mice in a mowed hayfield. He'd see a man run, but there wasn't time to shoot before the target disappeared again.

Ted dropped the 7mm and picked up the .243, screwed the scope down to 4 and checked his holdover notes; Yellow, +6. His peripheral vision kept catching glimpses flashing between trees.

He wished he could flush them into the open hillside. Then he thought of the bombs behind the gangsters. He triggered them all, then pulled his earplugs out. He didn't want to miss anyone sneaking up on him. The bombs succeeded in driving some gangsters into the open.

Ted fired the rockets; shrill whistles and flaming smoke trails announced; Ted screamed like a banshee. His war face gnarled and grimmacing...

"I'M HERE, MOTHERFUCKERS!
COME 'N GET ME! YAAAAAHHHHHH!"

The rockets intimidated them, but the scream redlined it; here was one crazy gringo. He actually WANTED them to know his location. On Ted's left, six or seven men broke out of thick cover and ran away, in the open hillside, where they could run faster.

Their flight was justified, but running in straight lines wasn't. Ted held over and four feet in front of the running man. He pressed the trigger, smoothly following through. He went down in a heap.

He put the next four rounds rapid-fire five feet in front of the running group. Two more dropped. Two seconds later, sound waves brought their howls of agony. He snapped in a fresh clip and swung to the right sideline. All he saw was one man's back, running straight away downhill... what a mistake; without having to lead him, Ted simply held three feet hihg and rolled him with a perfect spine shot.

Four men panicked and broke from cover, running toward the cars. Ted killed the second in the line with a great running shot at five hundred yards, blowing liver chunks out the front of his abdomen. He lived just long enough to wail some sort of half-assed prayer. The others dove into the low tumbleweed, terrorized.

He set the little rifle down to cool, since it shot high when hot. He grabbed the big rifle. Turning the scope down to six, he spotted a man belly-crawling on blue sand, toward the cars. Ted put the lowest dot on his chest and fired, but he jerked the trigger. The bullet exploded, shearing off the gangster's right femur above the knee. Ted tried to put two more through him, but missed, because the gangster writhed too much. Then he was out of sight.

Looking to the nearby ravines, he hadn't seen or heard anything, but his hackles were bunching. He slung the .243 and grabbed the riot gun. He dumped the box of spreader rounds in his vest and stood up, when the sand started dancing; from bullets.

One caught him in the left biceps, near his chest. Ted swung the riot gun to the only bush big enough to hide a man; he fired twice. The bush came alive with high-pitched screams from a young man or maybe a boy.
"Ay! OJOS... MIS OJOS!!!"
Ted hosed the brush with spreader loads. This time, larger buckshot found vitals and the punk went quiet.

Ted ran down the back of the knoll on his escape route, stuffing more rounds while running; it wasn't easy with one gimpy arm. Lungs burning for thin air, he'd only gone a hundred yards before he heard someone yelling, maybe 100 yards away.
"The gringo got away. Manuel's down! Andale, hermanos... we finish heem!"
The tone said they were hot for blood.
Ted bolted for the junipers, then wondered.
'Why yell? They're trying to drive me!'
He stood still, evaluating his status... wounded left arm. One spare clip, five in the rifle. 20 rounds, shotgun. He probed his wound; a neat hole through the muscle, bleeding profusely. He couldn't feel any bone shards. The hole seemed to be of the same size on both sides; a pistol round, no doubt.

Ted knew his enemies couldn't say the same. Some of their exit holes were as big as beer cans. He gave thanks that he still had an arm left, tore off a sleeve and quickly bandaged it.

On his right came the unmistakable sound of a hard sole on gravel, maybe forty yards out. Ted pointed the shotgun in the general direction, waiting for confirmation. Just then he heard the big snake buzz.

"Madre Dios!"

Ted fired three rounds through the junipers. A loud grunt and body crashing told him what he needed to know. What he didn't know was that the big old rattler already bit the bastard, making him give away his position; one could say he'd been killed twice.

Ted sprinted sidehill forty yards inside the tree line, stopping to listen for pursuit, but the only sounds were his panting and blood dripping onto dry leaves. He skulked back to camp, took the first aid kit and treated the wound.

Then he realized it was almost over. He stalked downhill to the gulch where his four-wheeler was still concealed in cedars. He never heard a sound while hiking downhill.

He fired up the four-wheeler and jacked a round into the riot gun. He slung the .243. Charging down the two-track at top speed, Ted bore down on the smoking carnage in the gulley. He spotted three gangsters running as hard as they could, straight for the interstate, so many unreachable miles away.

Ted closed on them easily, while he realized he couldn't shoot with his left hand, because of the wound; he'd have to let go of the throttle. So he placed the shotgun butt against his belly, barrel resting on the headlight.

They whirled. The middle gangster held a large chrome-plated pistol, the right, a shotgun. The man on the left, reaching into a pocket.

Ted dropped the throttle and fired the riot gun while inertia kept the four-wheeler rolling straight. The recoil kicked Ted squarely in the stomach, temporarily disabling him.

Two buckshot spined the man holding the saw-off; he dropped without a whimper. His buddy on the left dropped the pistol and started screaming. Ted couldn't hear it because he, too, was screaming from the recoil kicking his nuts and guts. The third youth writhed in the dirt, legs pumping him around in tethered circles.

With one shot of his spreader loads, he'd managed hits on all three luckless gangsters. Ted crawled off the four-wheeler. The boy rolled over to his knees, just as he pulled his pistol from that pocket. He would have killed Ted, except for one thing; the smallest shot pellets blinded him.

With his gun waving, head tilted to discern the slightest noise, the blind gangster looked pretty brave. Ted hid behind the four-wheeler and taunted.
"What are you going to do now, punk?"
"Kill you, motherfucker!"
The punk shot three rounds in rapid succession. One bullet hit the mechanical horse dead center in the headlight.
"That's pretty good shooting, for a punk... why don't you try again, only a little higher?"
"Fuck you!"
He emptied the wheelgun, cutting only sky. Then the gun kept clicking impotently.
As Ted walked up, the one with the big pistol let out a feeble moan and expired. Two tiny holes in his chest told the story; buckshot found the edge of his aorta, draining all his blood inside the thorax. He was a tidy corpse.

Ted went to the blind gangster with the empty pistol.
"Boy, did you rape... and cut up my wife?"
The boy looked small and weak, now that he was on the other end of the violence. He tried to act bold.
"No... but I would have, you bastard! Even if I did, I wouldn't rat my homeboys, chingado!"
Ted raised the shotgun, speaking in a faraway voice.
"That's what I thought you'd say."

He noticed that this particular boy was Caucasian, just before he shot him. The twelve-gauge sawed a one-inch hole right through his chest. At three feet, even a spreader load couldn't open up. Ted reloaded and drove to a high spot to scout survivors.

He killed the engine at the base of the knoll, to keep from broadcasting his location. He hiked up the small hill. Almost immediately he saw two gangsters standing on another hillock, barely two hundred yards away. They were pointing in different directions, apparently debating their escape route. The one on the left held a machine pistol with a large curved magazine; a close-range weapon with extreme firepower. The other held a rifle; he would shoot him first.

With his biceps burning, a pure offhand was impossible; Ted rested the barrel on a small juniper branch. The first bullet struck high, exploding the calvarium. Swinging fast to the pistol-toter, Ted held a foot lower and fired two rapid shots. Ted couldn't see the hits, but he heard one. Machine gun man went down; the bushes kept moving.

He rode over and got off the quad. Grabbing the shotgun, he found the head-shot punk immediately. The bullet turned his brains into a fine, pinkish-white misty cloud, part of which still drifted in the air. A large fragment of scalp and right ear swung from nearby bushes.

Twenty yards away, the bushes moved.
"Hey, puto...I am glad to spare your life for one answer... How 'bout it?"
The bushes stopped moving.
"This shotgun can hurt you bad, and I don't even have to aim... You want MORE bullets or see a doctor and get some killer drugs?"
"No more shooting... I tell you what you wanna know."
Ted smiled coldly... he had him pegged.
"Come out; I won't hurt you any more."
Groggy from blood loss, the punk wasn't thinking right, grasping at hope where none exists. He crawled into the open. His left hand lagged behind, hiding something.
"Who raped my wife and cut her up like a hog?"
"I don't know, but my friend can find out for you!"
His right hand jerked to pull the hidden Uzi into play. The twelve-gauge sawed off his right forearm.

"Wrong answer, Cabron... *Wrong answer.*"
He died while Ted stuffed shells in the tube. The rage didn't let up. He went back to the ambush knoll to look for others to kill. It took a few minutes to spot a large dark spot, very far out. He couldn't make it out with hand-held binoculars and a bad arm, but at that distance, a dark blob that big just had to be gangsters.

He caught them in ten minutes. Three gangbangers quickly turned around. Then the dazed pair turned slowly, vacant expressions, blood trickling from noses and ears.

The alert ones had terror in their eyes but tried to look tough. Ted raised the .243 to his hip, still astride the four-wheeler. Then something jolted his memory. Sure enough, two of them were the bastards that glared at him in court, but now they didn't look so cocky. He scanned the two vegetables and found the other courtroom face, which looked almost angelic from bomb shock.

His voice sounded strangely shrill and far away, like a red-tailed hawk screeching to scare a covey into staying still.
"Before I shoot... you pricks got anything to say?"
The middle gangster pissed his pants, fell to his knees and put his hands together for a prayer.

"Please, mister; don' shoot! I deedn't wanna do it, you know? I deedn't mean to do... I mean..."

The bullet caught him below the stomach, but it didn't really matter. At such close range, hydrostatic shock exploded his organs into a homogeneous gray-brown ooze. His guts, liver, heart and lungs were all the same; structure-less, shit-gray, stinking pulp. He slumped back on his heels, head slumped forward and that was that, for the rapist, wife-cutting motherfucker.

The other two started pleading, but Ted couldn't hear any of it. His mind saw only his cut-up, bandaged bride and her failing vital signs. He felt her pain as the knives cut her skin. He tasted their stinking sweat and his ass felt their infected dicks ramming her unwilling body.

He wanted to kill them slow; a bullet in the knee, the balls, one to the arm... kill 'em over a week, so they could share some of the pain they'd caused his wife, his kids and him. But rage consumed him; he just wanted them off his planet. He wanted to be able to tell her the world was safe again. With two quick blasts, the two rapists had no more need to plead.

Ted reloaded while the two bomb-shocked gangsters milled around aimlessly. He shot them both through their backs, literally dead before they hit the sand. He went to a nearby high spot to look for more gangsters. He couldn't find any. It took a while to register. He had killed them all...

It was over.

## Thirty-five

## CLEANUP

Ted's rage slowly melted, then transformed into survival mode. He drove to camp, loaded the trailer and pulled it down to the scene. With the .243 over his shoulder, he hopped on the tiny tractor, then went about the grisly task. It was fairly simple; drive up to a body/part, scoop it with the bucket, dump in the nearest grave-site. Then, repeat.

In two hours, he had located and buried every body part he could find. With the exception of a hand here or maybe a foot there, some scalp and skull fragments dangling in the brush where he couldn't see it, the desert was fairly clean. The blood, spatter and smaller parts would soon go away. The late afternoon saw him sculpturing the bomb-blasted grave sites, his landscaping tools perfectly suited to the task, just as he had planned.

Each finished site got the same final treatment; the box scraper smoothed out the surface to blend with the terrain. Then he would hit it with the leaf blower, to hide the scraper marks. Finally, he gave each site with a little drought-resistant seed and fertilizer, then a blast with the spray wig to wet it, so it wouldn't blow away, and soon that site would almost pass for native soil. It wasn't perfect, but it wasn't bad.

Finally he became aware of the dead cars. He hadn't planned on them. Chalk up one more mistake in his perfect plan. But since the cars held no clues pointing at him, he decided to forget about them. True, the lead car probably had some bullets in it, but those rifling marks would never match his new barrels waiting back at home.

Ted idled toward the interstate, processing a great deal of pent-up emotion while checking for footprints or survivors. Through his rear view mirror, the first buzzards arrived. He could relax about the smaller body parts now; soon they'd be soaring around in buzzard bellies, a thousand feet up.

A dozen miles later, he found what he sought. An old dirt road led off the interstate. The trail was little more than an old wagon train scar, left in the desert almost 150 years before. Little had changed since those early prospectors first cut the trail. In some places, the original wagon ruts could still be seen.

In the past fifty years, the two-track had seen just a few passersby; the silver mine long played out, little of human interest remained in the dry mesa. But for a few naive hunters or perhaps a displaced trapper, the road lay dormant. This mesa had white dirt, and few game animals cared for plants that grew in that nutrient-poor soil.

Ten miles out and one mile up brought him to what he wanted. Removing the barrels and bolts was fairly hard. He took them over to an inconspicuous little hole in the side of the mountain. He stood over the hole for a moment and savored the cool air as it sucked into the ventilation shaft.

He dropped his bolts into the shaft. He heard no noise. Almost eighteen hundred feet below, the bolts hit bottom. Both barrels followed. With forty feet of water in the bottom, it was unlikely they'd be seen again. Likewise, the remaining spreader rounds found the dark water a third of a mile below; nothing could forensically tie him to the shootings.

He turned it around to leave. Then he remembered his shotgun; his empty hulls were strewn all over the desert. Since he forgot to order a bolt face for the riot gun, he dropped the old faithful shotgun into it. Later on, he'd report the shotgun missing. Ted idled back to the interstate. His trip home was uneventful.

## Thirty-six

## EPIPHANY

The second morning found Amelio Macias fifteen hard miles from the bloody scene. Such fast progress was due to adrenaline-fueled legs and mind-numbing fear. The youth couldn't recall the run. All he knew was that he needed to put distance between himself and that murdering, psycho gringo fucker.

What saved him was his youth and low status; he was in the last car in the convoy. When the shit started, the last car became the first to haul ass. They barely made it over the bomb when the car behind them turned to superheated plasma. Amelio turned his head in time to see the front half spinning high in the air, flailing heads and torsos fifty feet into the blue sky.

Then they got stuck, so he sprinted for the trees. Climbing up into the lowest branches, Amelio shut his eyes and wept in stark raving terror while bombs exploded. He heard several people take bullets, one within mere yards of his hideout. Each incident further galvanized his fear into a complete inability to do anything but freeze absolutely still. He couldn't explain it or overcome it.

The first time he heard a bullet slap meat, he instinctively knew what it was. The sharp supersonic 'crack' came first. Four seconds later, he heard the muffled roar of the distant rifle. He saw a compatriot writhing and kicking in the sand and he heard the rattle as the youth's lungs alternately sucked clean desert air in and sprayed frothy bloody orange mist back out. He heard the death moan; the punctuation mark at the end of a death sentence carried out by a tiny supersonic emissary. Such a small noise, carrying such grisly consequences, from such a long distance. It was like a bullet from God. Amelio could not have been more afraid. He lost his bladder and anal control right on the spot.

Soon after the explosions and gunfire subsided he heard the four-wheeler riding down survivors. He heard one man,

Nestor, maybe, plead with the gringo. He heard the sickening 'plop' of bullets slamming into flesh. Then he heard the gunman drive off to shoot more people.

Then, after what seemed like an eternity, the four-wheeler surprised him when it swooped down onto Amelio's position. Through the thick branches, the youth watched the man stare intently into the thick trees; a grim stare, from glazed eyes, like Terminator. Apparently satisfied the tracks belonged to dead gangsters nearby, he drove off in pursuit of other survivors.

Even though he had the tiny pistol, Amelio was unaware of it... and even if he'd thought of it, he would have been unable to move enough to shoot. The man's death-look finished what the bombs, gunshots and carnage started, permeating the youth's soul to the core.

It was only after sunset that he dared to venture from his hide. Although the highway lay to the west, he ignored the lights from occasional vehicles; the gringo might still be out there, hunting down cripples. Amelio headed south, paralleling the highway.

He walked in darkness, using the late-rising full moon for light. Sometime around 2 A.M., the boy collapsed. He was too tired to notice the lumpy ground, hunger or even to recount the savagery he'd witnessed. He was in emotional vapor lock. His was the sleep of the battle-weary soldier. Amelio's travel resumed at sunup. The day was a blur, with the drive to get further from danger.

However, bodily needs ultimately replaced his fear. He awoke very hungry. He checked his pockets; his left front held his Bic lighter, a pair of wrinkled twenty-dollar bills and nothing else. The right front pocket held a melted, mashed up candy bar and his knife; a gangland knife, practically useless in the woods. The thin stiletto's cheap steel was made to entice customers, rather than do any real cutting work, but the boy knew nothing of that when he stole it.

His back pockets held only the purse pistol, but he couldn't eat that, so it seemed of little immediate use. He checked to make sure it was still loaded; if that maniac found him, he'd use it. The mashed-up Snickers went down in two bites. He ate it; wrapper and all, instead of trying to separate the mess, but eating the bar had the adverse effect. It merely awakened his hunger, without putting it back to sleep.

With nothing else to do, he started walking; parts of his brain started working. Soon he had his wits about him, in large part due to the magic of the open desert. Gradually, the boy's eyes opened.

Everything about the desert was completely foreign. The city noise was replaced by wind music. Where he'd previously seen level concrete he saw irregular, undulating, wild terrain. Every footstep was uncertain, requiring visual inspection. Where he'd seen only skyscrapers and brown smog, the new backdrop was vast mountain ridges and powder blue sky. The unending terrain testified to its awesome expansiveness. One stride at a time, he began to learn the desert.

Growing up in the barrio, Amelio had only seen a few cats, dogs, pigeons and rats. Desert wildlife contrasted heavily; ny noon of that second day, his eyes were totally opened to the cornucopia of fauna that calls the high desert home.

He'd seen his first coyote, just a buff and yellow blur running down a jackrabbit. Rabbits and quail flushed from practically every other bush. One mule deer doe spooked twenty yards away. After she bounded to the top of a hillock, the doe stopped and swung her face at the youth. It was the first human she'd ever seen. Amelio could smell the deer's musky, sweet tarsal scent as he watched in awe. She snorted and vanished as quickly as she'd appeared. Amelio could relate to that, since he'd escaped the same way at first hiding, then bolting into the desert.

In the city, the youth was always on display. Whether he committed a crime or a kind act, it was always subject to study and punishment. Between TV, his abuela and his peers, there was never any solo time, so his thoughts were never his own. It was always rules, boundaries and gangs. In short, his life back in L.A. was totally smothering.

But the desert didn't care whether he lived or died or which direction he went. Its laws were simple. Live or die by your own hand. Nowhere was there a mouth to curse nor a hand to harm. He was alone; it intoxicated the boy.

As he walked along, his mind drifted to his grandmother and her incessant stories about growing up in New Mexico. The parables held meaning, now that he found himself in a similar setting. She used to talk about building fires and how important fire is to life. Fortunately, Amelio had his butane lighter, so fire starting shouldn't be a problem.

The boy was way past mere thirst by then, which triggered an old parable; her grandfather told the story to her father. He told her daughter, then she told Amelio. That was how the Indians taught, through parables and allegories.

Apparently, her grandfather got chased way out into strange territory, back when White Man still hunted the Indian for sport. He ran for three days and two nights. When they finally lost his trail and gave up, the grim nature of his predicament set in; Standing Buck was alone in a hostile tribe's territory, with no provisions other than his knife. It was live or die... by his own wits.

Standing Buck spent a full day hiding in a shallow, sun-baked arroyo. As he lay there parching from thirst, he studied birds flying over; Swallows or mud daubers, as the white man called them. When flying south, their bills were open. When they flew north, their bills were closed, holding mud for nest building. At dark, he headed south.

By morning, it was time to again lay up again, where no eyes could see him. He was close to water, because the swallows tittered excitedly as they flew toward it. He looked at every crack in the distant rocks for the telltale sign.

Finally he saw a small bit of green at the base of a rocky cliff. Against better judgment but driven by extreme thirst, grandfather made a run for the water in broad daylight. After an hour he made the spring. For the last fifty yards, he could smell it. The brave drank his fill and replenished his strength. He lived, to pass the survival story on.

And, so Amelio found water; it gave off a surprising amount of scent in the clear desert air. All it took was for the boy to associate the strange smell with water. Purged by the clear air, his nose began to sniff things better than ever before.

Naturally, no swallows over-flew him with mud in their beaks, but he had quail to help. If he flushed quail early, they invariably flew towards water. Most of it was barely fit to drink, but it was drink it or die.

Tina's stories about killing and cooking game animals came back as he trudged along, stomach rumbling. He recalled the story about throwing sticks. But he had a pistol, so he pushed that story aside. Having never fired a pistol, Amelio assumed it was just like he'd seen on TV; it would be easy.

He decided to shoot some game. A young jackrabbit lay in the shade, dusting itself. Totally unaware of the boy, it kept rolling and wiggling in the dust bowl. 'Melio pointed the pistol and fired; the harsh report made him blink. He didn't see where the bullet struck.

Not acquainted with guns or people, the rabbit resumed its dusting. Amelio tried his second shot, vowing to keep his eyes open. He focused on the cheap forged sights, wavering all over the hare and the sandy bowl. When the sights came near the rabbit, Amelio yanked the trigger. This time, he saw dust rise, six feet behind the jack.

The hare stood erect, ears pointing towards the bullet impact, then took a few bounds toward the stalker. Amelio tried his third shot, being more precise with his sight picture. That bullet struck precisely ten inches under the rabbit. Sand kicked up and stung the jack. It was gone in a flash. Amelio had learned a lifetime of marksmanship in just three shots. He only had four left. He was still hungry.

An hour later, he located a covey feeding on seeds in a dry creek bed, clucking and calling quietly as they foraged. Amelio belly-crawled to fifteen yards, learning from his prior busted stalk. The sentry cock perched in a bush; a tempting target, but since the boy wouldn't see the bullet's impact, he'd have no way to correct for the next shot, so he passed on the sentry.

Soon, five quail fed around a bush, barely ten yards in front of him. He aimed at the five birds. The bullet went high and left. The entire covey flushed. Amelio's hunger intensified. His burning stomach drove home the next hunting lesson; pick out a single target... NEVER shoot at the whole group!

After four hours of hard hunting, he managed to flush three coveys before seeing them. He spooked three jackrabbits and five cottontails. The midday sun dominated everything. Most animals would lay up. He had the sense to do the same; lie in the shade and listen to his burning stomach rumble. He went to sleep hungry again.

In the evening the desert came alive with game. Since he was still holed up, he got lucky and had the advantage. He learned much. Animals that avoided the moving lad were suddenly everywhere; hawks, snakes, lizards, rabbits, quail and deer.

On hands and knees, senses alert to every noise, the persistent youth finally closed on a covey of feeding quail. When he got within fifteen yards, he lay still. With his last three rounds, the boy intended to eat. Arms extended, gun butt resting on the sand for stability, he held the little semi-auto ready.

Soon a pair of males fed around the bush, eight yards from the muzzle. He held the sights on the closest bird, took an unconscious breath and tightened on the trigger. By then he had learned a thing or two about squeezing a trigger.

Squirt guns had better triggers. The birds kept calmly feeding, getting closer. He kept pulling the trigger, tracking the little cock; suddenly, the gun went off. The lead male flipped over and on its back, obviously hit. Instead of flying, the others hid in the brush. The bird flipped over and over, fluttering its wigs; an obvious sign of a brain or neck shot.

He could scarcely believe his luck. But before he could get up, he got his next lesson in desert survival. A brown blur dropped out of nowhere; Amelio watched in shock as his meal flew off in the talons of another hungry hunter.

In frustration, he shot his last two rounds at the departing hawk; who, by the way, flew up to a nearby perch and proceeded to tear off pieces of quail breast; as if to show off, maybe. Amelio threw the worthless gun at the raptor.

He went to sleep hungry again. His last thoughts were of that fucking hawk. The desert winds came up, sandblasting anything foolish enough to remain exposed. Amelio crawled deeper under the branches and fell into a deep sleep. He dreamed, for the first time since the massacre.

The last dream was a recanted tale of his grandmother's. It came to him in startling clarity. One of her jobs as a child was to gather small game for food. The children used the throwing stick... a healthy chunk of branch, trimmed of all sharp protrusions. Thrown at just the right moment, a throwing stick could topple into a covey of quail, breaking wings and legs with ease. Whereas a bullet could only cut a killing swath a quarter of an inch wide, the throwing stick had a lethal swath twenty inches wide, increasing the odds. Rabbits, snakes and gophers fell to throwing sticks too.

Amelio awoke before sunrise, so close to the last dream that he recalled it vividly. It seemed so real that he actually looked around for his abuela. Little did he know that she had seen his quest... And sent him the dream. He was excited; went to work at once to build a throwing stick.

He chose a growing branch, but it was too hard to break. His cheap knife wouldn't cut the dense wood. Next, he chose a blown-down branch that was old and dry. After carving its bumps off, it broke the first time he threw it.

When the sun got high in the sky, he finally found a good weathered branch. Apparently it fell the year before. The wood was good. The stick withstood a few experimental throws before he invested his efforts in whittling the bumps off. Soon he set out with the primitive weapon and a grim determination to eat.

His third stalk netted him success. He'd heard a band of quail calling, drinking in the runoff from a played-out silver mine. Closing to fifteen yards, using bushes and mine tailings for cover, he raised his arm to throw, but the covey instantly flushed. His hunger and frustration forced him to throw anyway.

He wasn't experienced at  throwing things; his stick went left by six feet, but luckily the covey broke to the left. The stick flew through the flying covey. Most of them swerved, but two birds fell. He was on them in a second.

Lying in the sand, the beautiful male with its blue, black and slate coloration stood out, its cock feathers curled forward in perfect alignment. Ten feet away, a female fluttered helplessly... its back broken. The boy didn't know how to kill well, so he just struck it with his stick. It stopped moving. Picking up his prey, he walked to a dead bush.

He didn't know anything about cleaning and cooking, but hunger is an excellent teacher. He gathered some large branches and tried to light them. It didn't work. Apparently, fire starting wasn't so simple either, just like shooting a pistol wasn't.

He tried progressively smaller twigs and soon got a fire going. Then he added larger wood too soon; the fire went out. With his stomach rumbling, he persisted, but this time he got it right; smaller twigs first, then slightly larger ones, then medium branches. Soon the fire popped and snapped happily; it felt great.

He decided to cut off the feathers, but his dull little city stabbing knife wouldn't do it. Next, he tried pulling the feathers off, but the skin came off with them. That was easier. Moisture steamed up with each torn off strip of skin, just as he'd seen with the hawk. Soon he had a pair of denuded quail. He skewered them on cedar branches.

He showed amazing will power, leaving the searing birds near the heat for almost ten minutes. Finally, the brazed quail scen overcame his last vestige of civilization; he couldn't stand it any longer. At first, the outer layer of breast meat tasted dry, hot and fantastic. Halfway through, it was wet, pink and raw. No matter; he was too famished to care. When he got beyond the breast meat, the entrails stench gagged him. Had it not been for overwhelming hunger, he would have passed on the guts.

There were plenty of firsts; his first fire and the first time he'd ever cooked anything. It surely was the first time he'd ever killed anything. And, it was his first successful stalk, after a shitload of bad ones; he learned persistence.

The strong sense of empowerment fueled him, perhaps more than the meager little half-cooked birds did. After that meal, everything changed for the boy.

Throughout the evening, he improved his stalking. He managed to kill another quail and a jackrabbit. Amelio's night fire held a stick with the quail and crudely cut chunks of jackrabbit meat. The cooking meat scent fueled him with an intoxicating thought; he was in charge. He could survive like this for years, if he had to.

For any twelve year-old, this would be heady news. Yet alone in the open expanses of the desert, it was even more astonishing. Amelio felt totally self-contained. In his belly was hot food that he had caught. His skin felt the warm glow of a fire he created. To make matters better, he spied evidence of a good spring just before sundown.

More importantly, his mind was his alone; he was free to think and feel his thoughts... NOT those of others. He made a decision.

After the massacre he paralleled the highway, keeping two or three miles away from the pavement. Now he didn't feel the need for the umbilical cord. He was, after all, a desert man. The magic continued to work on the boy.

He thought about his grandmother's explanation, who had simply shown up in LA, after his mother was killed.
... 'I saw it.'
It smacked of spirit worlds and voodoo.
'I saw it. I am here.'
Such was her faith. No logical explanation required.

Amelio lay on the desert sand, feeling guilty for the way he treated her. By the time he was ten, he knew her stories by heart and was sick of them. The street beckoned. Soon she became an embarrassment.

Scratching a desert flea off his waist, he found himself wishing that he'd listened more to that wrinkled old woman. When he saw her again, he would hug her tight and treat her right. With that vow, he drifted off to sleep.

The days settled into a natural rhythm; He'd wake up at sunrise, stalk until eight or nine. Then he'd cook his catch. Then he'd hike during the afternoon. Just before dark, stalk, cook his catch and sleep with a full belly, near a hot fire, under awesome starlight. This rhythm soaked into his being so effortlessly that he barely noticed it happening.

The desert had worked its purgative magic on the youth. By the third week of solo survival, Amelio could barely recall the importance of the gang. He found it harder to recall the faces of the heroes that he once worshipped. But when he did recall them, he couldn't see macho. He saw only primal fear; terrorized people, fleeing and pleading for their very lives.

His hunting skills had grown to the point that he could eat practically whenever he wanted to. On this night, Amelio had been especially lucky; he had six quail. Time improved his cleaning technique. Without the disgusting guts, the little birds tasted fantastic.

Quail became more than a staple; they were gourmet cuisine. He'd found several types of bushes that enhanced flavor. He didn't know Sage by name, but he knew it by taste. The few scrub oak branches he found gave a tantalizing smoky flavor to the tiny game birds. As he watched the meat cook, he thought about how killing had changed him.

First there was the massacre, a huge crossroad; he'd never be involved in a gang again. There was no safety in them. After all, one lone stranger chopped down all of his gods with one hand... no, with one finger.

He thought back on his first quail, snatched away in sharp talons; that hawk *didn't want to kill,* either. Perched up above Amelio, the Red-tail showed no anger or boast. It was just trying to make a living, the same as Amelio.

The hunting and killing was never easy or guaranteed. With each stalk, his prey could elude him. With each toss of the throwing stick, they could veer or swerve. His quarry always had a fair chance to escape. Most of the time, it did escape.

While pulling a hen from his favorite Sage skewer, he noticed a far-away light, gradually gaining brightness against the deepening darkness. It could be a convenience store... maybe he'd go there tomorrow. After all, his lighter was almost empty. It had been so long since the massacre that the psycho gringo *had to be gone.* He fell asleep near the fire. The rains came an hour later.

Amelio didn't sleep that night. Each raindrop from the near-freezing clouds felt like fire as it pierced his thin clothing. By the end of the cloudburst he was cold and soaked. He couldn't get a fire going; everything was soaked. With nothing left to do, he set out towards the distant light. After a few miles, his body warmed up from. The sun finally rose and dried his clothes.

After the rain, quail were hard to come by. He spent the morning hunting lizards, snakes and a gopher. Amelio thought the little guy foolish when it left its tunnel. Actually, it wasn't a mistake; the gopher smelled a rattler entering his burrow and had to leave or die. One quick thump with his throwing stick and the rodent stopped defiantly showing her sharp yellow teeth to the human.

He didn't like eating lizards or snakes; they were too dry and burned easily. Yet without quail, a man had to eat. He found some sun-dried kindling and finally got a fire going. His fingers nimbly dressed the gopher; a task unknown to him a month earlier.

He spent the rest of the day walking toward the highway. Before bedding down, Amelio ate the cottontail he'd taken in the evening. When darkness fell, the light seemed just as far away as the night before. Only a few weeks ago, that would have bothered him, but the desert changed him.

To the feral boy, time and distance were no longer the enemy; they weren't to be conquered, managed or measured. If it took a day or year to reach the store, it was all the same to the yearling buck. His last thoughts that night were of the game he would hunt in the morning. Maybe he'd hunt over by the short brush, where the cottontail rabbits thrived. He liked cottontails.

Amelio awoke before sunrise, the best time to kill cottontails. His two current throwing sticks were his best revision so far, worn smooth from countless abrasions and bloodstained from many kills. The boy had thrown them so much that he could hit without thinking. He had no need to improve on these two sticks.

He had first started with just one stick, but sometimes a missed animal wouldn't spook after he threw. That left Amelio in a frustrating position; he'd have to go fetch his stick, which meant spooking his prey and going hungry.

He tried carrying several sticks, but they were too cumbersome. So he settled on two sticks; one for throwing, the other a backup in his rear pocket. In the desolated terrain, where game hadn't seen humans, second chances were common, so he stayed with two sticks; it worked. Still, he had no desire to throw them after a fruitless morning hunt.

As the distance closed, the highway noises increased and beckoned. At noon he made it. The store was converted from an old barn after the interstate forced itself upon the landowner. Eminent domain knows no conscience.

After so many weeks of breathing clean desert air, the thick, sticky smell of doughnuts, pastries and second-hand cigarette smoke gagged him. He hurried past the pastry display to the rack of tee shirts. There were football logos and wildlife prints. He pulled a wildlife scene from the rack. It was a woodland white tailed buck.

He also chose two new lighters, two candy bars and a can of soda. Paying with one of his wrinkled twenties, he got his change and asked for the bathroom key and went to find the john.

Unlocking the restroom, Amelio flinched at the reflection in the mirror; he looked older, taller, thinner, stronger. His mouth and eyebrows had a white, crusty alkali lining. After washing up, the boy tossed the grimy purple gangster shirt in the trash and donned his wildlife motif.

He sat in the shade and opened the soda, but after so many weeks of eating naturally flavored game and drinking from bittersweet springs, his palate was purged; the sweet, syrupy soda was undrinkable.

He went back in and bought a cup of black coffee. He sat down outside to gorge on the candy and coffee, while he watched a dilapidated old Chevy truck drive up to the pumps. It was full of Native Americans wearing colorful clothing. One got out and walked past Amelio to pay for the gas. His kind, warm eyes washed over the boy.

Amelio watched them pump gas. He finished his snack. He got up and started heading back to his desert. He walked past the truck.
Unexpectedly, one spoke to him.
"Hey, you wanna ride?"
It stopped him cold. He hadn't even considered a ride. He looked carefully at the men; four in back, three up front. His voice sounded odd to his own ears; it had been a long time since he spoke out loud.
"Are you going to L.A.?"
"No."
Amelio smiled.
"Yeah... a ride... Sure."

The driver pointed his mouth to the open window, while watching the kid in the rear-view mirror. He spoke loud enough to be heard past the tailgate squeak and engine noise.
"What's your name?"
Amelio looked toward the cab, speaking loud enough.
"My friends call me... Jackie."
"Hop in, Jackie."
He climbed up into the truck bed. In order to sit down, he had to pull the pair of worn throwing sticks out from his pocket.
The oldest one spoke in a Navajo dialect. Several heads nodded agreement. One man chuckled softly. Amelio sat down and asked the chuckler.
 "What did he say?"
"He said; welcome Jackie Two Sticks."
They drove off into the desert.

Jackie Two Sticks didn't care WHERE they were headed; as long as it wasn't LA.

## Thirty-seven

# AFTERMATH

State Trooper Lance Forrest had patrolled this section for all of his twenty years on the force. For the most part, his job was routine; write speeding tickets, escort the locals home when they got drunk, bust out-of-state drivers for doing the same thing. He had five more years to pension, and he couldn't wait for it. Busting drunks and trapping speeders had long since lost its allure.

But this call was far from routine; apparently, some hunter claimed he heard an explosion. The cloud allegedly looked off-color. Of course, the call got delayed, while troopers answered more important ones, so nobody could verify the clouds at the time.

The hunter had no cell phone, so naturally his call was made the next day, when he got back to civilization. And, since it wasn't important, it got delayed further.

The Silver State troopers were spread pretty thin. They had better things to do than go looking at clouds. Besides, it was probably some prospector blasting a fruitless hole in the desert. But in the days since 911, terrorism could no longer be ruled out, even in the vast expanses of Nevada.

So he found himself eighty miles from nowhere, close to where the hunter reported suspicious clouds. He knew this desert section fairly well; there were only a handful of such roads to check, for at least forty miles. The first few got nothing more than a slow-down and glance.

Then he came to the trail that Ted and the Campesinos took. Tracks indicated a whole group of vehicles took that old road. He tried to recall precisely where this particular road went, but couldn't. He had a vague memory of an old silver mine, some ten miles out, but... Hell, half those old roads led to exhausted mines; this trail didn't ring any bells.

When he got to the first gulley crossing, the soil had been worked to allow better passage; that was weird. Scrapes from cars or trailers or SOMETHING; too low for any self-respecting four-wheel drive rig to make... Curiouser and curiouser, with each passing mile.

Then he came to the wreckage, unsheathed his service pistol and unhinged the riot gun; it was a lonely spot. Stepping into the wind, he pumped a round in the shotgun and walked uphill to Ortega's Mercedez; three neat bullet holes in the windshield, well spaced, head level. He spoke aloud, for confidence.
*'Windshield ain't shattered... GOOD!'*
That ruled out low-velocity bullets, such as machine pistols or shotguns, so it wasn't a mob hit, thank God. He didn't want to get mixed up in one of THOSE again.

He looked at the other low riders; all good, except for one that looked like it was hit it with a bazooka... Definitely odd. He hiked several hundred yards uphill, turned and looked back at the water-colored ranges.

He roved and found some odd looking spots; OK to the casual eye maybe, but not to the trooper's keen gaze... No bushes on them. The topsoil was off-color and they had a sculpted appearance. He had a hunch what was underneath. He went to the squad car and keyed the mike.

"Hey, how 'bout it, Lonnie... got your ears on?"
In a few seconds, the tentative voice of someone illegally transmitting on a law frequency answered.
"UH, YEAH, what's up?"
It wasn't exactly LAW talk, but it worked well enough in the high, lonesome plains.
"Mile marker 262. Got a job for you. Get here as quick as you can, ten four?"
Lonnie perked up.
"I'm leavin' now... OVER."
Almost as an afterthought, Lance re-keyed the mike.
"OH, LON? Bring the *BIG TRUCK, copy?"*

"BIG TRUCK... TEN FOUR. We're out."

He dropped his hot pastrami sandwich and grabbed the keys for the mammoth tow rig.

Lonnie met the trooper two hours later, then followed him to the scene.

"Holy, shit! What happened?"

Wherever he looked, he saw low riders. Most were still in perfect shape to drive away, worth tens of thousands, in parts alone.

Lance had rehearsed while waiting, to get it right.

"Well, near as I can figure, they drove out here to have a spiritual communion, got religion, and just walked off... leaving their material possessions behind. But as you can plainly see, these abandoned vehicles are blocking a Nevada thoroughfare. I hereby authorize YOU to tow them away and dispense with, as you see fit."

Lonnie smirked. He knew the drill. Murders in the desert were just like murders anywhere else, only with less paperwork. He had towed some expensive cars from mob hits before, but this current scene was just a cheaper grade of car and criminal.

He knew a guy that knew a guy... they could part out the low riders. He'd clear maybe thirty grand. And that didn't include the Mercedes; with new plates, windshield and some seat covers over the blood stains, it would be all his.

He went to work winching cars onto the big rig. They both knew the unwritten law of the desert; the three "S's"; Shoot, Shovel and Shut up. Someone already beat them to the shooting and shoveling.

Trooper Forrest drove off, his services required elsewhere. He thought about the victims; a bunch of gangsters from California... and the Nevada boys were already sick of "Californicaters," a bunch of loud, arrogant assholes, with too much money and not enough horse sense.

They acted like they owned Nevada, like it was just another playground for flatlanders. The idiots had too much attitude and too little respect. For all he cared, the whole fuckin' state could slip into the ocean.

Lonnie and Lance were in perfect accord with their anti-Californian sentiment. So they turned their eyes from the crime scene and went about their business. Lonnie would haul them off. Lance would file the paperwork; a few abandoned vehicles found on a give-a-shit piece of back-road two-track.

Only the well-sculpted mounds would remain, semi-permanent monuments to the stupidity of God-knows how many arrogant Mexican-American gangbangers. They probably deserved it. For all he cared, all the world's gangsters could get buried out there. There was plenty of desert ready for it.

He hit the freeway, stomped the gas and muttered aloud.

"Won't be the first or last such monument. Sumbitches had it coming or they wouldn't have got shot. No sense in wasting resources on the self-evident truths of the universe."

The West's most philosophical short-timer called it a night. Five years to retirement and the sweet life.

## Thirty-eight

## KEYNOTE

The speaker cleared his throat. The crowd respectfully grew silent. Soon a nervous vacuum awaited his words of truth.

"An ancient wise man once said...

*'Assassination is the highest form of public service.'*

"In other words, although killing is unacceptable most of the time, it is clearly called for, in certain extreme situations. The difficulty, as with all other facets of human ethics, lies in discerning the differences.

"Sometimes we have months to ponder the ethics of taking a life, as in a murder trial. In other situations, we only have split seconds, maybe less, to choose. Few of us have ever been in that position, but three years ago, on a desolate ridge, strangers started shooting at me. I only had seconds to decide... would I kill or be killed? I made the right choice. You see, I killed all three of the men who tried to kill me."

The crowd didn't murmur, because the grapevine already told them about the speaker.

"Of course, constitutional protection allows me to tell it now. I was judged Not Guilty on all charges, but as God is my witness, I've re-lived those hours when I was alone and bleeding, trembling with fear on that hilltop. I still can't see any other alternative to my decision."

"Do I regret it? Hell yes! I have nightmares. My life will never be the same; and I regret that, too... But at least I have a lifetime to regret it. Those dope-dealing thugs could have stolen that from me."

He sipped some water.

"If I tried to REASON, if I tried to run, they would've killed me. If I would have HESITATED... or tried ANY OTHER option, *I'd be dead.* But I didn't have time for deliberating; I barely had time to react. In fact, it was only MY WOODSMANSHIP, MY SURVIVAL INSTINCTS, AND GOD... that saved me.

"That's why your leaders asked me to come and speak to you today... Some of you already know what it's like to be in a firefight. I pray to God that you never have to deal with a similar incident... but if you do, I pray mightily that my words today will help you make the right choice... *LIFE!"*

The peace officers stood and applauded Ted Morgan's opener for the assembly of peace officers, in Remo, Nevada, the Silver State... his new residence.

## Thirty-nine...
## IMPACT

Eight hundred miles southeast of the peace officers' conference, Jackie Two Sticks completed his quest to become a blood brother of the Navajo human beings.

Six hundred miles to the Southwest, the newest CEO, Victor Saldivar chaired the meeting of the largest video store chain in California.

The four corrupt deputies retired from the Mendonesia Sheriff's Department, just before it came under indictment. Talvez and Engard went to work as security consultants for the largest video chain in California. Null disappeared completely; nobody knew if he was killed or if he beamed the planet, but Ted Morgan made sure he an alibi for the time frame; his jailhouse tutoring hadn't been wasted.

Thompkins retired to a small Caribbean island... but just as he'd planned, nobody knew which one. His bearer bonds would keep him in a moderate lifestyle of fine women and good wine, as long as he doesn't abuse either.

Three thousand, one hundred sixty-miles away, the only two Purple massacre survivors settled into their new life as Boston dockworkers. For these two, the desert encounter with Ted Morgan truly was a religious experience. It remains a mystery how Chessy and Alberto escaped, 'cuz they ain't talkin'.

Dave Semple still lives in Hidden Crest. He married his longtime sweetheart, finally. He continues to hunt big mule deer in several western states. When they get together, Dave and Ted hunt. They drink fine ale. They talk about old times. But they *never* talk about Ted's solo trip.

Jo Morgan surprised her doctors when she came out of her coma of eight months. Her physical scars gradually disappearing, with ongoing dermabrasion and laser therapy, but her prognosis; not so good regarding the nightmares, chronic depression, and failed marriage.

AJ and Kelly deeply resent their father divorcing her, then running off like some coward. Some pains can't fade, and some wrongs can't be undone. That's just how it is.

In Cell Block C, Soledad, California, Hector Alonzo Corazon carefully worked over his fledgling's tatt... He had to get it right, this Madonna.

After all, the fledgling was his only living homeboy. The Campesinos... They stick together, *verdad?*

Well, I hope you liked Turnabout; my fictional story, which might very easily come true. You see, in my neck of the woods, the danger is real. Hidden marijuana patches abound in my beloved mountains, ruining my hunting, messing with tranquility... *got it?*

And, although most folks who grow a few plants for private use are peaceable citizens, the incredibly lucrative Pot industry also attracts hardened career criminals and cartel types. In fact, just last summer a friend went to check on his spring, since his water suddenly quit. He lives in very rugged terrain; hiked two hundred yards uphill, planning to unclog his gravity-flow water supply.

Imagine his surprise when instead of a few leaves, a frog or mouse clogging the line, three illegal Mexican nationals pointed rifles at him. They had the audacity to cut his house line, divert his water to plants that they'd secretly planted on his property.

Fortunately, they didn't kill him. He went home and dialed 911 on a cell phone. In three hours, the choppers showed, took the plants, but failed to find the scampering illegals.

Thanks to Marijuana, there's a lot of weird shit happening up here in God's country... on both sides of the law.

OH, yeah; all of it is... fictional, by the way.

➢ COURT OF LAW; to catch a serial pedophile, three young cops must think outside the profile. Filled with sub-plots, quirks, sex, depravity and corruption... Pretty good twist ending, too.

➢ CHAMELEON; a young serial killer with father issues; his dad's a famous profiler. Just as chameleons use camouflage, Vincent stays invisible by exploiting profiling data. A few twists, weird sex & bizarre ending.

➢ TURNABOUT; a hunter stumbles upon a cartel Pot patch, high up in the coastal mountains. A gunfight ensues, which sets Ted Morgan on a grisly quest for revenge; it's not wise to piss off the average American hunter! Turnabout's such a bitch.

➢ Urik-Tah, the Death Rose; Majesty travels at Hawk Speed to see what happened to a mining colony. She finds something that will change the balance of power in the universe. If you like Star Trek, you'll like this. Has the mother of all unexpected endings.

➢ Mother saves Majesty; Read the Death Rose first, then this prequel. It might warp your mind. Key ingredients; theoretical speeds, black holes, primitive life-form weaponry, insoluble conundrum.

* Owing to various online production glitches, books are in print or will be online shortly at the biggest book site; can't say which, but it's... amaz...ingly big. Search author or title; hell, you'll figure it out.

BTW; I'm receptive to ideas from readers, for stories. I welcome ideas, love praise... and scoff at criticism.

Feel free to email me; lanceksteele@yahoo.com